CITY OF OTHERS™

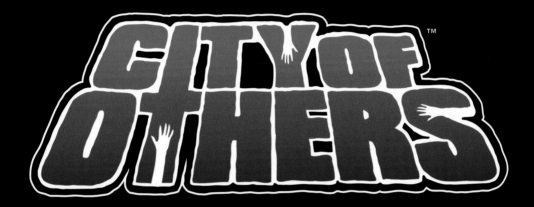

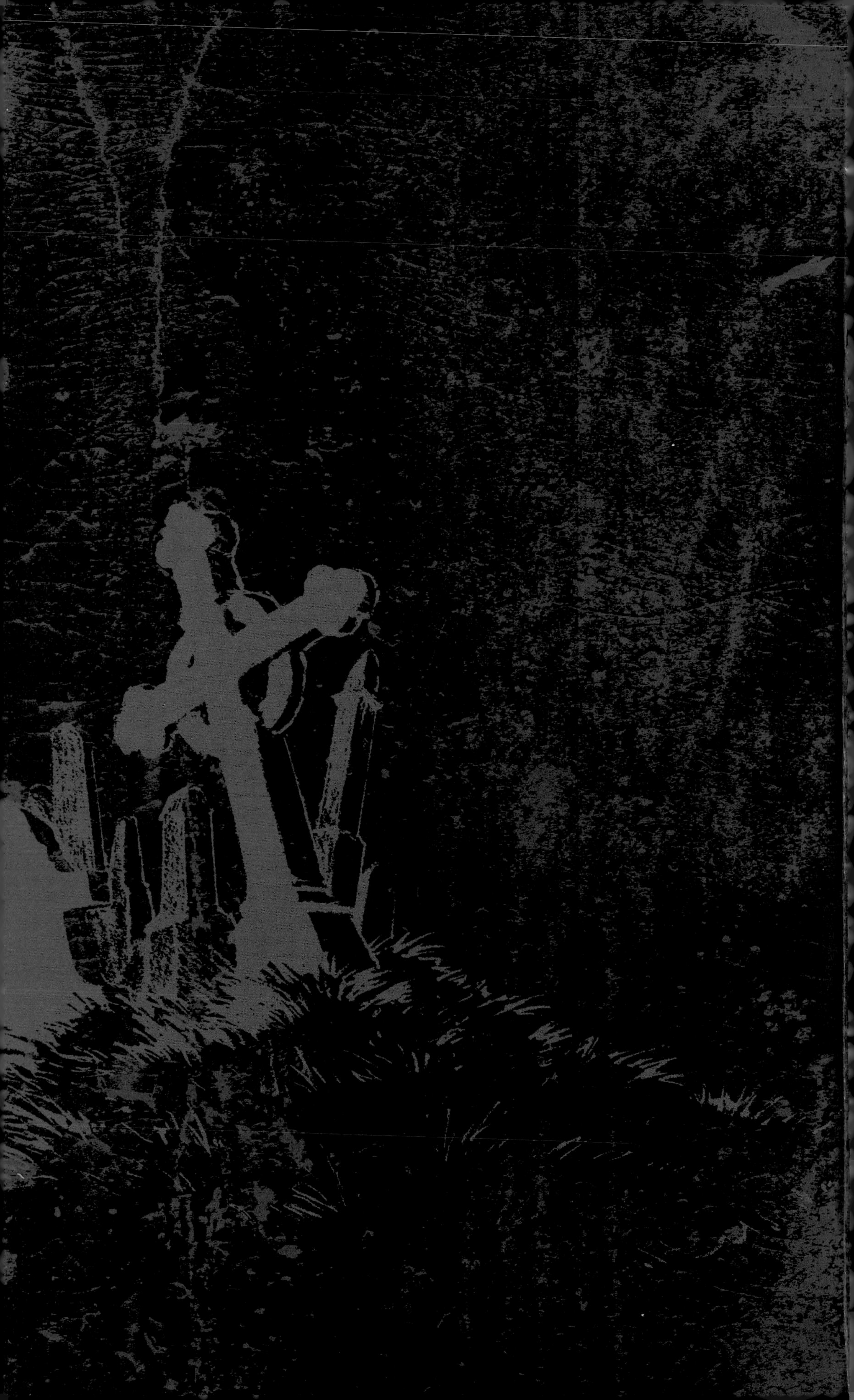

CITY OF OTHERS ™

STORY BY
STEVE NILES AND
BERNIE WRIGHTSON

COVER AND INTERIOR ART BY
BERNIE WRIGHTSON

COLORS BY
JOSÉ VILLARRUBIA

LETTERED BY
MICHAEL DAVID THOMAS

DARK HORSE BOOKS®

EDITOR
SHAWNA GORE

ASSISTANT EDITOR
JEMIAH JEFFERSON

DESIGNER
DAVID NESTELLE

PUBLISHER
MIKE RICHARDSON

SPECIAL THANKS TO
TIM BRADSTREET

Published by Dark Horse Books,
A division of Dark Horse Comics, Inc.
10956 SE Main Street Milwaukie, OR 97222

This book collects issues 1–4 of *City of Others*,
published by Dark Horse Comics.

February 2008 First edition

ISBN 978-1-59307-893-5

1 3 5 7 9 10 8 6 4 2
Printed in China

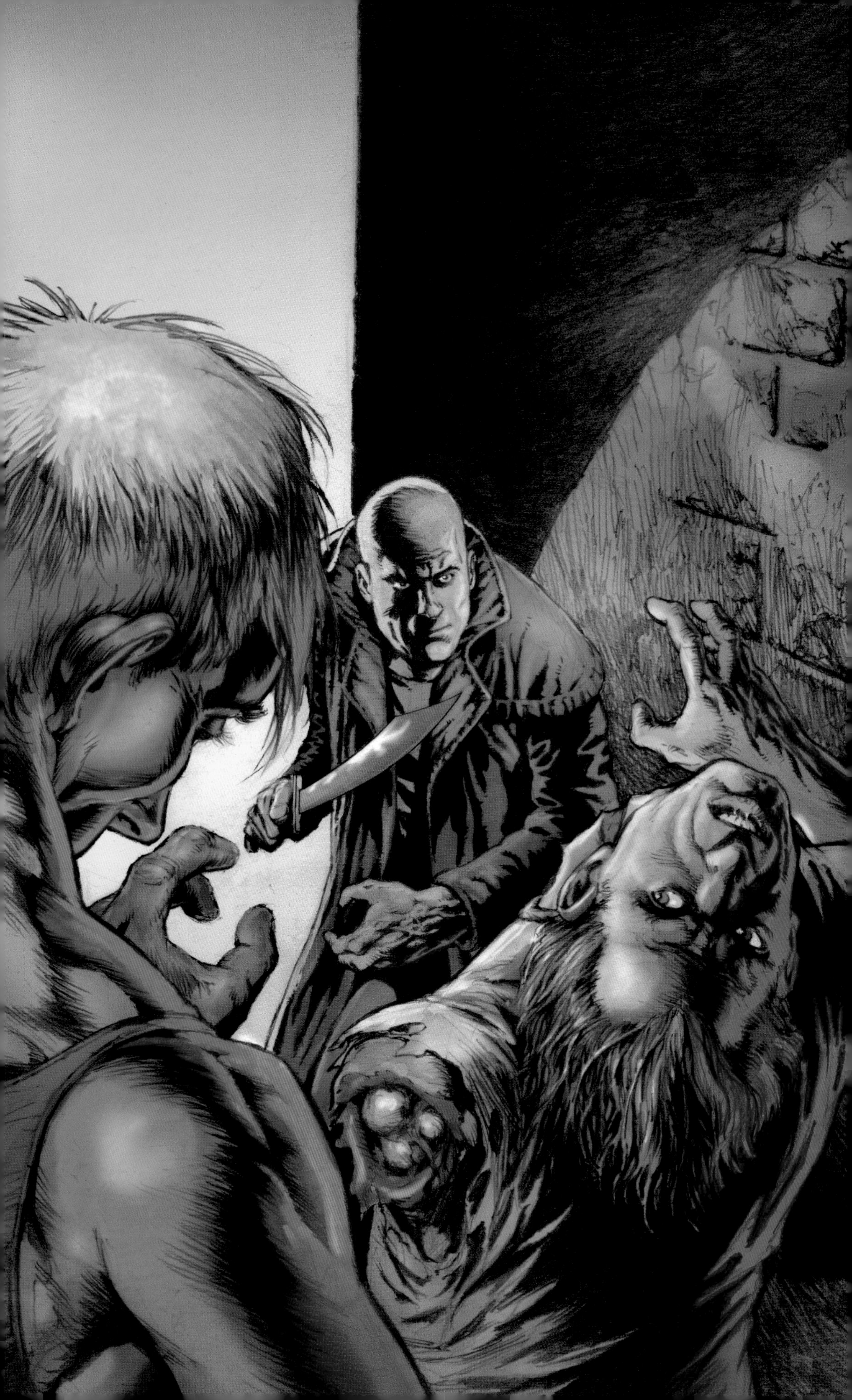

ONE CHAPTER

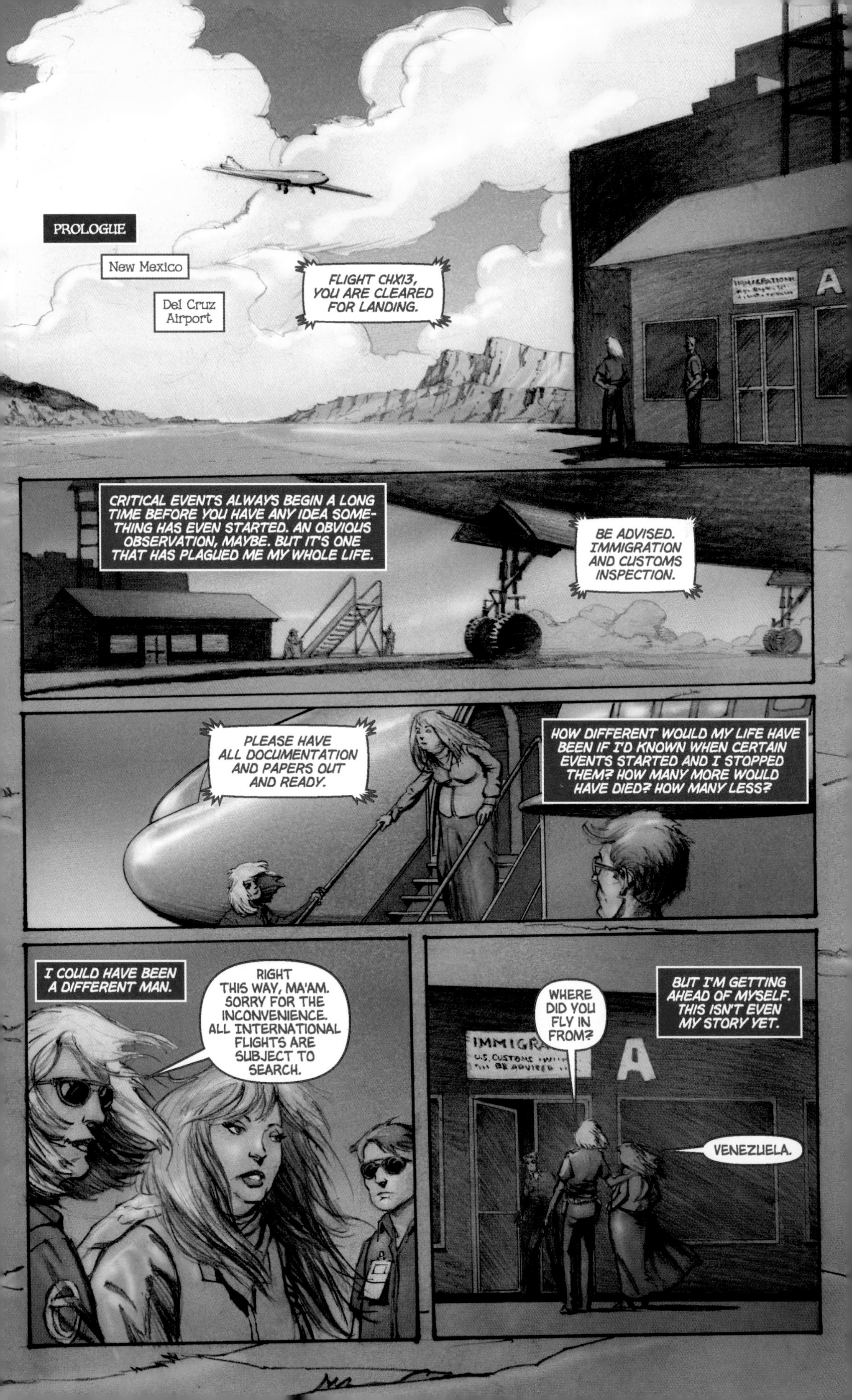
PROLOGUE
New Mexico
Del Cruz Airport
FLIGHT CHX13, YOU ARE CLEARED FOR LANDING.
CRITICAL EVENTS ALWAYS BEGIN A LONG TIME BEFORE YOU HAVE ANY IDEA SOMETHING HAS EVEN STARTED. AN OBVIOUS OBSERVATION, MAYBE. BUT IT'S ONE THAT HAS PLAGUED ME MY WHOLE LIFE.
BE ADVISED. IMMIGRATION AND CUSTOMS INSPECTION.
PLEASE HAVE ALL DOCUMENTATION AND PAPERS OUT AND READY.
HOW DIFFERENT WOULD MY LIFE HAVE BEEN IF I'D KNOWN WHEN CERTAIN EVENTS STARTED AND I STOPPED THEM? HOW MANY MORE WOULD HAVE DIED? HOW MANY LESS?
I COULD HAVE BEEN A DIFFERENT MAN.
RIGHT THIS WAY, MA'AM. SORRY FOR THE INCONVENIENCE. ALL INTERNATIONAL FLIGHTS ARE SUBJECT TO SEARCH.
BUT I'M GETTING AHEAD OF MYSELF. THIS ISN'T EVEN MY STORY YET.
WHERE DID YOU FLY IN FROM?
VENEZUELA.

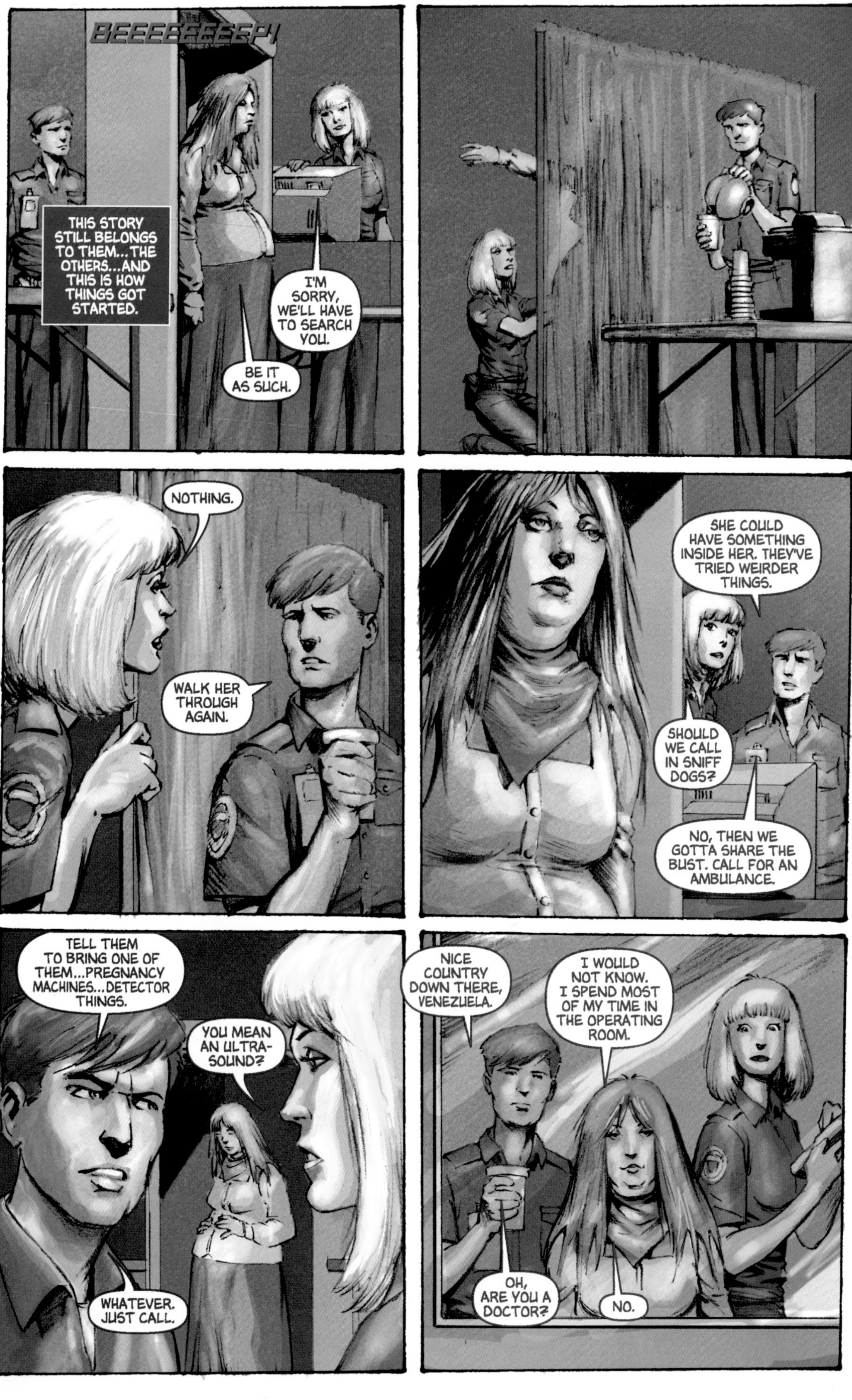
BEEEEEEEEP!
THIS STORY STILL BELONGS TO THEM...THE OTHERS...AND THIS IS HOW THINGS GOT STARTED.
I'M SORRY, WE'LL HAVE TO SEARCH YOU.
BE IT AS SUCH.
NOTHING.
WALK HER THROUGH AGAIN.
SHE COULD HAVE SOMETHING INSIDE HER. THEY'VE TRIED WEIRDER THINGS.
SHOULD WE CALL IN SNIFF DOGS?
NO, THEN WE GOTTA SHARE THE BUST. CALL FOR AN AMBULANCE.
TELL THEM TO BRING ONE OF THEM...PREGNANCY MACHINES...DETECTOR THINGS.
YOU MEAN AN ULTRA-SOUND?
WHATEVER. JUST CALL.
NICE COUNTRY DOWN THERE, VENEZUELA.
I WOULD NOT KNOW. I SPEND MOST OF MY TIME IN THE OPERATING ROOM.
OH, ARE YOU A DOCTOR?
NO.

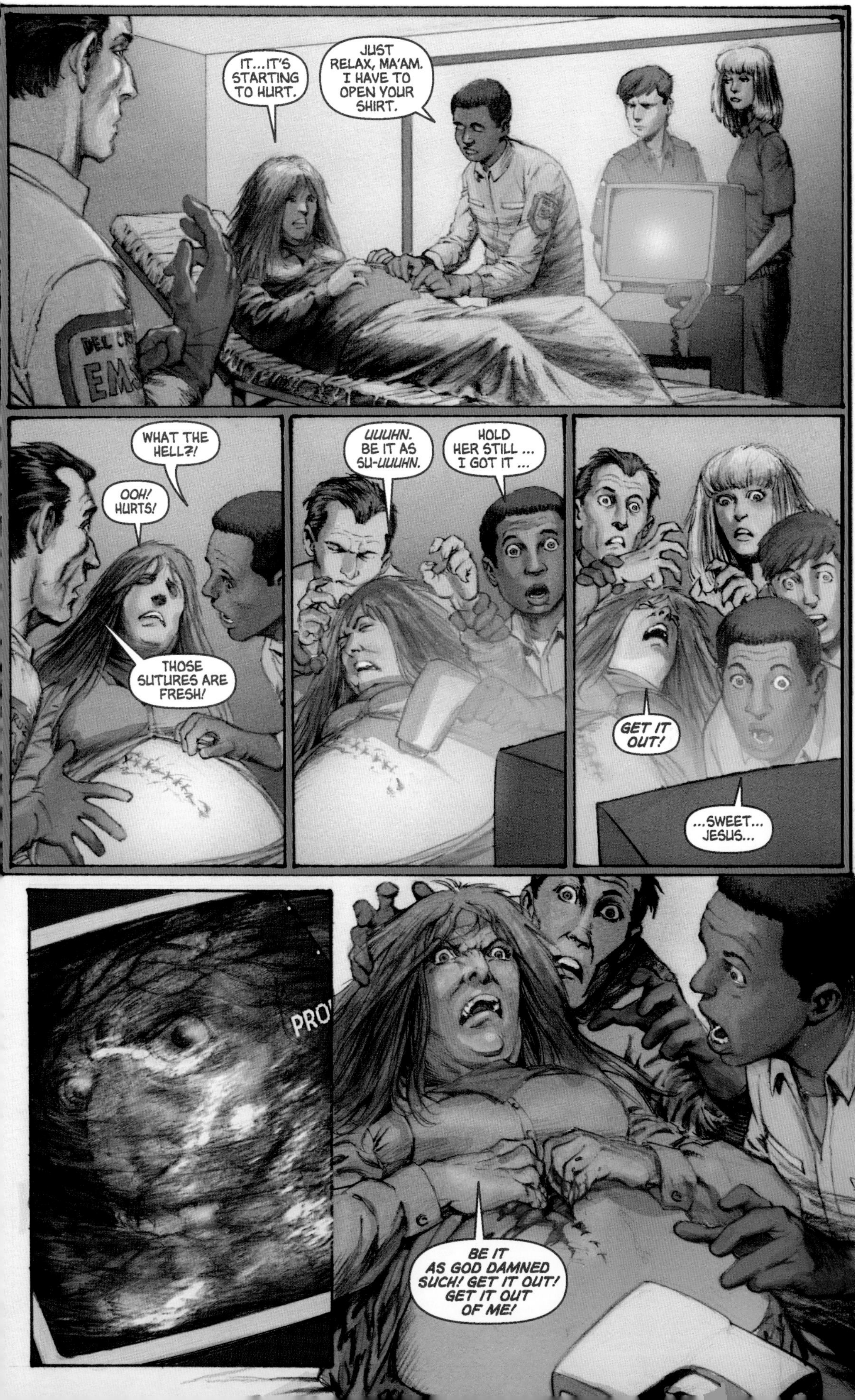
IT...IT'S STARTING TO HURT.
JUST RELAX, MA'AM. I HAVE TO OPEN YOUR SHIRT.
WHAT THE HELL?!
OOH! HURTS!
THOSE SUTURES ARE FRESH!
UUUHN. BE IT AS SU-UUUHN.
HOLD HER STILL ... I GOT IT ...
GET IT OUT!
...SWEET... JESUS...
BE IT AS GOD DAMNED SUCH! GET IT OUT! GET IT OUT OF ME!

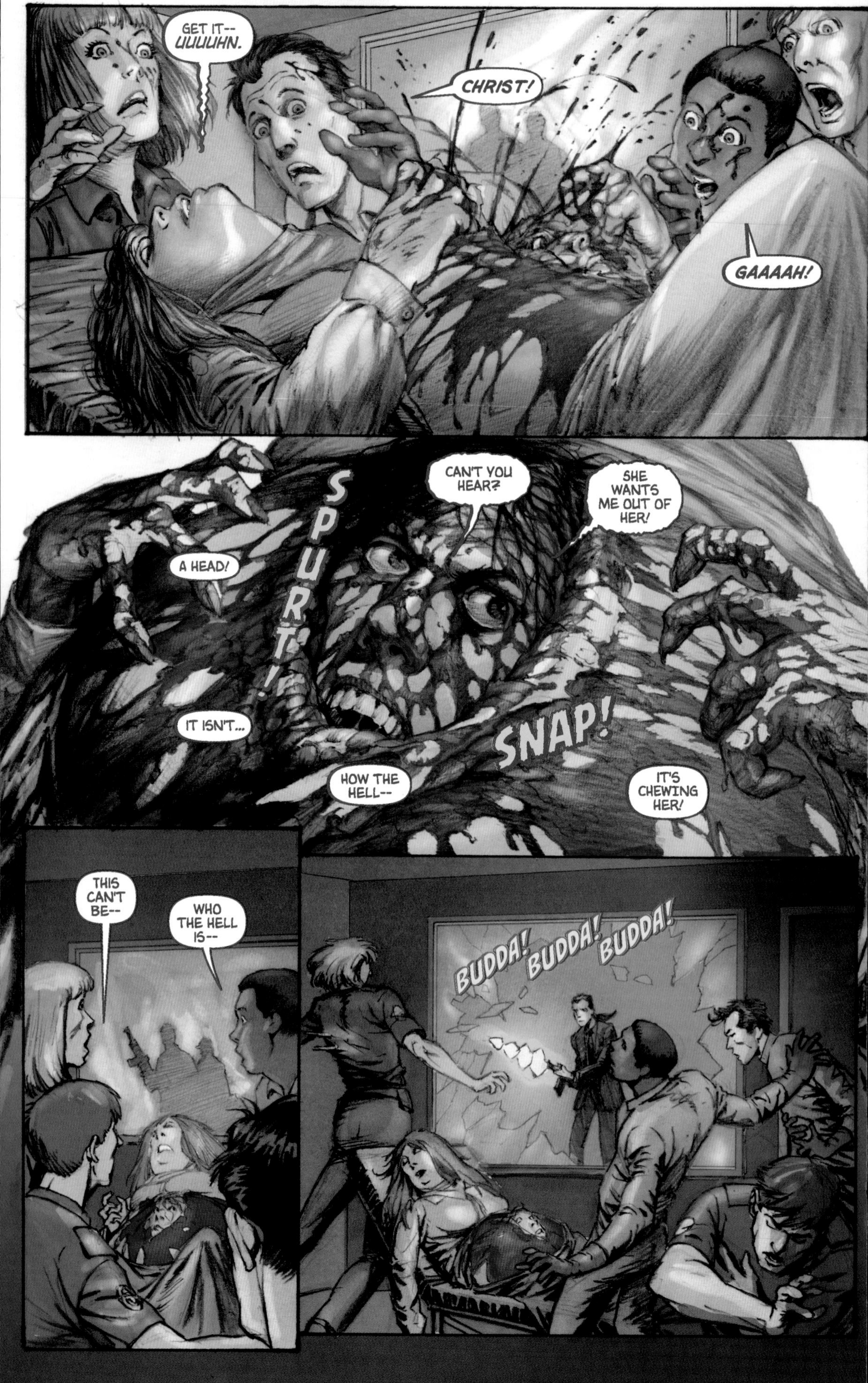
GET IT-- UUUUHN.
CHRIST!
GAAAAH!
CAN'T YOU HEAR?
SHE WANTS ME OUT OF HER!
SPURT!
A HEAD!
IT ISN'T...
SNAP!
HOW THE HELL--
IT'S CHEWING HER!
THIS CAN'T BE--
WHO THE HELL IS--
BUDDA! BUDDA! BUDDA!

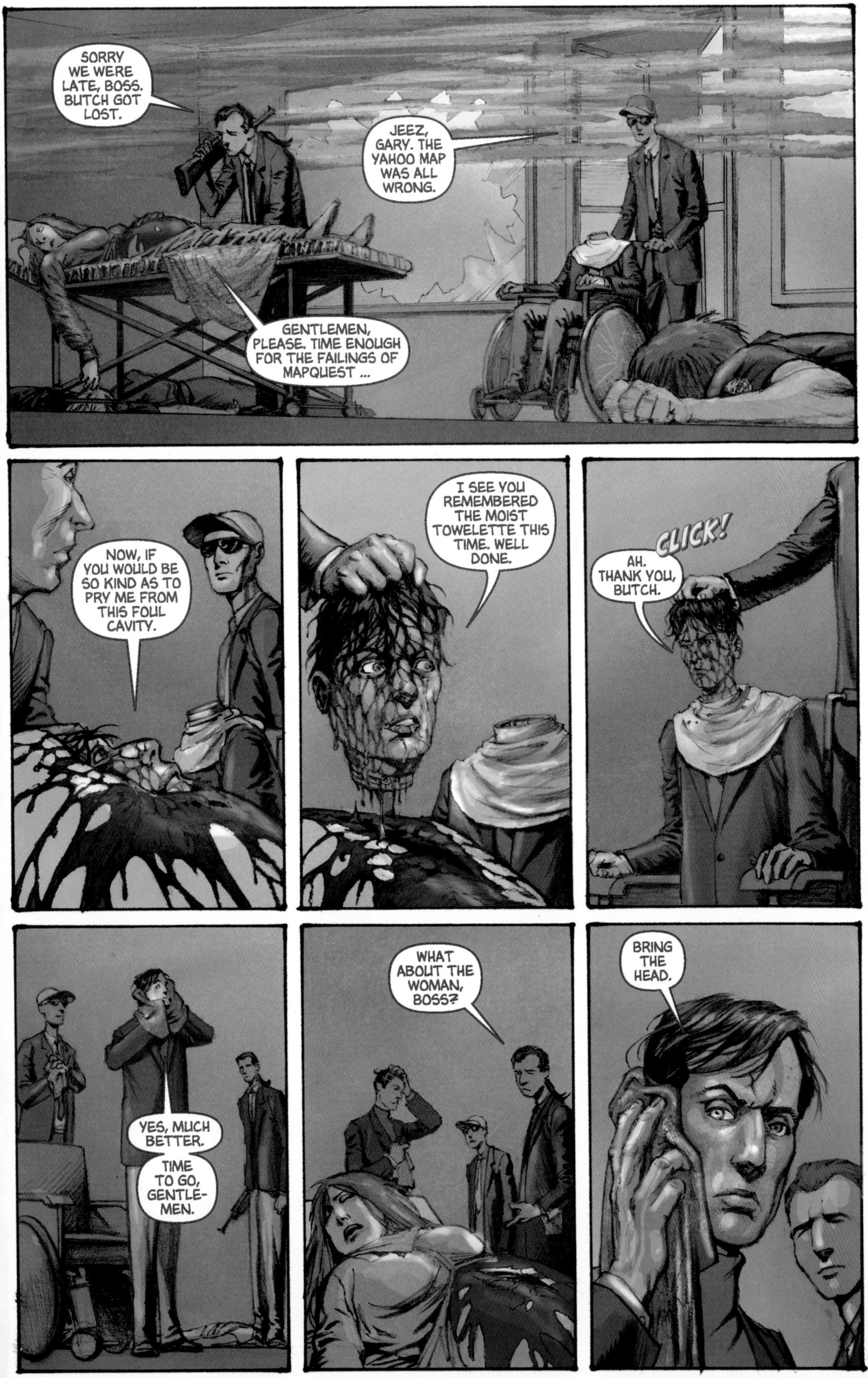
SORRY WE WERE LATE, BOSS. BUTCH GOT LOST.
JEEZ, GARY. THE YAHOO MAP WAS ALL WRONG.
GENTLEMEN, PLEASE. TIME ENOUGH FOR THE FAILINGS OF MAPQUEST ...
NOW, IF YOU WOULD BE SO KIND AS TO PRY ME FROM THIS FOUL CAVITY.
I SEE YOU REMEMBERED THE MOIST TOWELETTE THIS TIME. WELL DONE.
CLICK!
AH. THANK YOU, BUTCH.
YES, MUCH BETTER.
TIME TO GO, GENTLE-MEN.
WHAT ABOUT THE WOMAN, BOSS?
BRING THE HEAD.

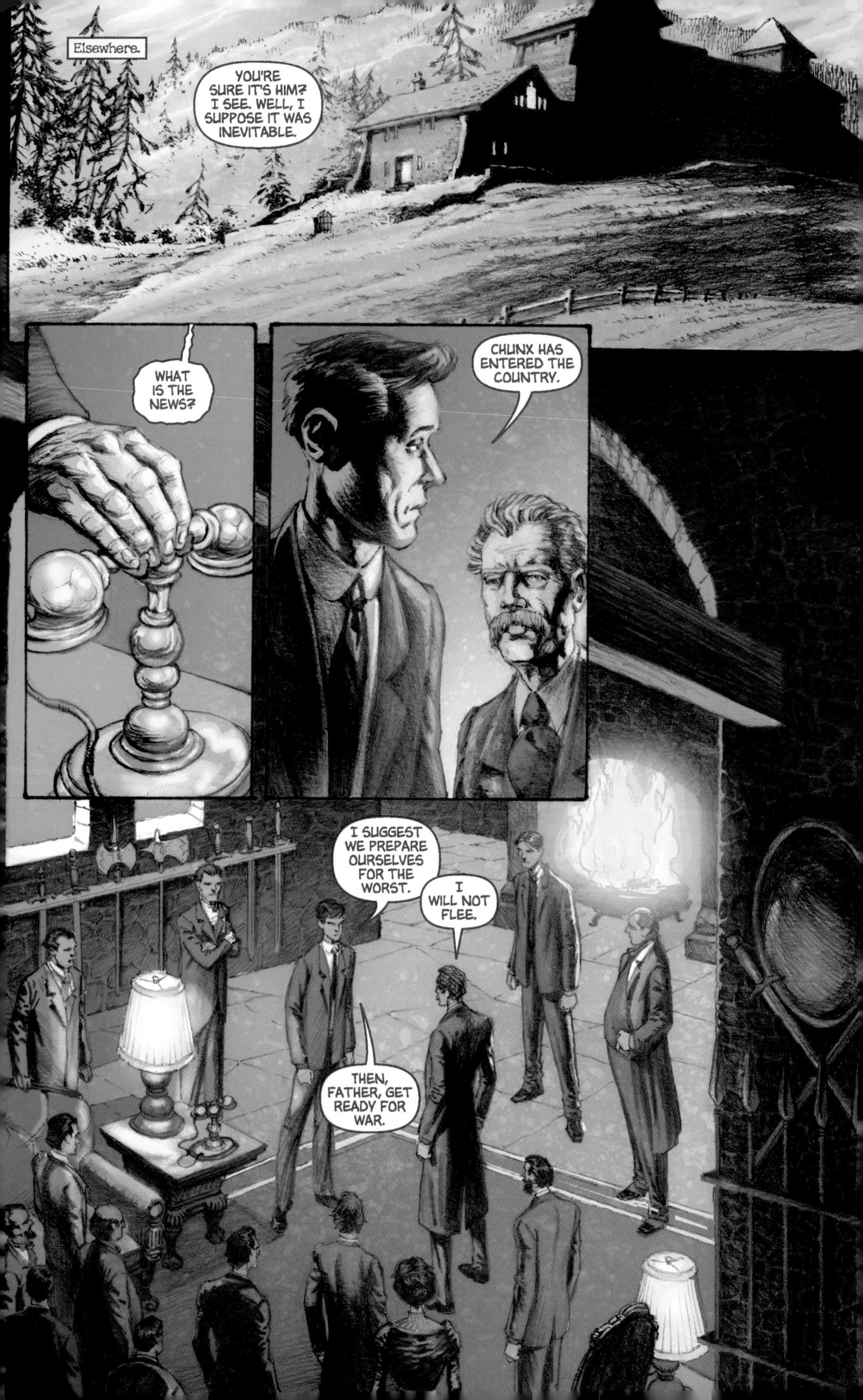
Elsewhere.
YOU'RE SURE IT'S HIM? I SEE. WELL, I SUPPOSE IT WAS INEVITABLE.
WHAT IS THE NEWS?
CHUNX HAS ENTERED THE COUNTRY.
I SUGGEST WE PREPARE OURSELVES FOR THE WORST.
I WILL NOT FLEE.
THEN, FATHER, GET READY FOR WAR.

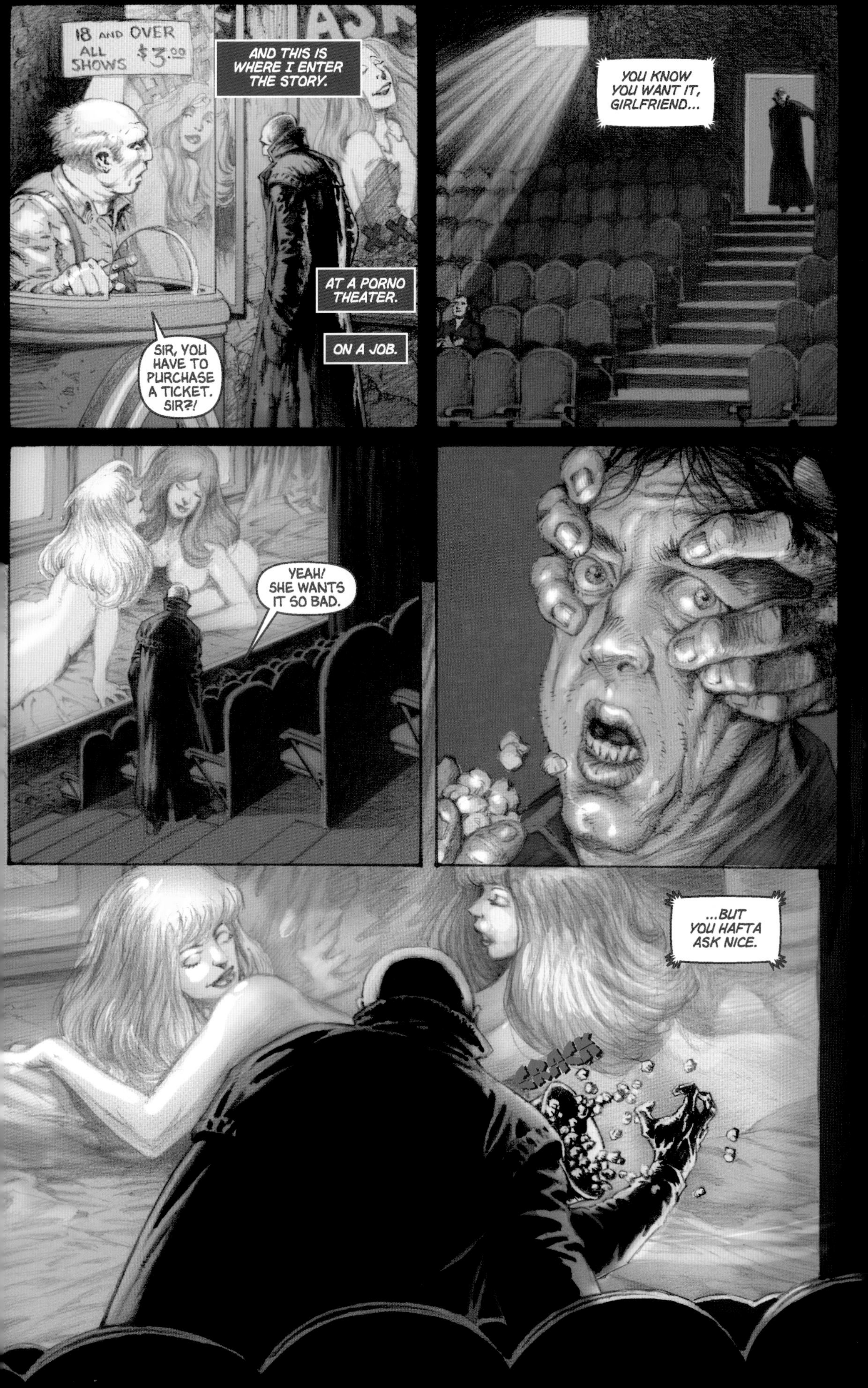
18 AND OVER
ALL SHOWS $3.00
AND THIS IS WHERE I ENTER THE STORY.
AT A PORNO THEATER.
ON A JOB.
SIR, YOU HAVE TO PURCHASE A TICKET. SIR?!
YOU KNOW YOU WANT IT, GIRLFRIEND...
YEAH! SHE WANTS IT SO BAD.
...BUT YOU HAFTA ASK NICE.
KRAK

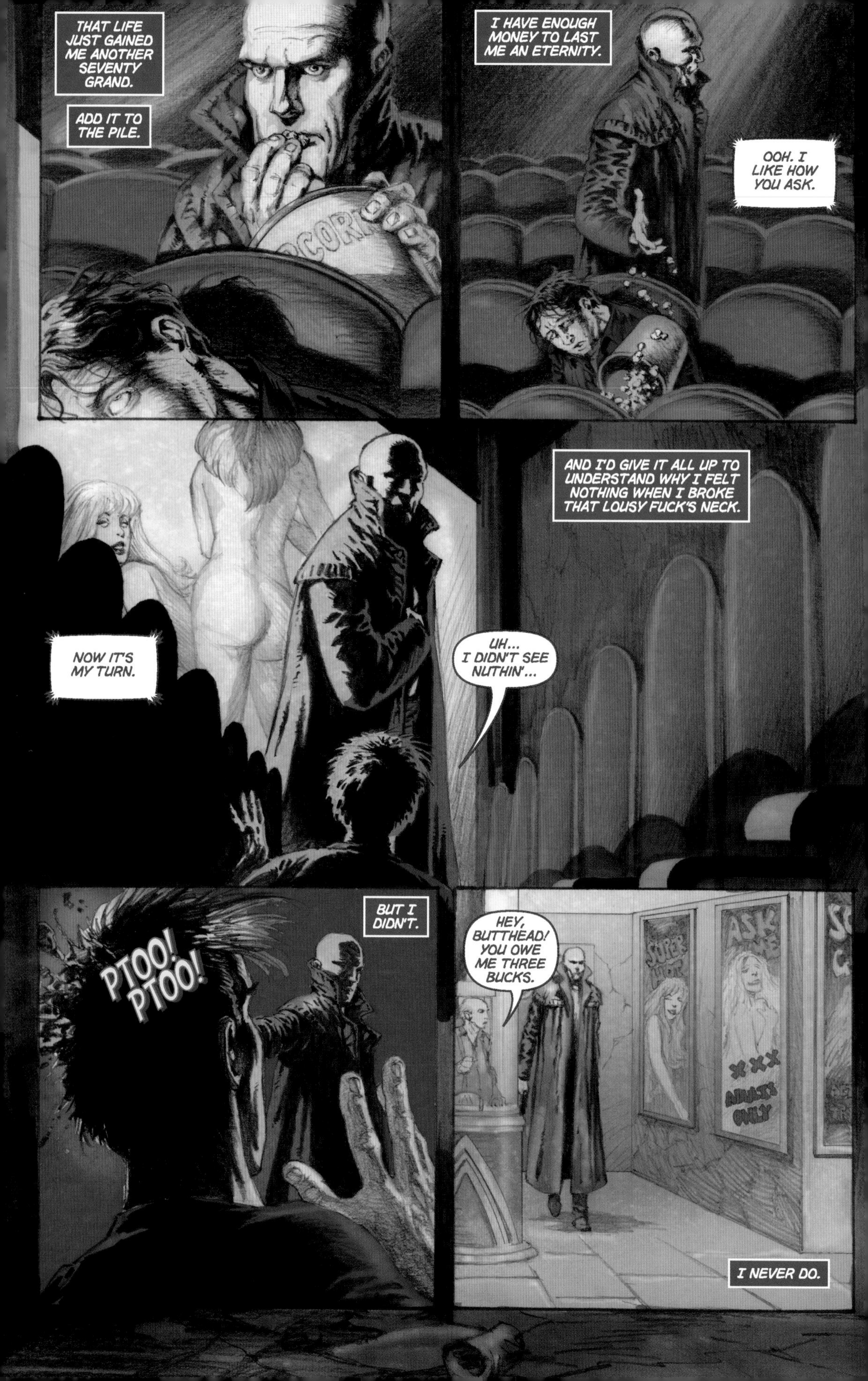
THAT LIFE JUST GAINED ME ANOTHER SEVENTY GRAND.
ADD IT TO THE PILE.
I HAVE ENOUGH MONEY TO LAST ME AN ETERNITY.
OOH. I LIKE HOW YOU ASK.
AND I'D GIVE IT ALL UP TO UNDERSTAND WHY I FELT NOTHING WHEN I BROKE THAT LOUSY FUCK'S NECK.
NOW IT'S MY TURN.
UH... I DIDN'T SEE NUTHIN'...
BUT I DIDN'T.
PTOO! PTOO!
HEY, BUTTHEAD! YOU OWE ME THREE BUCKS.
I NEVER DO.

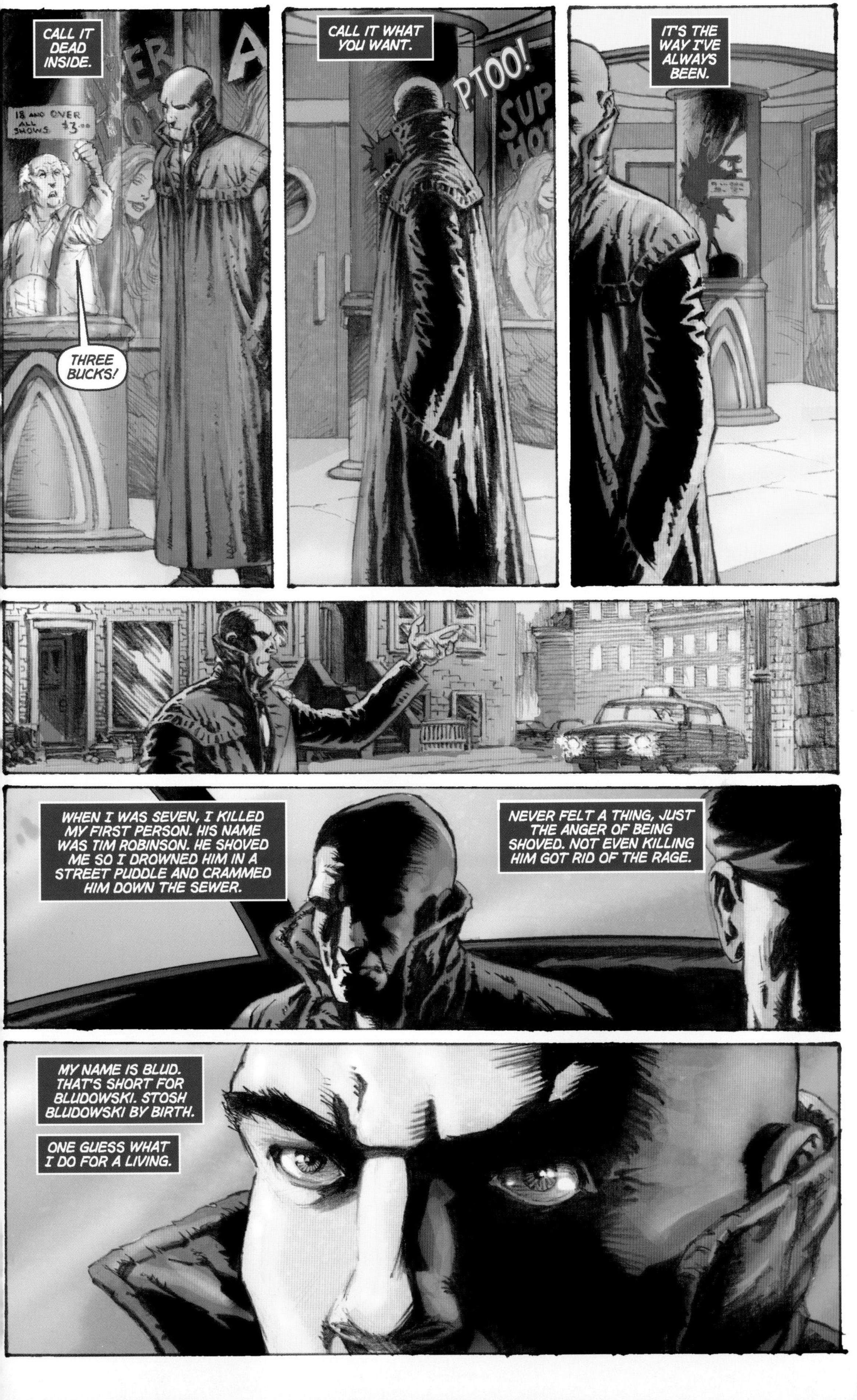
CALL IT DEAD INSIDE.
18 AND OVER ALL SHOWS $3.00
THREE BUCKS!
CALL IT WHAT YOU WANT.
PTOO!
IT'S THE WAY I'VE ALWAYS BEEN.
WHEN I WAS SEVEN, I KILLED MY FIRST PERSON. HIS NAME WAS TIM ROBINSON. HE SHOVED ME SO I DROWNED HIM IN A STREET PUDDLE AND CRAMMED HIM DOWN THE SEWER.
NEVER FELT A THING, JUST THE ANGER OF BEING SHOVED. NOT EVEN KILLING HIM GOT RID OF THE RAGE.
MY NAME IS BLUD. THAT'S SHORT FOR BLUDOWSKI. STOSH BLUDOWSKI BY BIRTH.
ONE GUESS WHAT I DO FOR A LIVING.

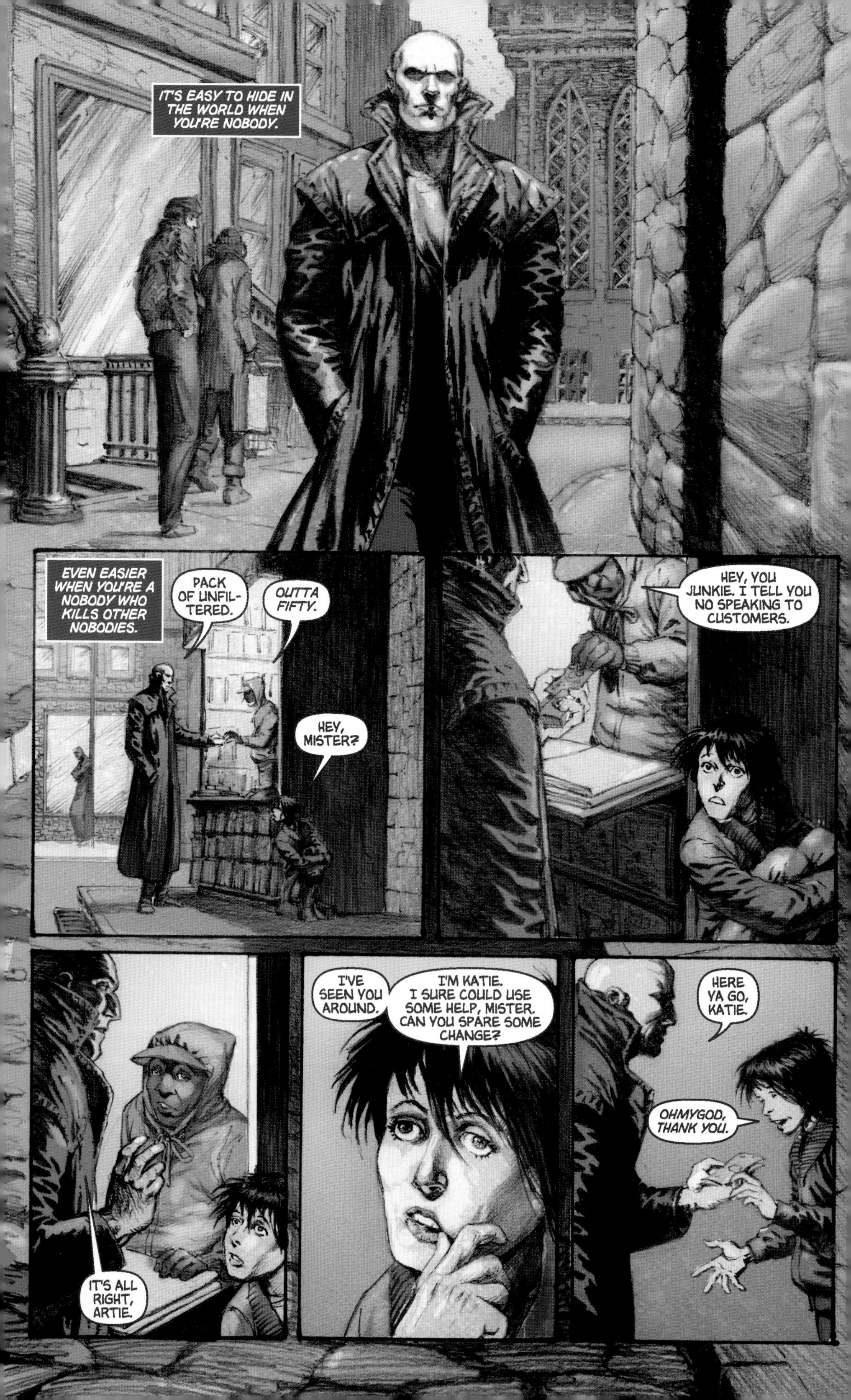
IT'S EASY TO HIDE IN THE WORLD WHEN YOU'RE NOBODY.
EVEN EASIER WHEN YOU'RE A NOBODY WHO KILLS OTHER NOBODIES.
PACK OF UNFIL-TERED.
OUTTA FIFTY.
HEY, MISTER?
HEY, YOU JUNKIE. I TELL YOU NO SPEAKING TO CUSTOMERS.
IT'S ALL RIGHT, ARTIE.
I'VE SEEN YOU AROUND.
I'M KATIE. I SURE COULD USE SOME HELP, MISTER. CAN YOU SPARE SOME CHANGE?
HERE YA GO, KATIE.
OHMYGOD, THANK YOU.

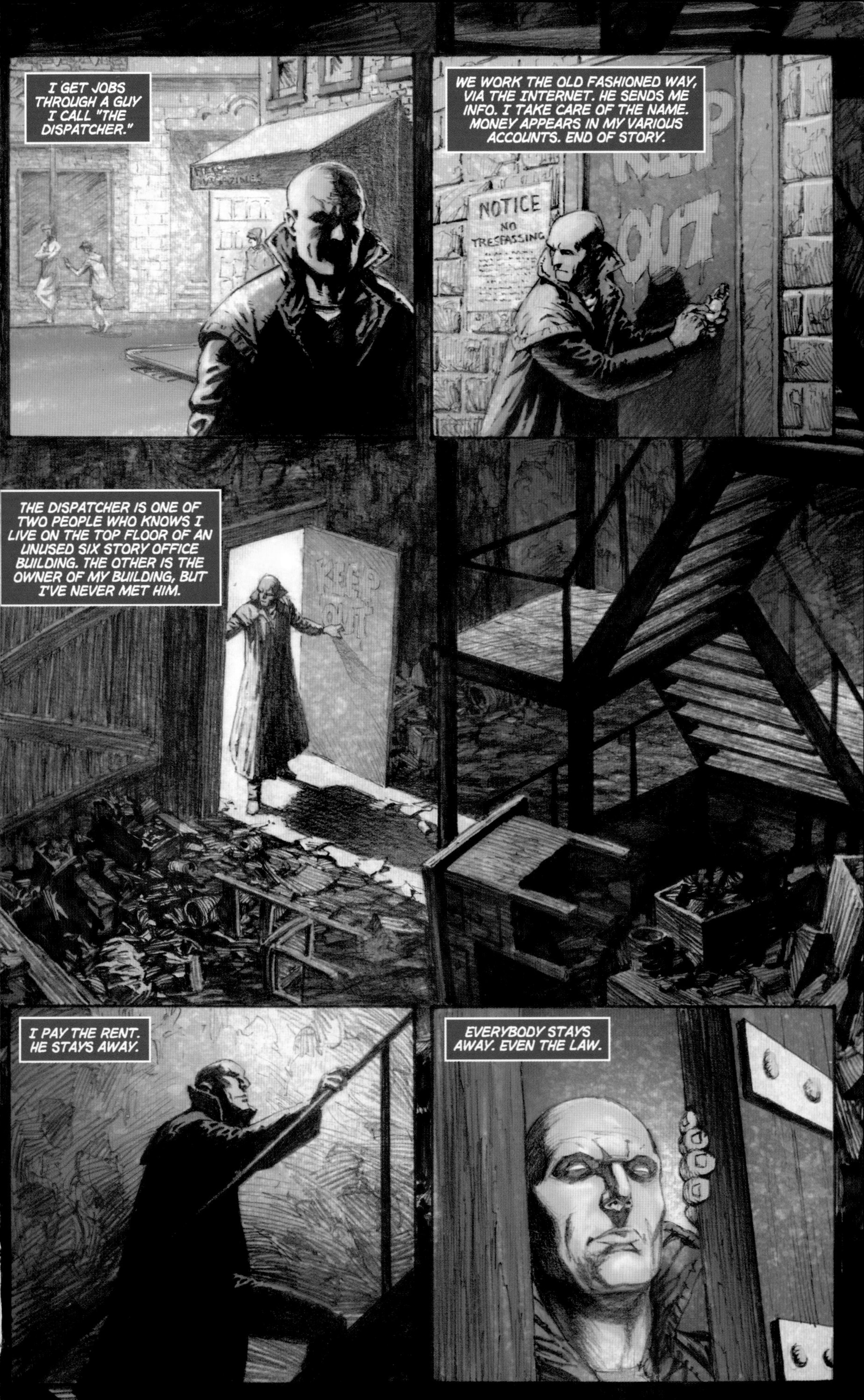
I GET JOBS THROUGH A GUY I CALL "THE DISPATCHER."
WE WORK THE OLD FASHIONED WAY, VIA THE INTERNET. HE SENDS ME INFO. I TAKE CARE OF THE NAME. MONEY APPEARS IN MY VARIOUS ACCOUNTS. END OF STORY.
NOTICE
NO TRESPASSING
THE DISPATCHER IS ONE OF TWO PEOPLE WHO KNOWS I LIVE ON THE TOP FLOOR OF AN UNUSED SIX STORY OFFICE BUILDING. THE OTHER IS THE OWNER OF MY BUILDING, BUT I'VE NEVER MET HIM.
I PAY THE RENT. HE STAYS AWAY.
EVERYBODY STAYS AWAY. EVEN THE LAW.

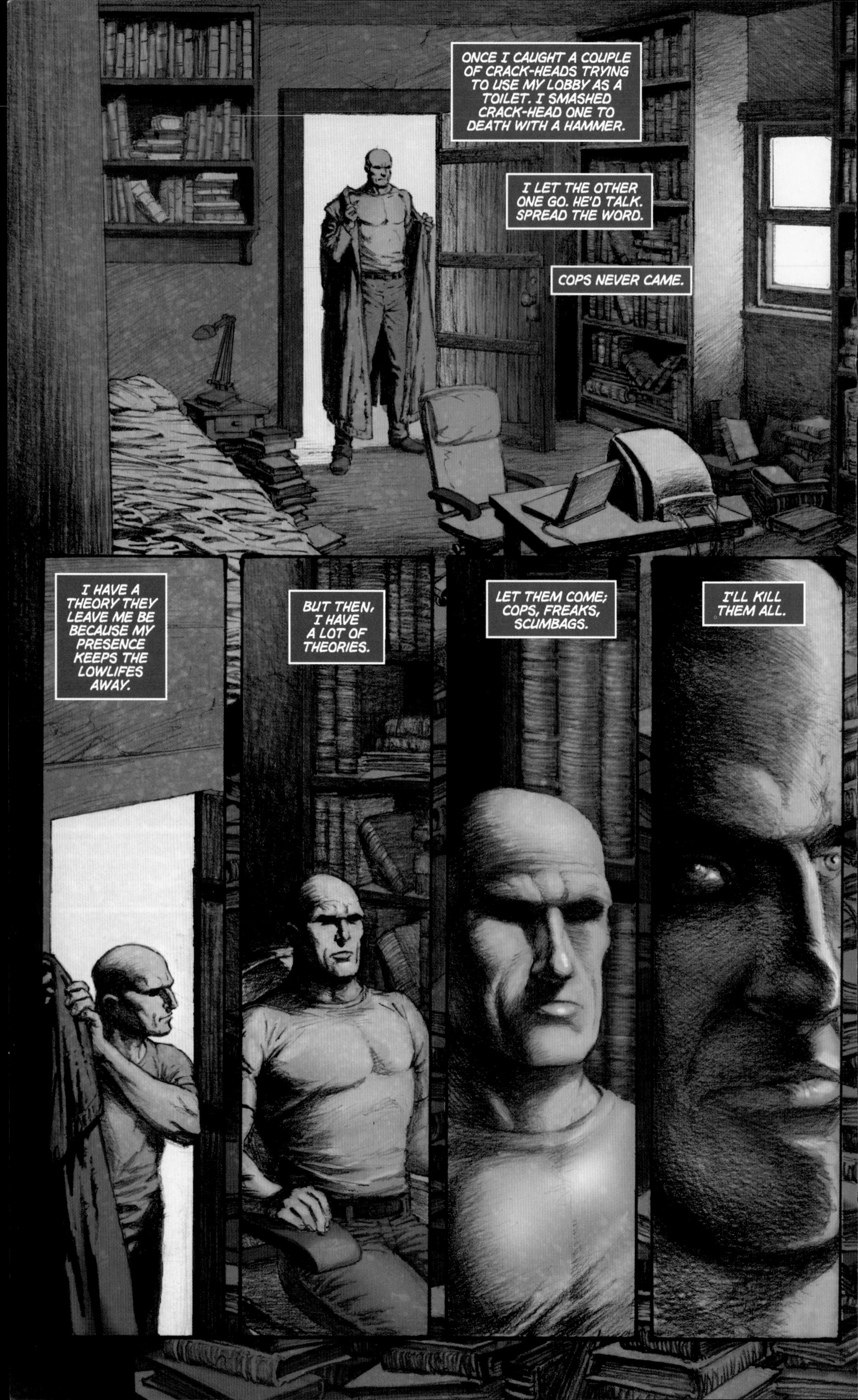
ONCE I CAUGHT A COUPLE OF CRACK-HEADS TRYING TO USE MY LOBBY AS A TOILET. I SMASHED CRACK-HEAD ONE TO DEATH WITH A HAMMER.
I LET THE OTHER ONE GO. HE'D TALK. SPREAD THE WORD.
COPS NEVER CAME.
I HAVE A THEORY THEY LEAVE ME BE BECAUSE MY PRESENCE KEEPS THE LOWLIFES AWAY.
BUT THEN, I HAVE A LOT OF THEORIES.
LET THEM COME; COPS, FREAKS, SCUMBAGS.
I'LL KILL THEM ALL.

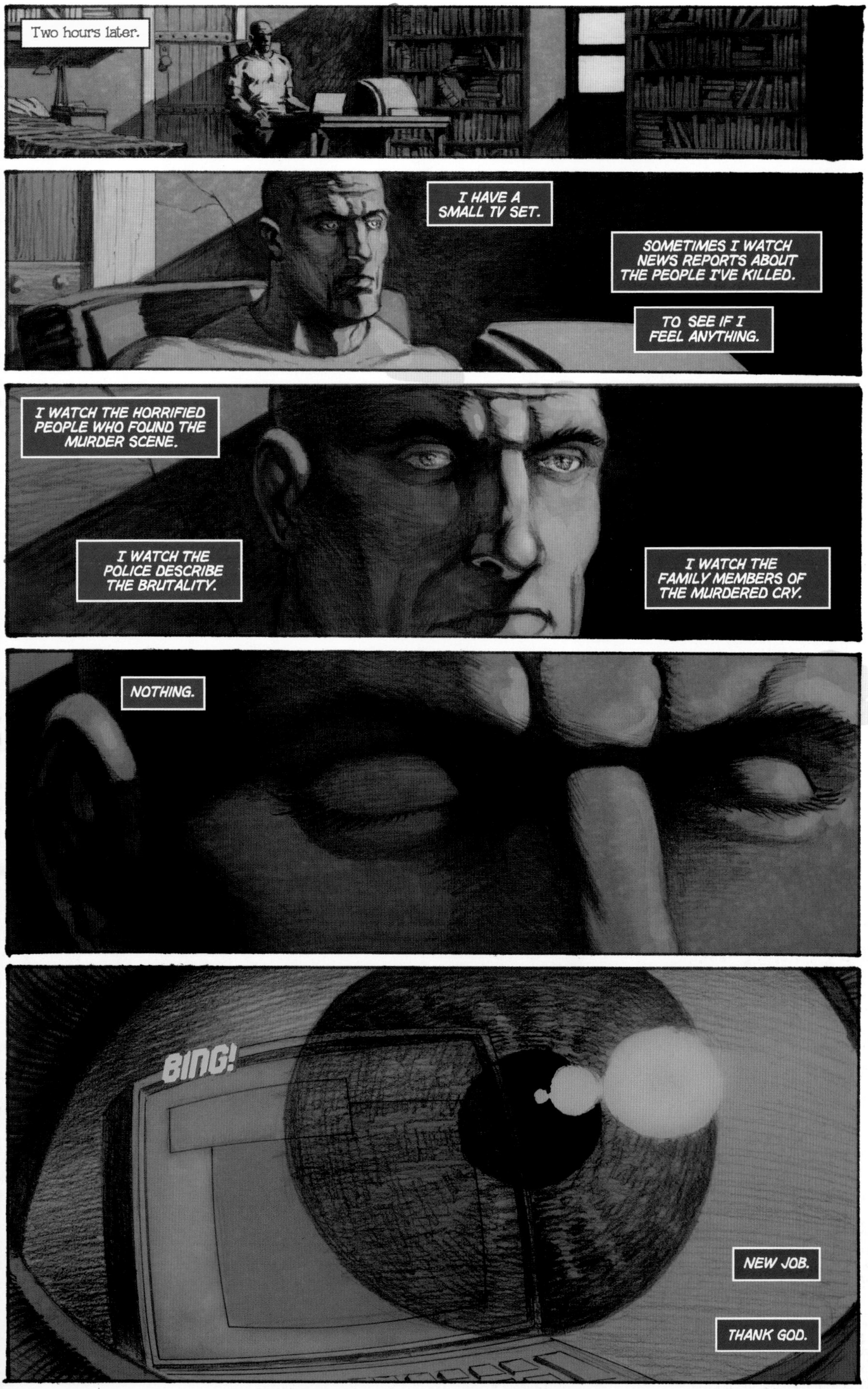
Two hours later.
I HAVE A SMALL TV SET.
SOMETIMES I WATCH NEWS REPORTS ABOUT THE PEOPLE I'VE KILLED.
TO SEE IF I FEEL ANYTHING.
I WATCH THE HORRIFIED PEOPLE WHO FOUND THE MURDER SCENE.
I WATCH THE POLICE DESCRIBE THE BRUTALITY.
I WATCH THE FAMILY MEMBERS OF THE MURDERED CRY.
NOTHING.
BING!
NEW JOB.
THANK GOD.

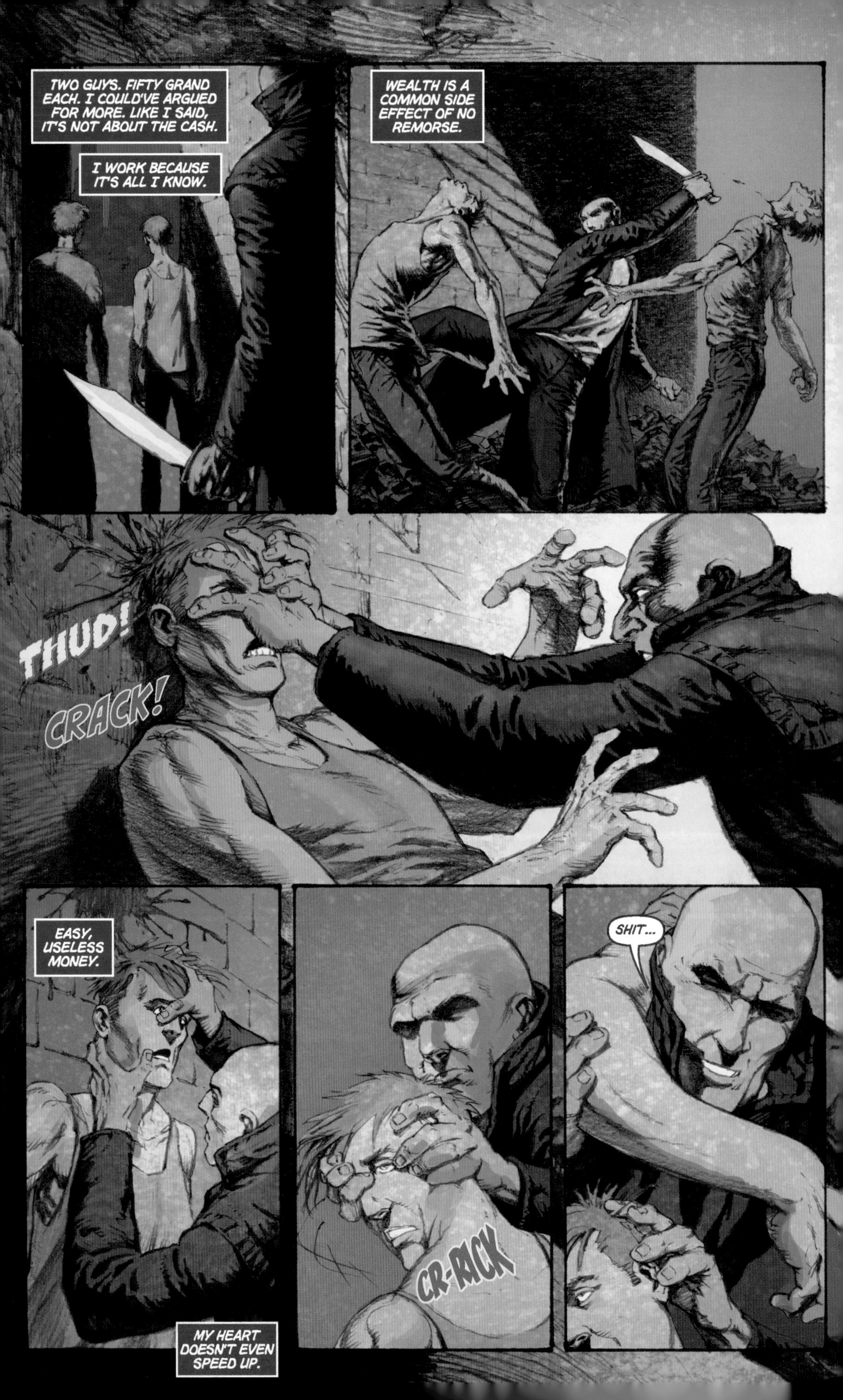
TWO GUYS. FIFTY GRAND EACH. I COULD'VE ARGUED FOR MORE. LIKE I SAID, IT'S NOT ABOUT THE CASH.
I WORK BECAUSE IT'S ALL I KNOW.
WEALTH IS A COMMON SIDE EFFECT OF NO REMORSE.
THUD!
CRACK!
EASY, USELESS MONEY.
CR-RICK
MY HEART DOESN'T EVEN SPEED UP.
SHIT...

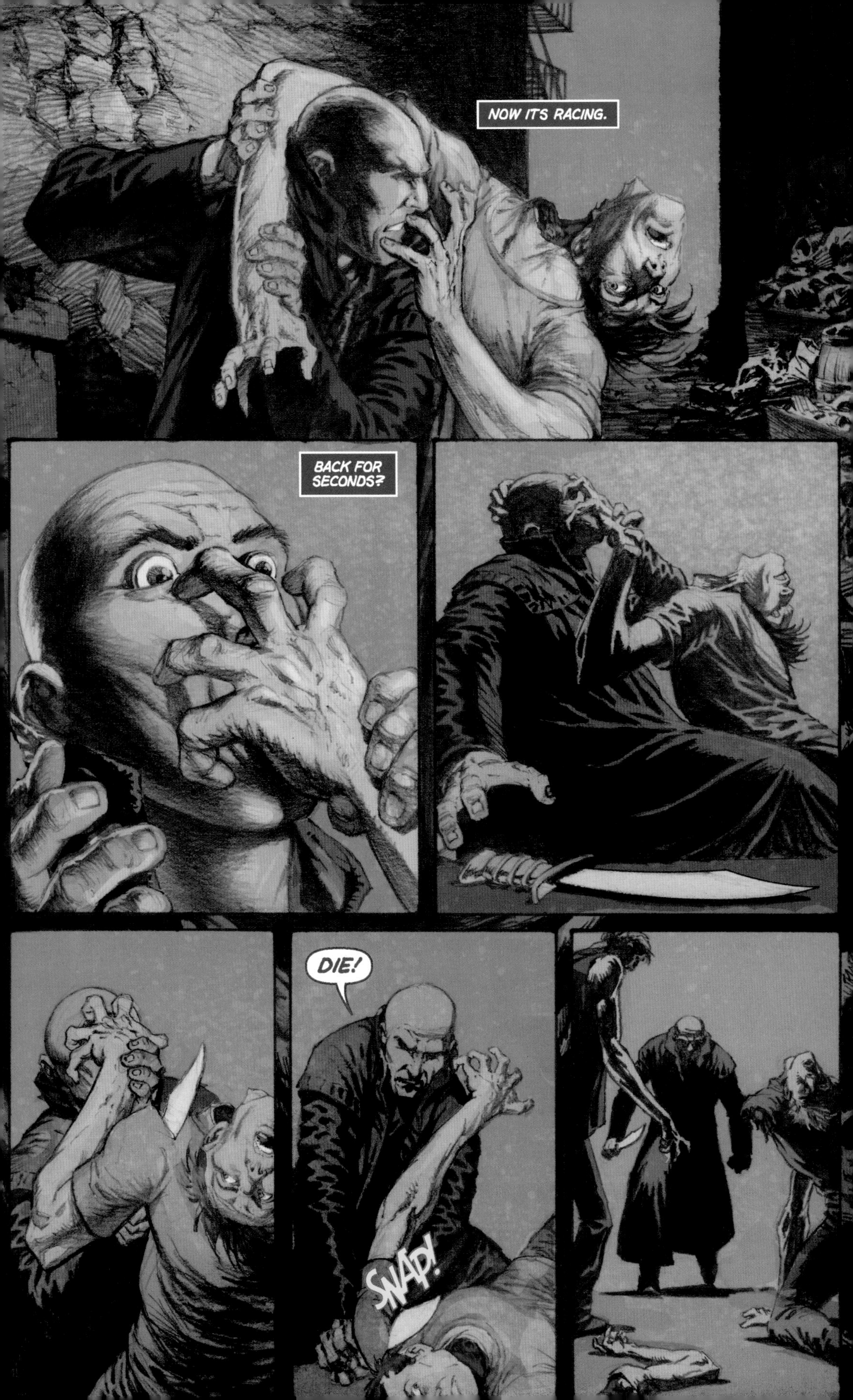
NOW IT'S RACING.
BACK FOR SECONDS?
DIE!
SNAP!

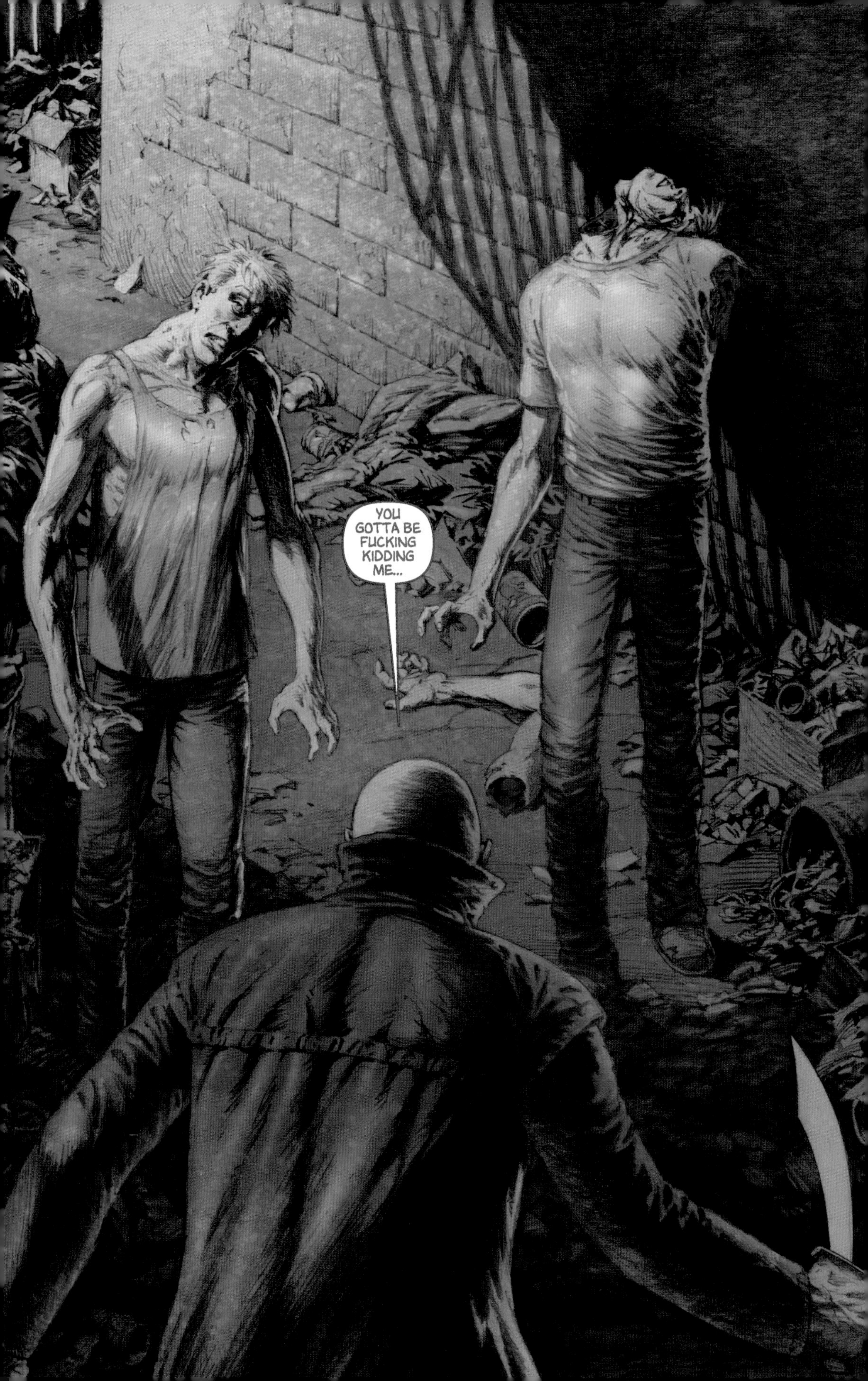
YOU GOTTA BE FUCKING KIDDING ME...

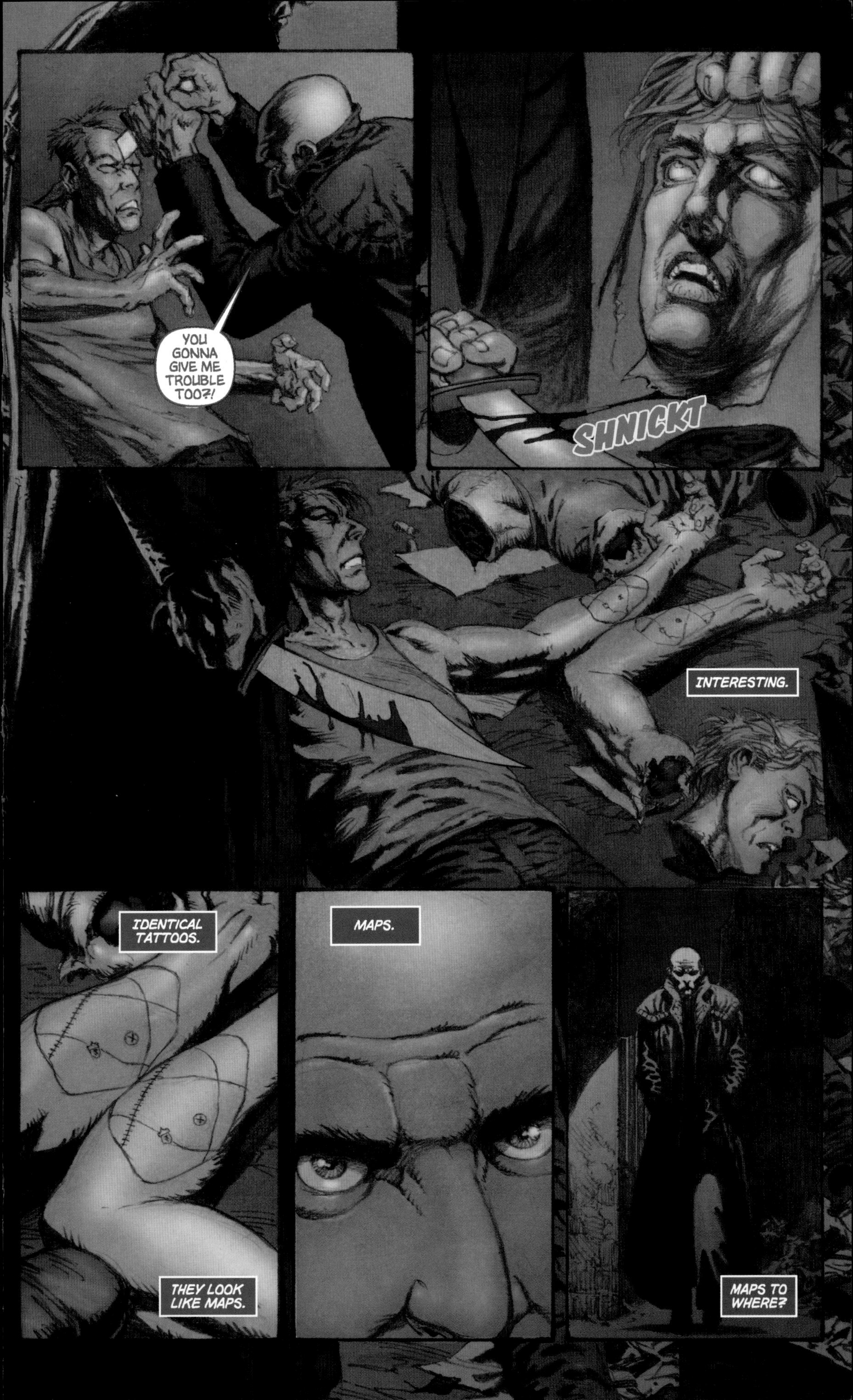
YOU GONNA GIVE ME TROUBLE TOO?!
SHNICKT
INTERESTING.
IDENTICAL TATTOOS.
THEY LOOK LIKE MAPS.
MAPS.
MAPS TO WHERE?

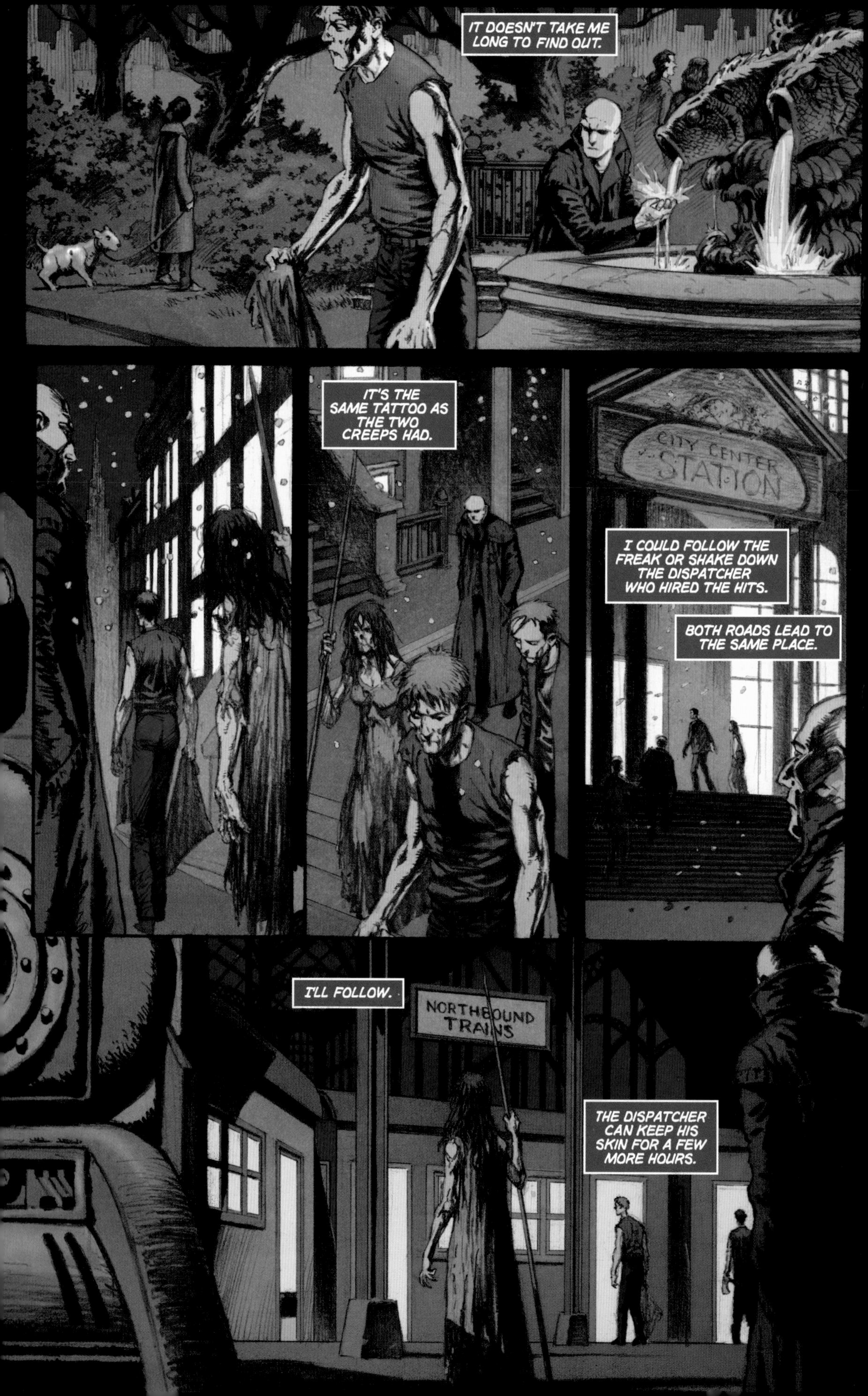
IT DOESN'T TAKE ME LONG TO FIND OUT.
IT'S THE SAME TATTOO AS THE TWO CREEPS HAD.
CITY CENTER STATION
I COULD FOLLOW THE FREAK OR SHAKE DOWN THE DISPATCHER WHO HIRED THE HITS.
BOTH ROADS LEAD TO THE SAME PLACE.
I'LL FOLLOW.
NORTHBOUND TRAINS
THE DISPATCHER CAN KEEP HIS SKIN FOR A FEW MORE HOURS.

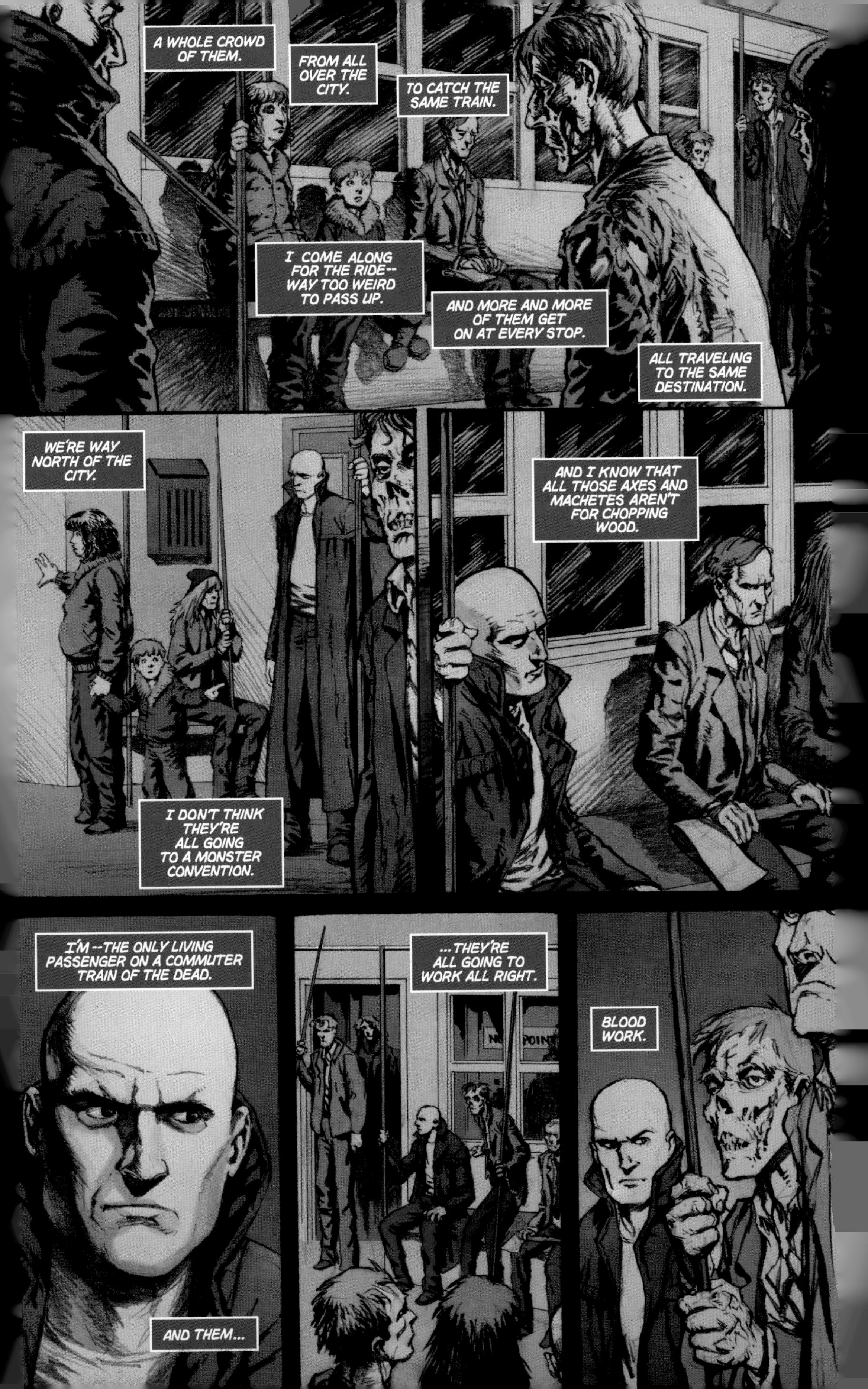
A WHOLE CROWD OF THEM.
FROM ALL OVER THE CITY.
TO CATCH THE SAME TRAIN.
I COME ALONG FOR THE RIDE-- WAY TOO WEIRD TO PASS UP.
AND MORE AND MORE OF THEM GET ON AT EVERY STOP.
ALL TRAVELING TO THE SAME DESTINATION.
WE'RE WAY NORTH OF THE CITY.
AND I KNOW THAT ALL THOSE AXES AND MACHETES AREN'T FOR CHOPPING WOOD.
I DON'T THINK THEY'RE ALL GOING TO A MONSTER CONVENTION.
I'M --THE ONLY LIVING PASSENGER ON A COMMUTER TRAIN OF THE DEAD.
AND THEM...
...THEY'RE ALL GOING TO WORK ALL RIGHT.
BLOOD WORK.

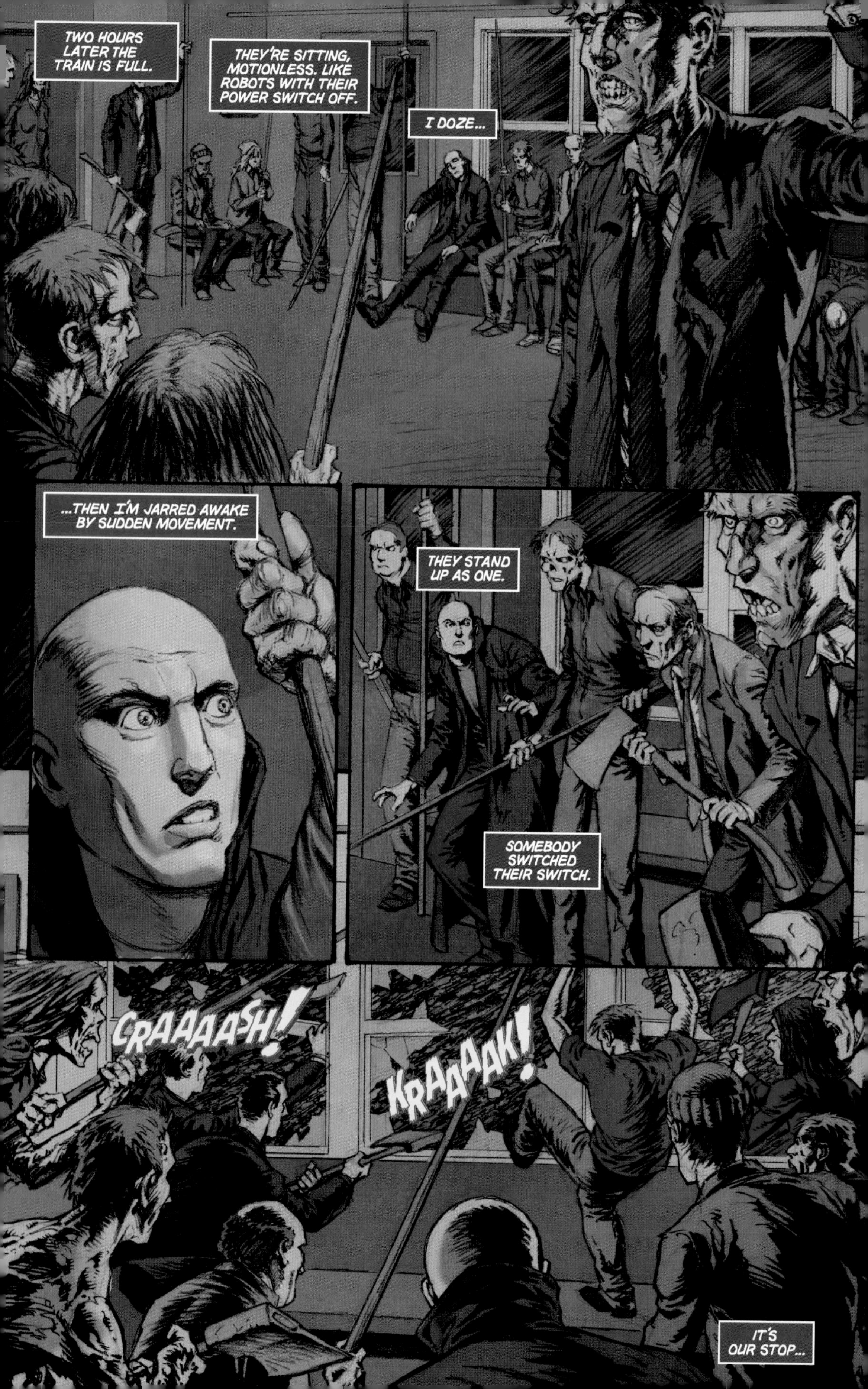
TWO HOURS LATER THE TRAIN IS FULL.
THEY'RE SITTING, MOTIONLESS. LIKE ROBOTS WITH THEIR POWER SWITCH OFF.
I DOZE...
...THEN I'M JARRED AWAKE BY SUDDEN MOVEMENT.
THEY STAND UP AS ONE.
SOMEBODY SWITCHED THEIR SWITCH.
CRAAAASH!
KRAAAAK!
IT'S OUR STOP...

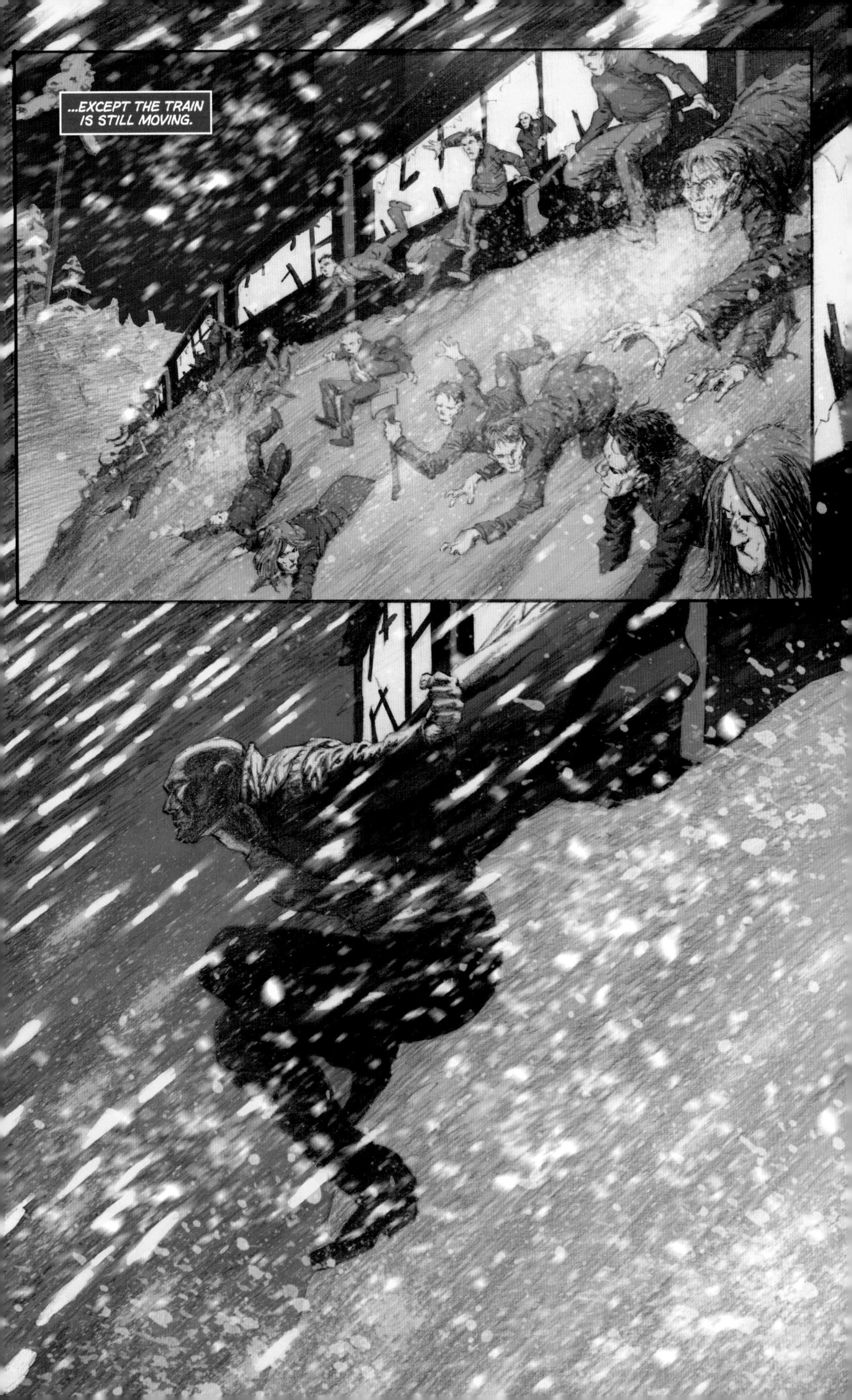
...EXCEPT THE TRAIN IS STILL MOVING.

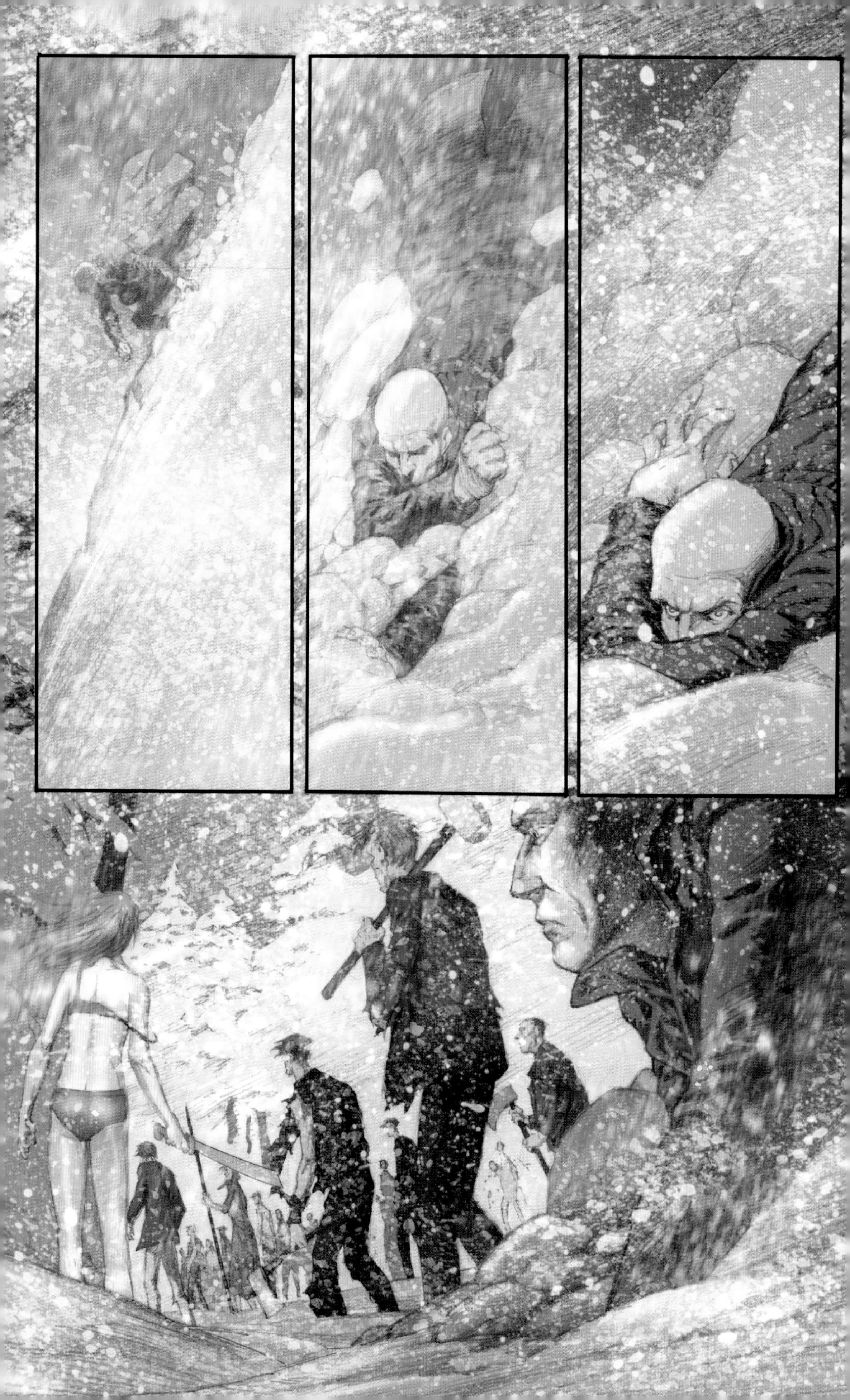

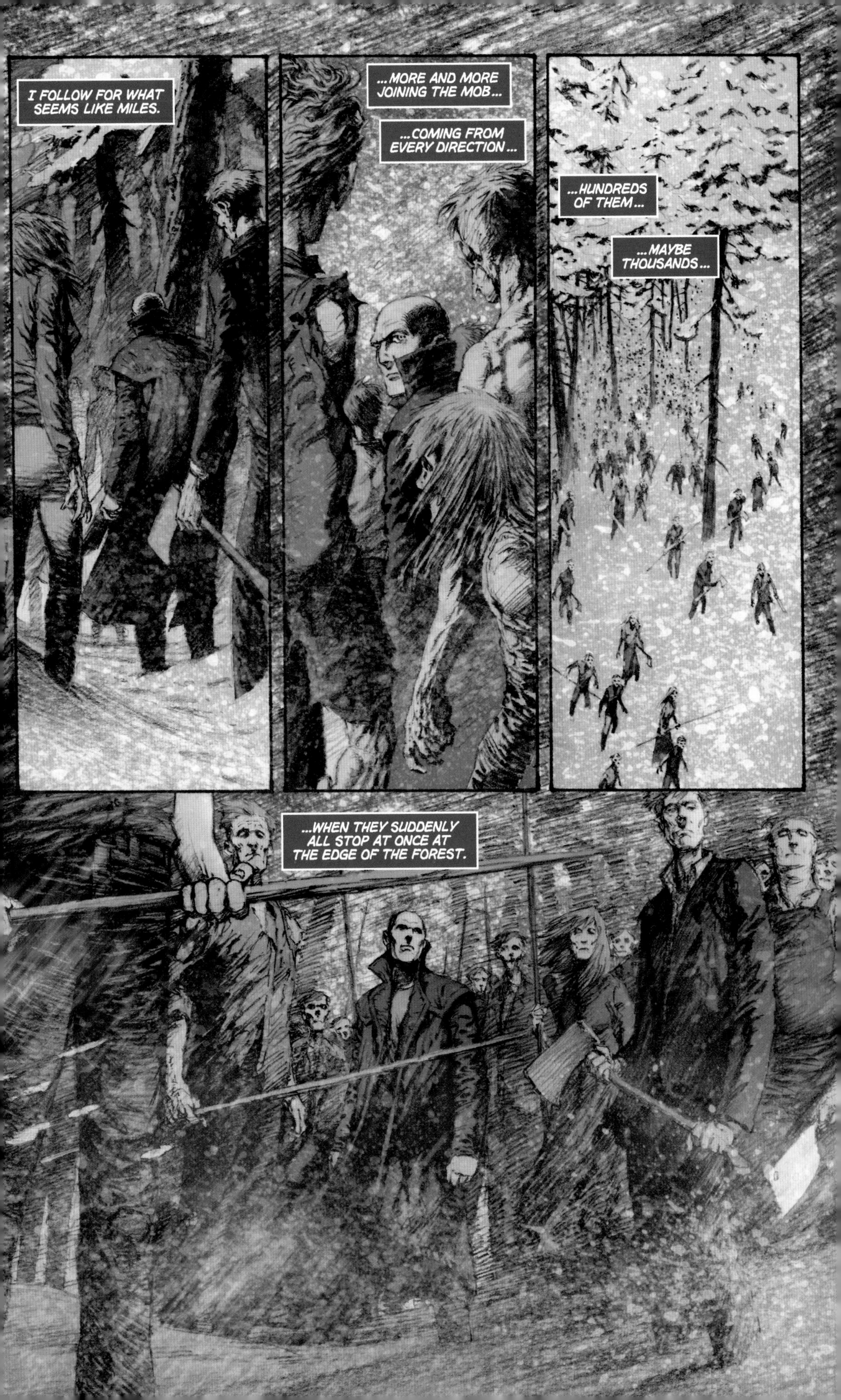
I FOLLOW FOR WHAT SEEMS LIKE MILES.
...MORE AND MORE JOINING THE MOB...
...COMING FROM EVERY DIRECTION...
...HUNDREDS OF THEM...
...MAYBE THOUSANDS...
...WHEN THEY SUDDENLY ALL STOP AT ONCE AT THE EDGE OF THE FOREST.

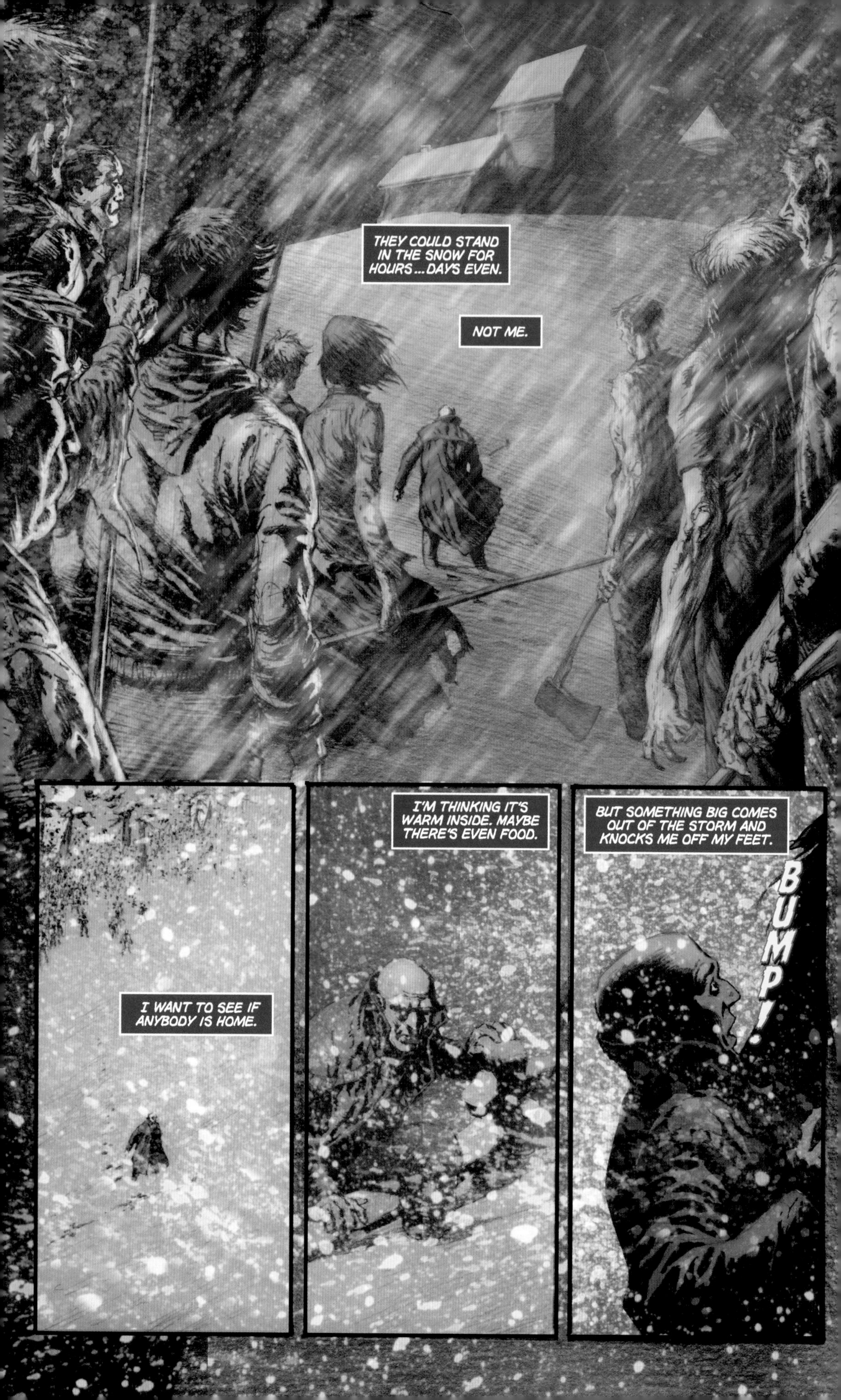
THEY COULD STAND IN THE SNOW FOR HOURS...DAYS EVEN.
NOT ME.
I WANT TO SEE IF ANYBODY IS HOME.
I'M THINKING IT'S WARM INSIDE. MAYBE THERE'S EVEN FOOD.
BUT SOMETHING BIG COMES OUT OF THE STORM AND KNOCKS ME OFF MY FEET.
BUMP!

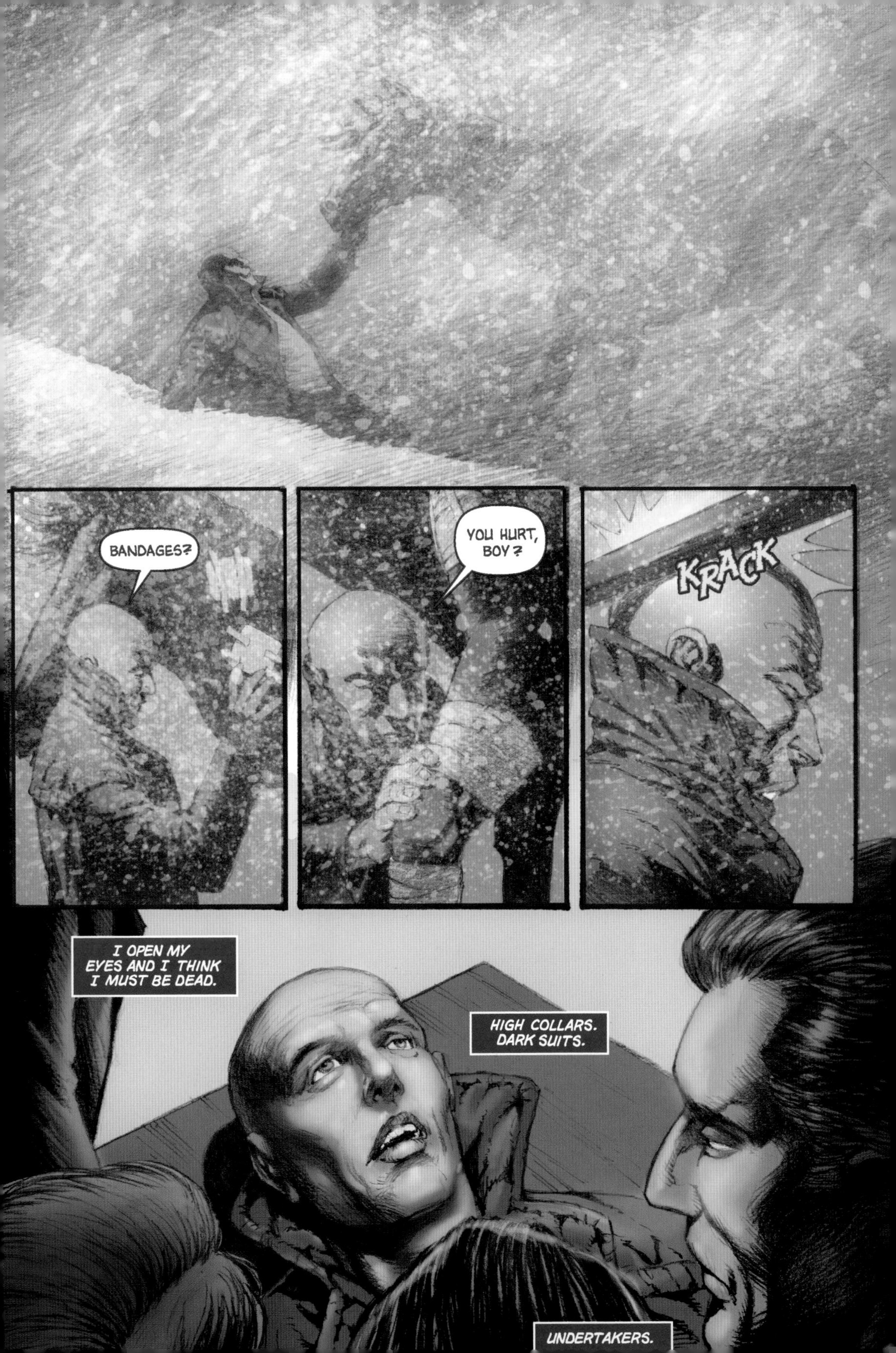
BANDAGES?
YOU HURT, BOY?
KRACK
I OPEN MY EYES AND I THINK I MUST BE DEAD.
HIGH COLLARS. DARK SUITS.
UNDERTAKERS.

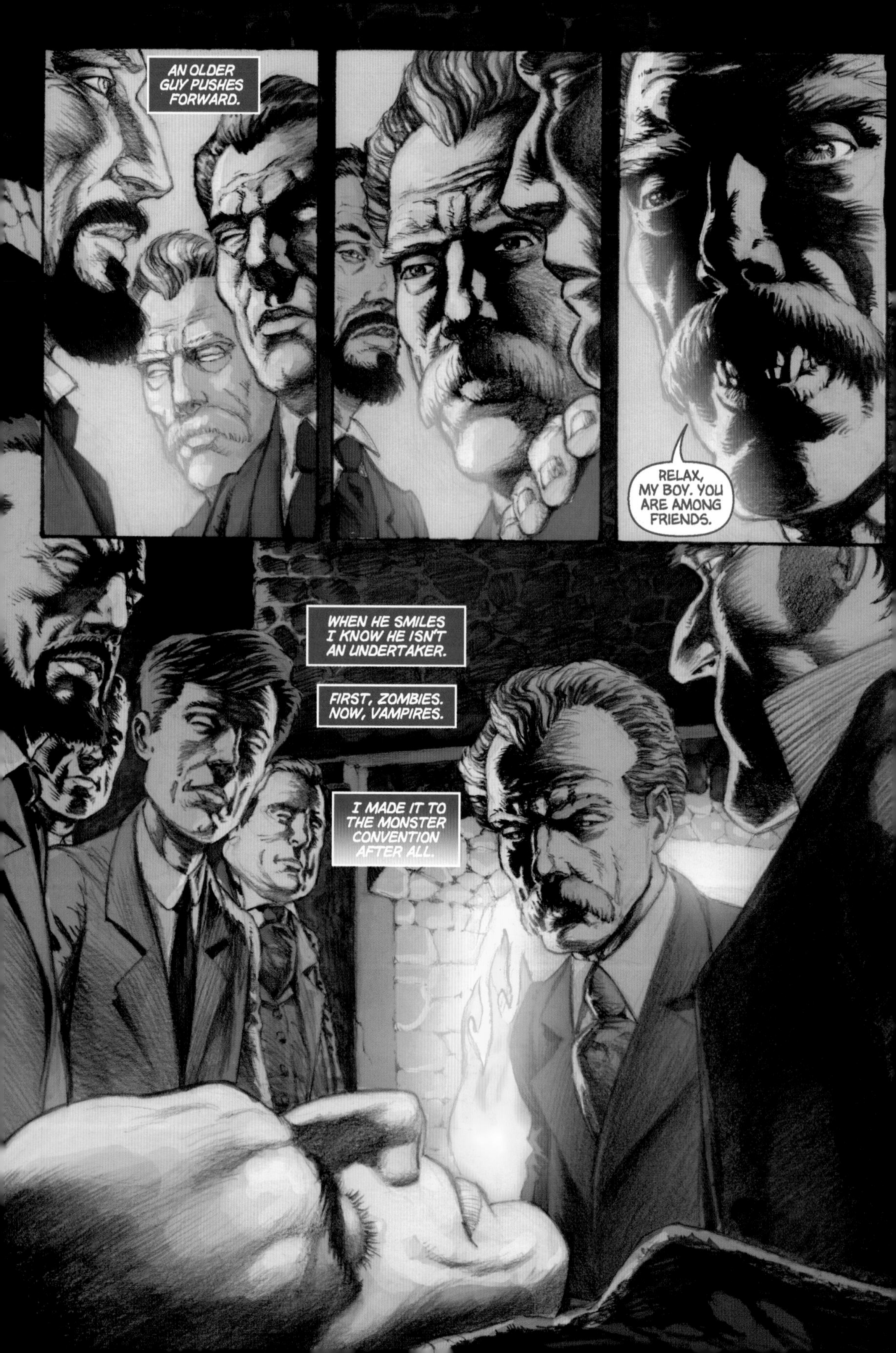
AN OLDER GUY PUSHES FORWARD.
RELAX, MY BOY. YOU ARE AMONG FRIENDS.
WHEN HE SMILES I KNOW HE ISN'T AN UNDERTAKER.
FIRST, ZOMBIES. NOW, VAMPIRES.
I MADE IT TO THE MONSTER CONVENTION AFTER ALL.

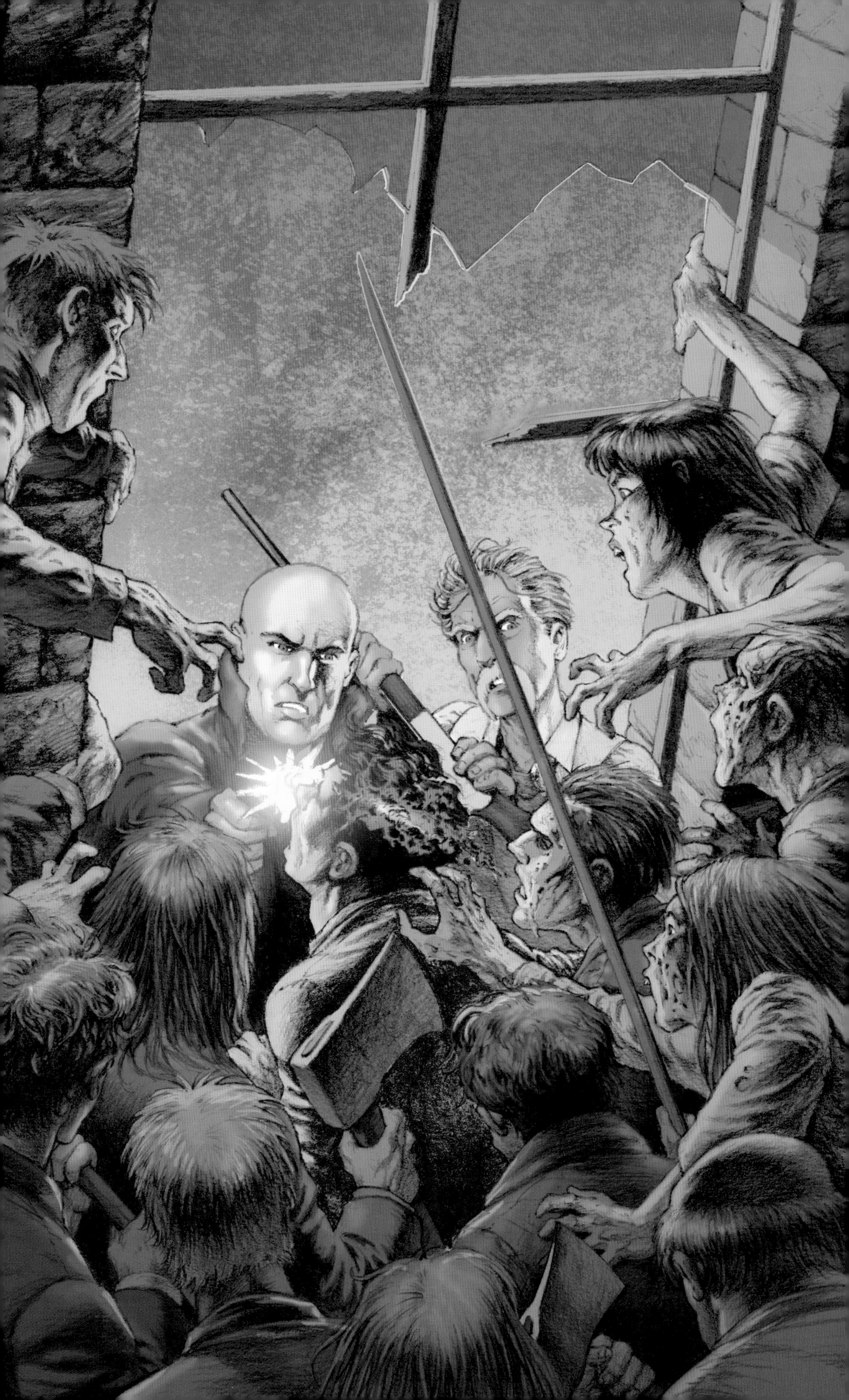

TWO CHAPTER

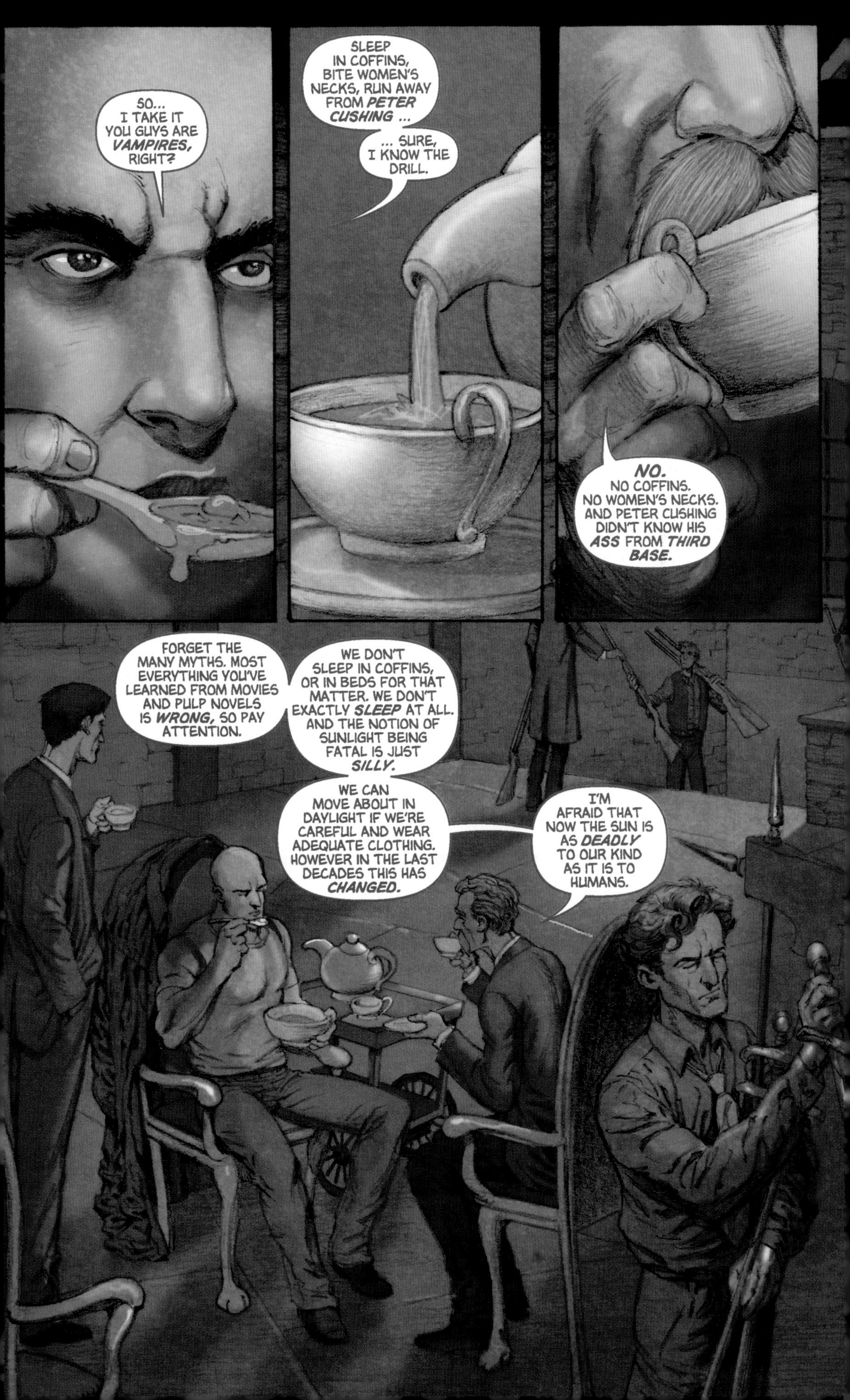
SO... I TAKE IT YOU GUYS ARE VAMPIRES, RIGHT?
SLEEP IN COFFINS, BITE WOMEN'S NECKS, RUN AWAY FROM PETER CUSHING ...
... SURE, I KNOW THE DRILL.
NO. NO COFFINS. NO WOMEN'S NECKS. AND PETER CUSHING DIDN'T KNOW HIS ASS FROM THIRD BASE.
FORGET THE MANY MYTHS. MOST EVERYTHING YOU'VE LEARNED FROM MOVIES AND PULP NOVELS IS WRONG, SO PAY ATTENTION.
WE DON'T SLEEP IN COFFINS, OR IN BEDS FOR THAT MATTER. WE DON'T EXACTLY SLEEP AT ALL. AND THE NOTION OF SUNLIGHT BEING FATAL IS JUST SILLY.
WE CAN MOVE ABOUT IN DAYLIGHT IF WE'RE CAREFUL AND WEAR ADEQUATE CLOTHING. HOWEVER IN THE LAST DECADES THIS HAS CHANGED.
I'M AFRAID THAT NOW THE SUN IS AS DEADLY TO OUR KIND AS IT IS TO HUMANS.

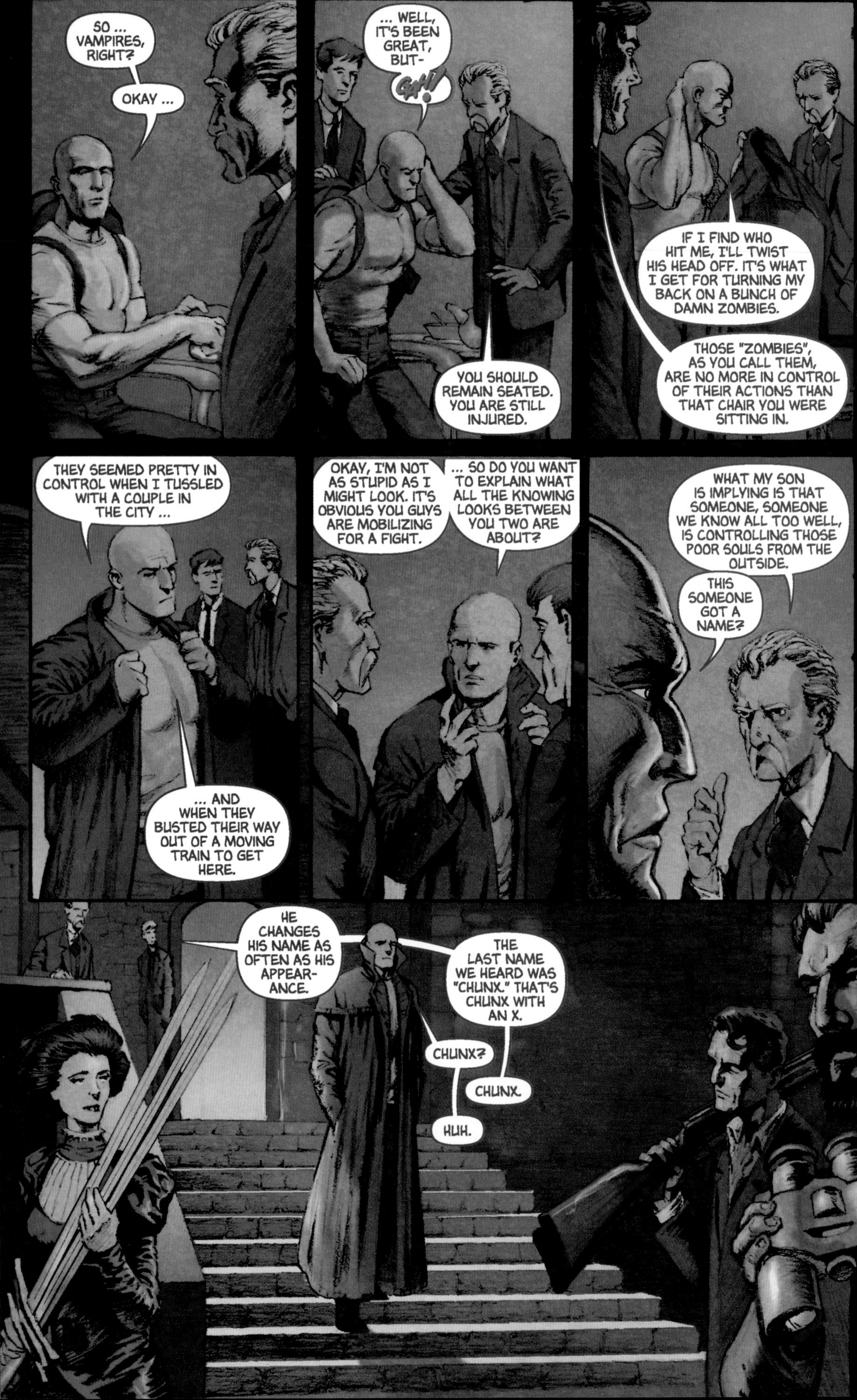
SO ... VAMPIRES, RIGHT?
OKAY ...
... WELL, IT'S BEEN GREAT, BUT-
GAH!
YOU SHOULD REMAIN SEATED. YOU ARE STILL INJURED.
IF I FIND WHO HIT ME, I'LL TWIST HIS HEAD OFF. IT'S WHAT I GET FOR TURNING MY BACK ON A BUNCH OF DAMN ZOMBIES.
THOSE "ZOMBIES", AS YOU CALL THEM, ARE NO MORE IN CONTROL OF THEIR ACTIONS THAN THAT CHAIR YOU WERE SITTING IN.
THEY SEEMED PRETTY IN CONTROL WHEN I TUSSLED WITH A COUPLE IN THE CITY ...
... AND WHEN THEY BUSTED THEIR WAY OUT OF A MOVING TRAIN TO GET HERE.
OKAY, I'M NOT AS STUPID AS I MIGHT LOOK. IT'S OBVIOUS YOU GUYS ARE MOBILIZING FOR A FIGHT.
... SO DO YOU WANT TO EXPLAIN WHAT ALL THE KNOWING LOOKS BETWEEN YOU TWO ARE ABOUT?
WHAT MY SON IS IMPLYING IS THAT SOMEONE, SOMEONE WE KNOW ALL TOO WELL, IS CONTROLLING THOSE POOR SOULS FROM THE OUTSIDE.
THIS SOMEONE GOT A NAME?
HE CHANGES HIS NAME AS OFTEN AS HIS APPEAR-ANCE.
THE LAST NAME WE HEARD WAS "CHUNX." THAT'S CHUNX WITH AN X.
CHUNX?
CHUNX.
HUH.

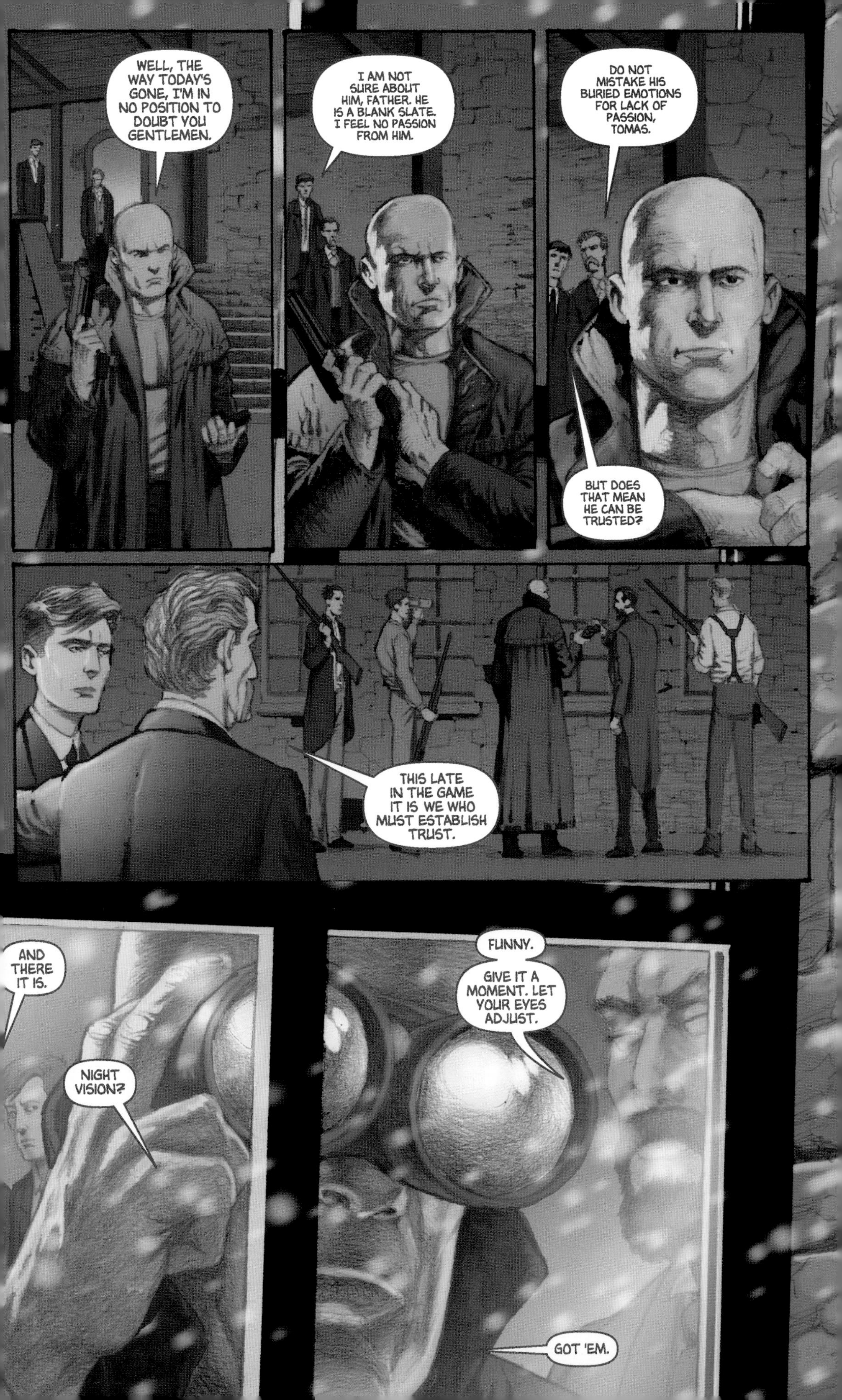
WELL, THE WAY TODAY'S GONE, I'M IN NO POSITION TO DOUBT YOU GENTLEMEN.
I AM NOT SURE ABOUT HIM, FATHER. HE IS A BLANK SLATE. I FEEL NO PASSION FROM HIM.
DO NOT MISTAKE HIS BURIED EMOTIONS FOR LACK OF PASSION, TOMAS.
BUT DOES THAT MEAN HE CAN BE TRUSTED?
THIS LATE IN THE GAME IT IS WE WHO MUST ESTABLISH TRUST.
AND THERE IT IS.
NIGHT VISION?
FUNNY.
GIVE IT A MOMENT. LET YOUR EYES ADJUST.
GOT 'EM.

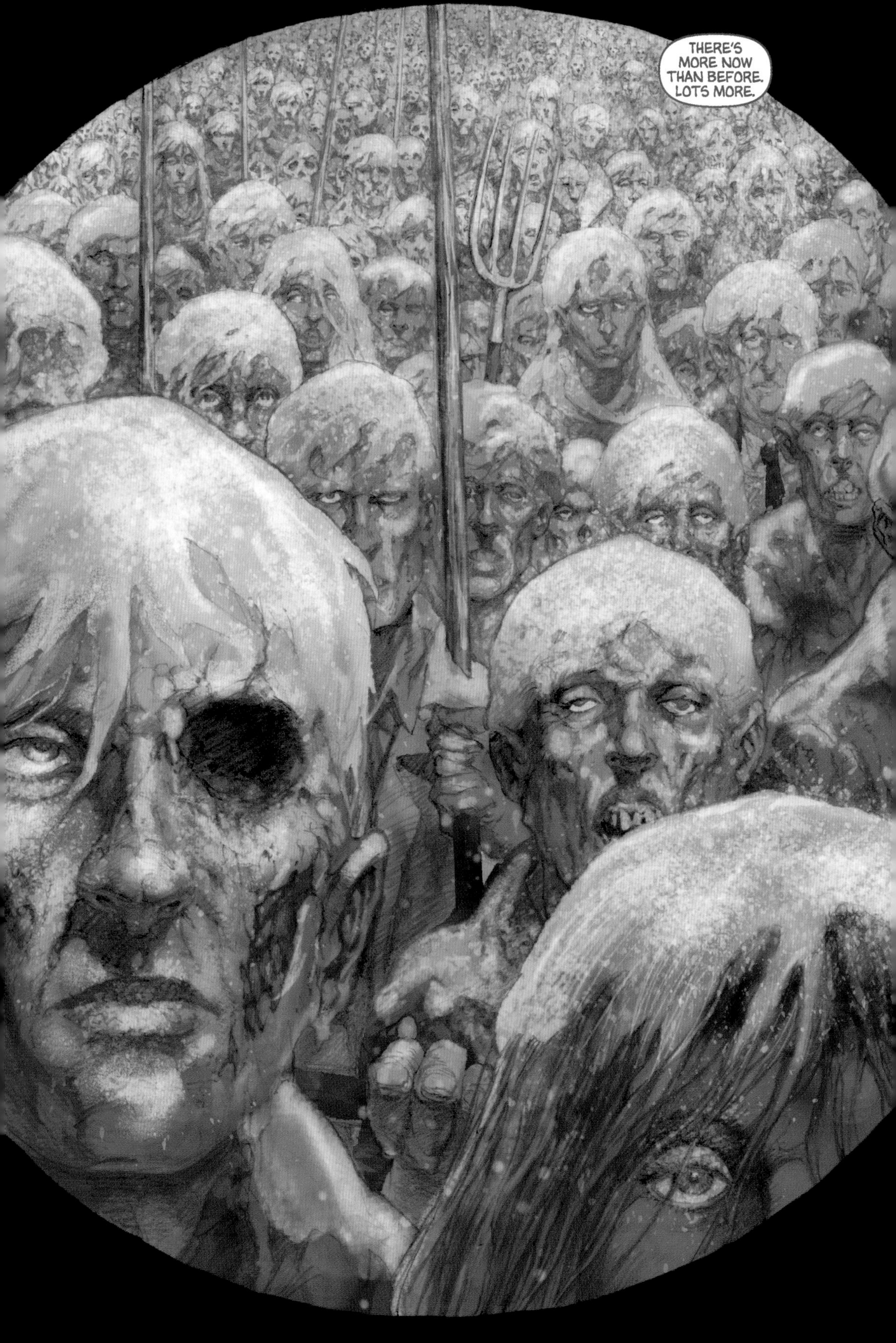
THERE'S MORE NOW THAN BEFORE. LOTS MORE.

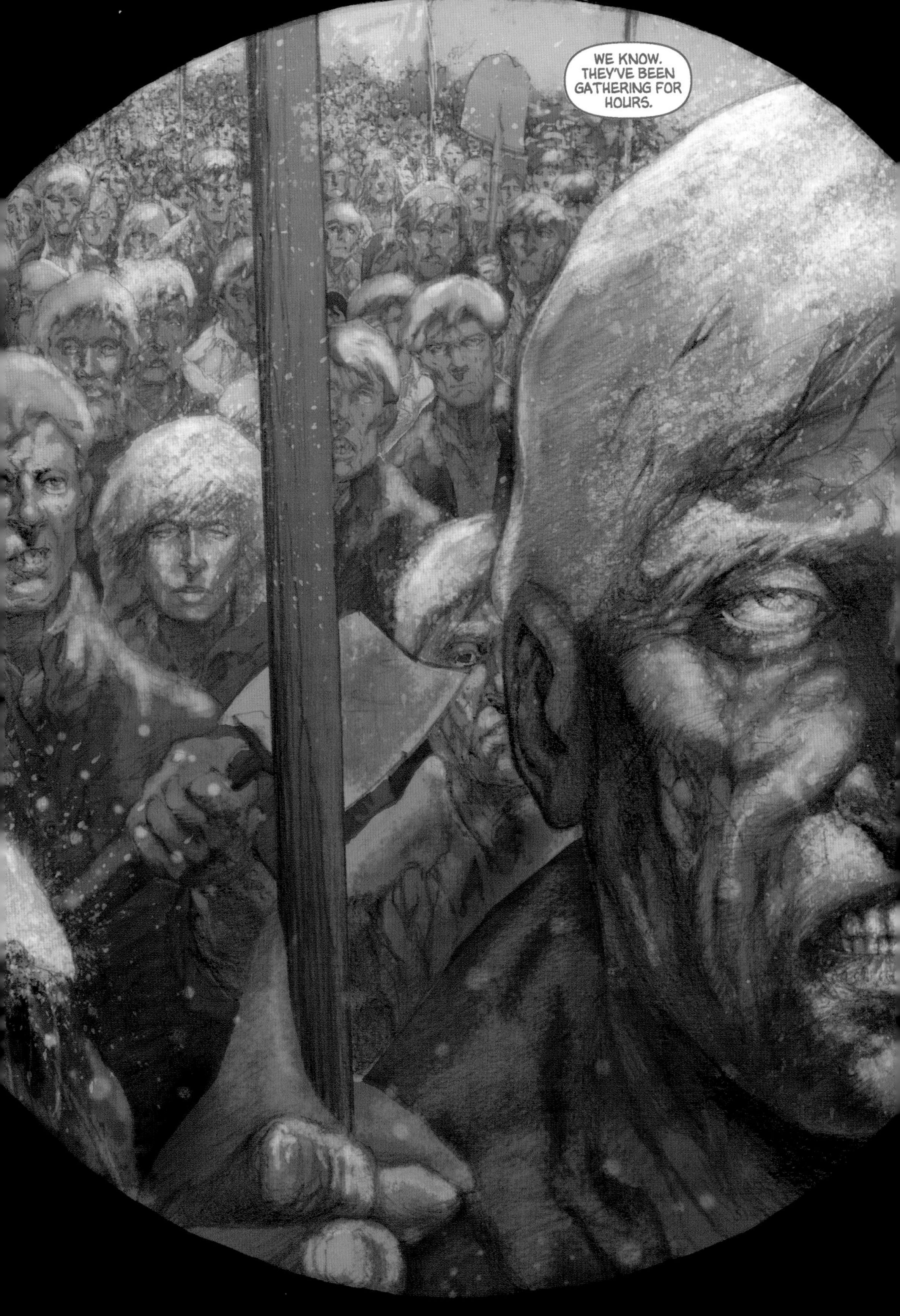
WE KNOW. THEY'VE BEEN GATHERING FOR HOURS.

HOW MUCH TIME, BUTCH?

A MINUTE TO GO. UH, I WAS WONDERIN', BOSS, WHEN YOU WERE PLANNIN' TO, UH ...

... I MEAN ...ME AND GARY WORKED OUR BUTTS OFF, IMPLANTING THOSE MICROCHIPS INTO ALL THOSE STIFFS.

YEAH. FOR A MONTH, UP TO OUR ELBOWS IN GORE AND ...

AH, YES, GENTLEMEN. ALL THOSE TINY COMPUTERS IN SO MANY DEAD SKULLS.

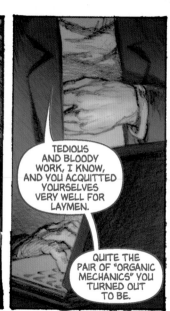

TEDIOUS AND BLOODY WORK, I KNOW, AND YOU ACQUITTED YOURSELVES VERY WELL FOR LAYMEN.

QUITE THE PAIR OF "ORGANIC MECHANICS" YOU TURNED OUT TO BE.

NOW, I DARESAY YOU ARE IMPATIENT FOR RECOMPENSE.

NAW, BOSS. WE JUST WANNA GET PAID.

PAYMENT IN FULL, GENTLEMEN.

POW! POW!

FIRST YOU, THE NEW DEBTS ...

... AND NOW THE OLD.

PROGRAM EXECUTE

CLIK!

THEY'RE MOVING.

MUST BE MIDNIGHT.

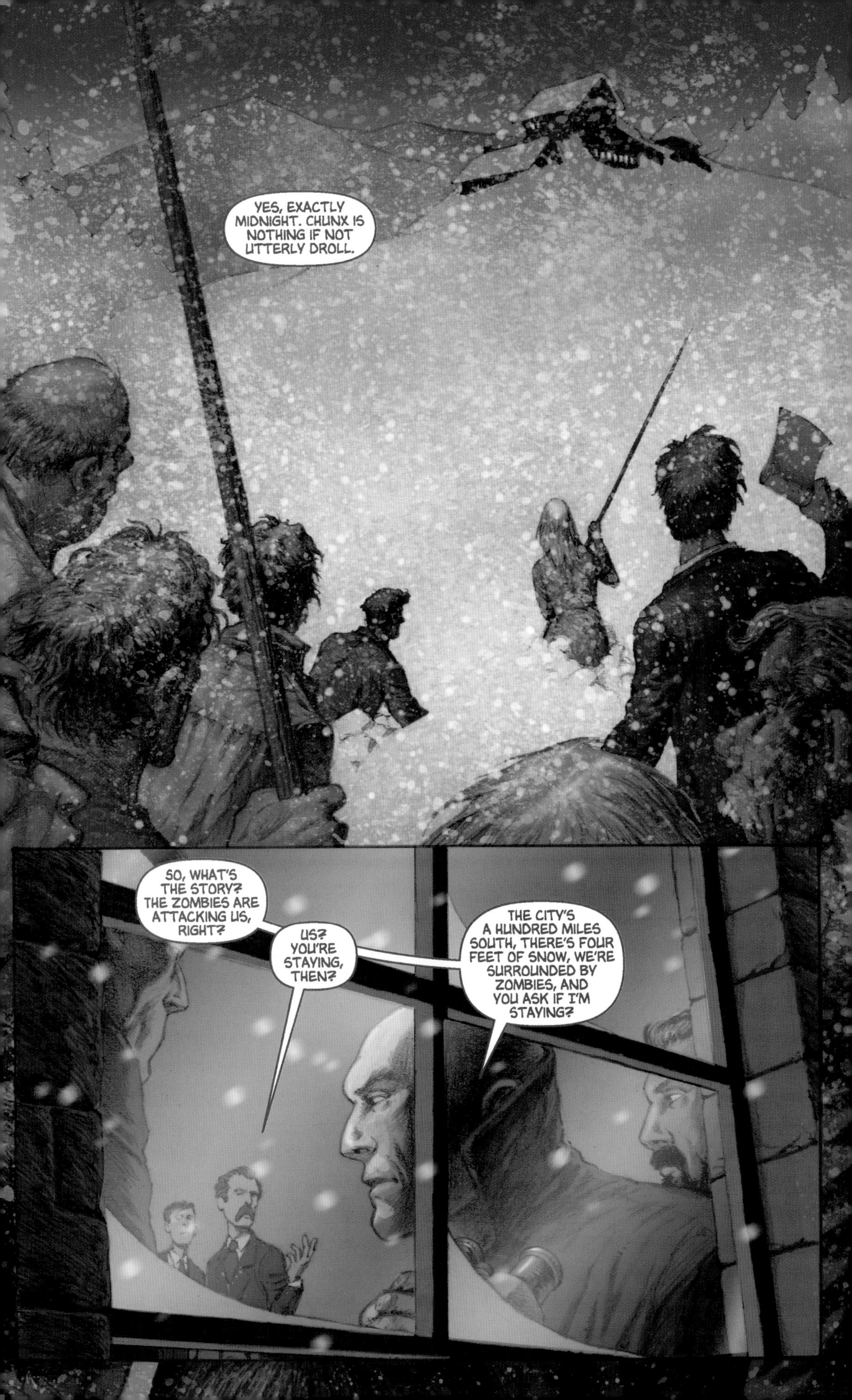
YES, EXACTLY MIDNIGHT. CHUNX IS NOTHING IF NOT UTTERLY DROLL.
SO, WHAT'S THE STORY? THE ZOMBIES ARE ATTACKING US, RIGHT?
US? YOU'RE STAYING, THEN?
THE CITY'S A HUNDRED MILES SOUTH, THERE'S FOUR FEET OF SNOW, WE'RE SURROUNDED BY ZOMBIES, AND YOU ASK IF I'M STAYING?

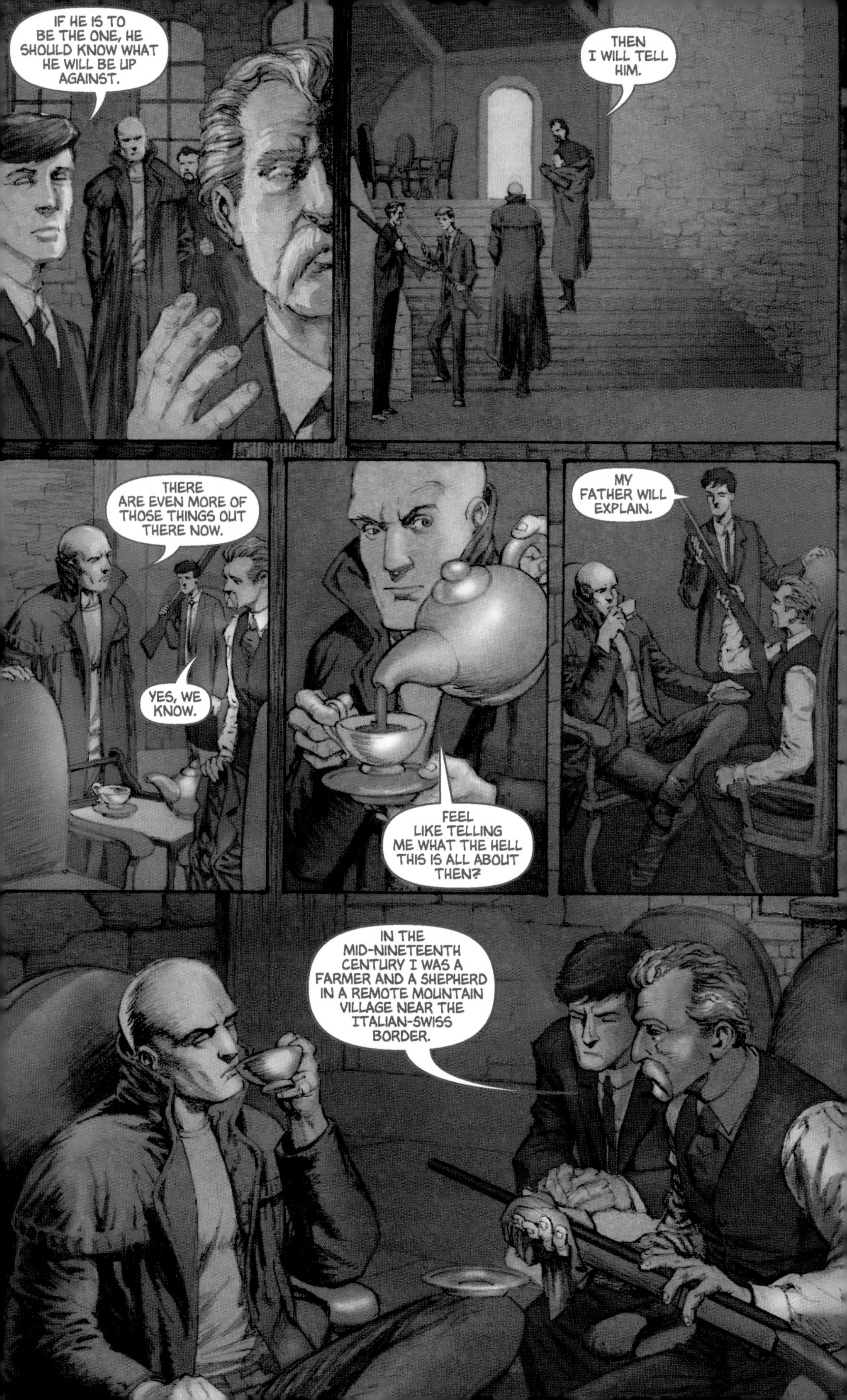
IF HE IS TO BE THE ONE, HE SHOULD KNOW WHAT HE WILL BE UP AGAINST.
THEN I WILL TELL HIM.
THERE ARE EVEN MORE OF THOSE THINGS OUT THERE NOW.
YES, WE KNOW.
FEEL LIKE TELLING ME WHAT THE HELL THIS IS ALL ABOUT THEN?
MY FATHER WILL EXPLAIN.
IN THE MID-NINETEENTH CENTURY I WAS A FARMER AND A SHEPHERD IN A REMOTE MOUNTAIN VILLAGE NEAR THE ITALIAN-SWISS BORDER.

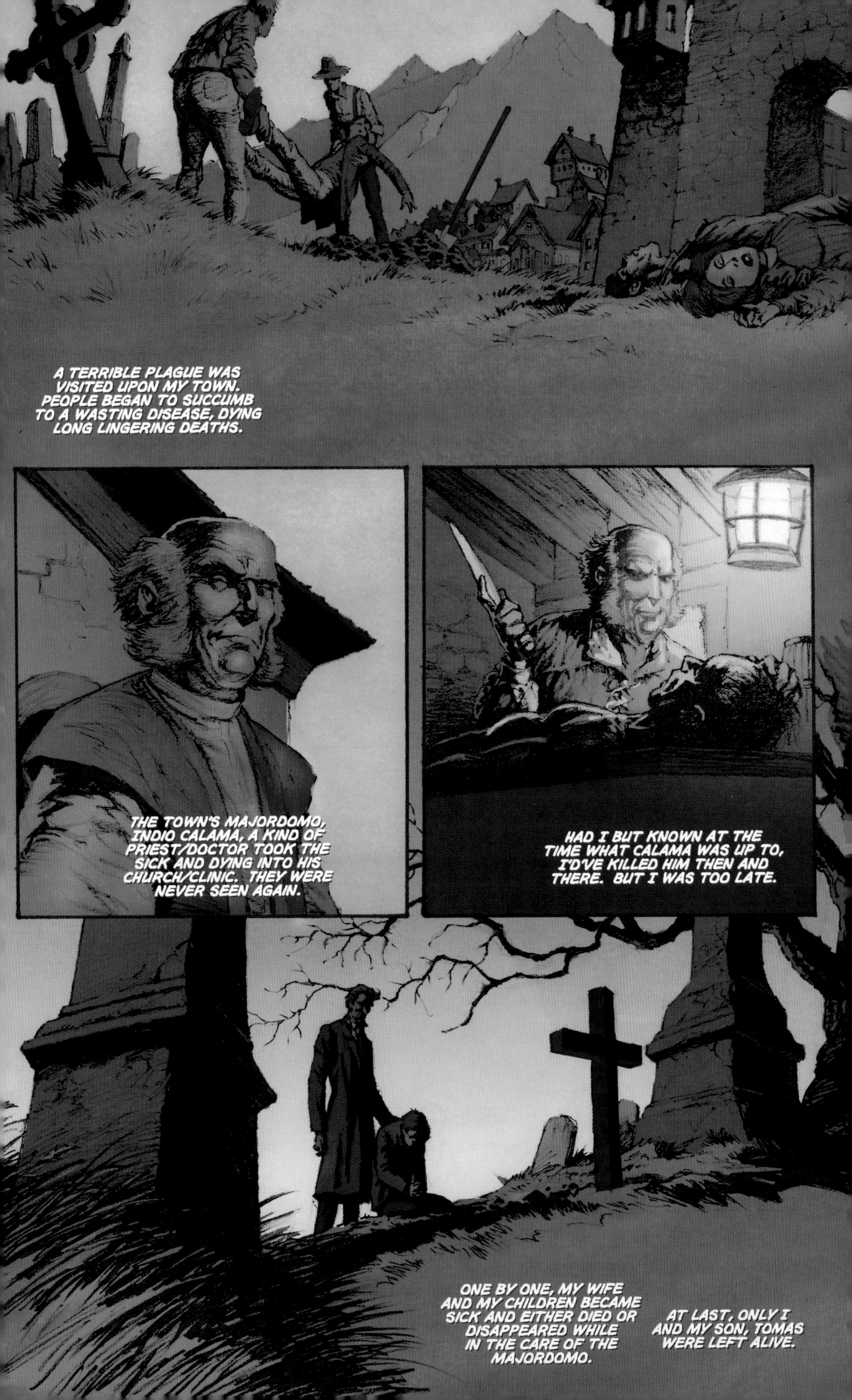

A TERRIBLE PLAGUE WAS VISITED UPON MY TOWN. PEOPLE BEGAN TO SUCCUMB TO A WASTING DISEASE, DYING LONG LINGERING DEATHS.
THE TOWN'S MAJORDOMO, INDIO CALAMA, A KIND OF PRIEST/DOCTOR TOOK THE SICK AND DYING INTO HIS CHURCH/CLINIC. THEY WERE NEVER SEEN AGAIN.
HAD I BUT KNOWN AT THE TIME WHAT CALAMA WAS UP TO, I'D'VE KILLED HIM THEN AND THERE. BUT I WAS TOO LATE.
ONE BY ONE, MY WIFE AND MY CHILDREN BECAME SICK AND EITHER DIED OR DISAPPEARED WHILE IN THE CARE OF THE MAJORDOMO.
AT LAST, ONLY I AND MY SON, TOMAS WERE LEFT ALIVE.

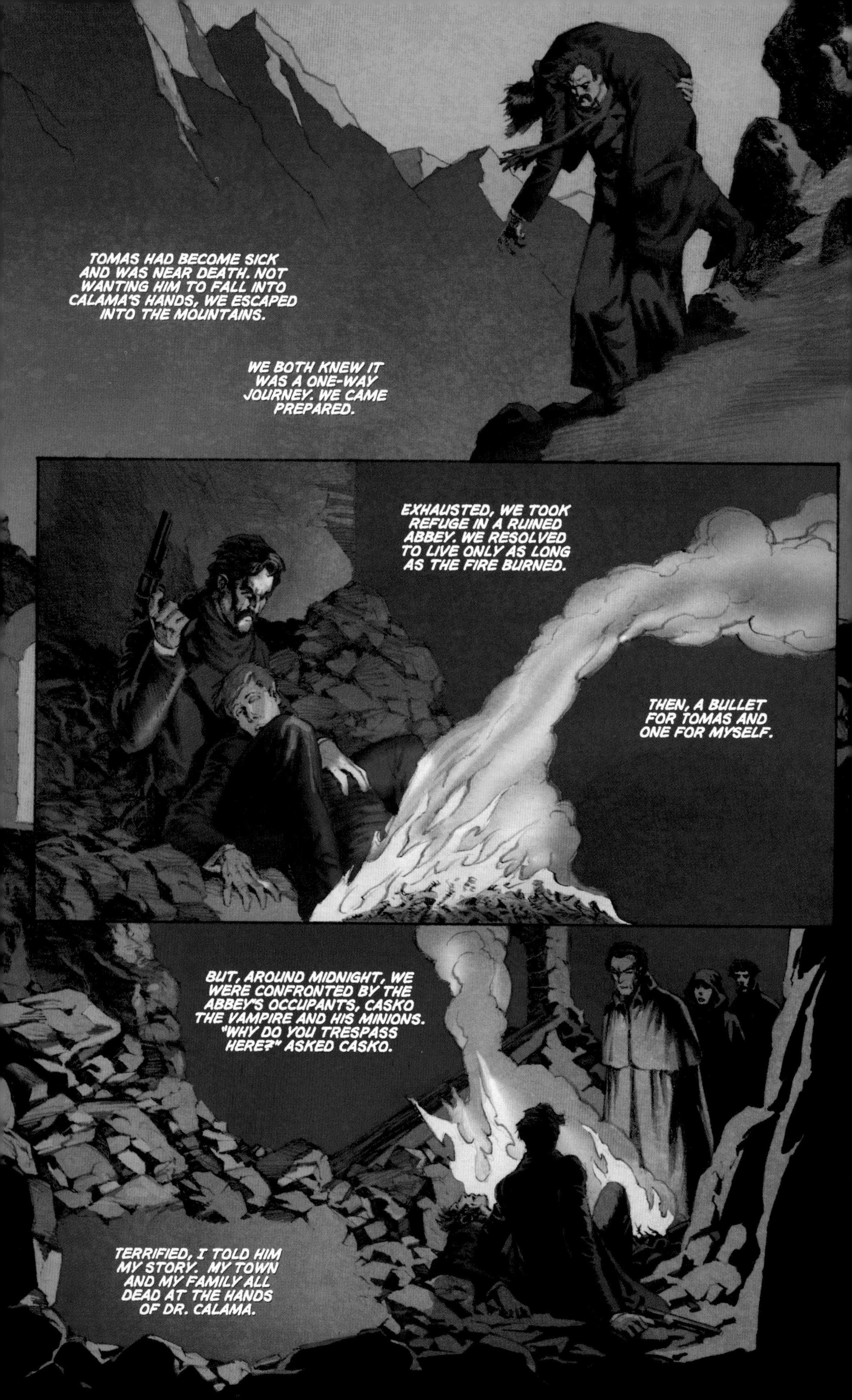
TOMAS HAD BECOME SICK AND WAS NEAR DEATH. NOT WANTING HIM TO FALL INTO CALAMA'S HANDS, WE ESCAPED INTO THE MOUNTAINS.
WE BOTH KNEW IT WAS A ONE-WAY JOURNEY. WE CAME PREPARED.
EXHAUSTED, WE TOOK REFUGE IN A RUINED ABBEY. WE RESOLVED TO LIVE ONLY AS LONG AS THE FIRE BURNED.
THEN, A BULLET FOR TOMAS AND ONE FOR MYSELF.
BUT, AROUND MIDNIGHT, WE WERE CONFRONTED BY THE ABBEY'S OCCUPANTS, CASKO THE VAMPIRE AND HIS MINIONS. "WHY DO YOU TRESPASS HERE?" ASKED CASKO.
TERRIFIED, I TOLD HIM MY STORY. MY TOWN AND MY FAMILY ALL DEAD AT THE HANDS OF DR. CALAMA.

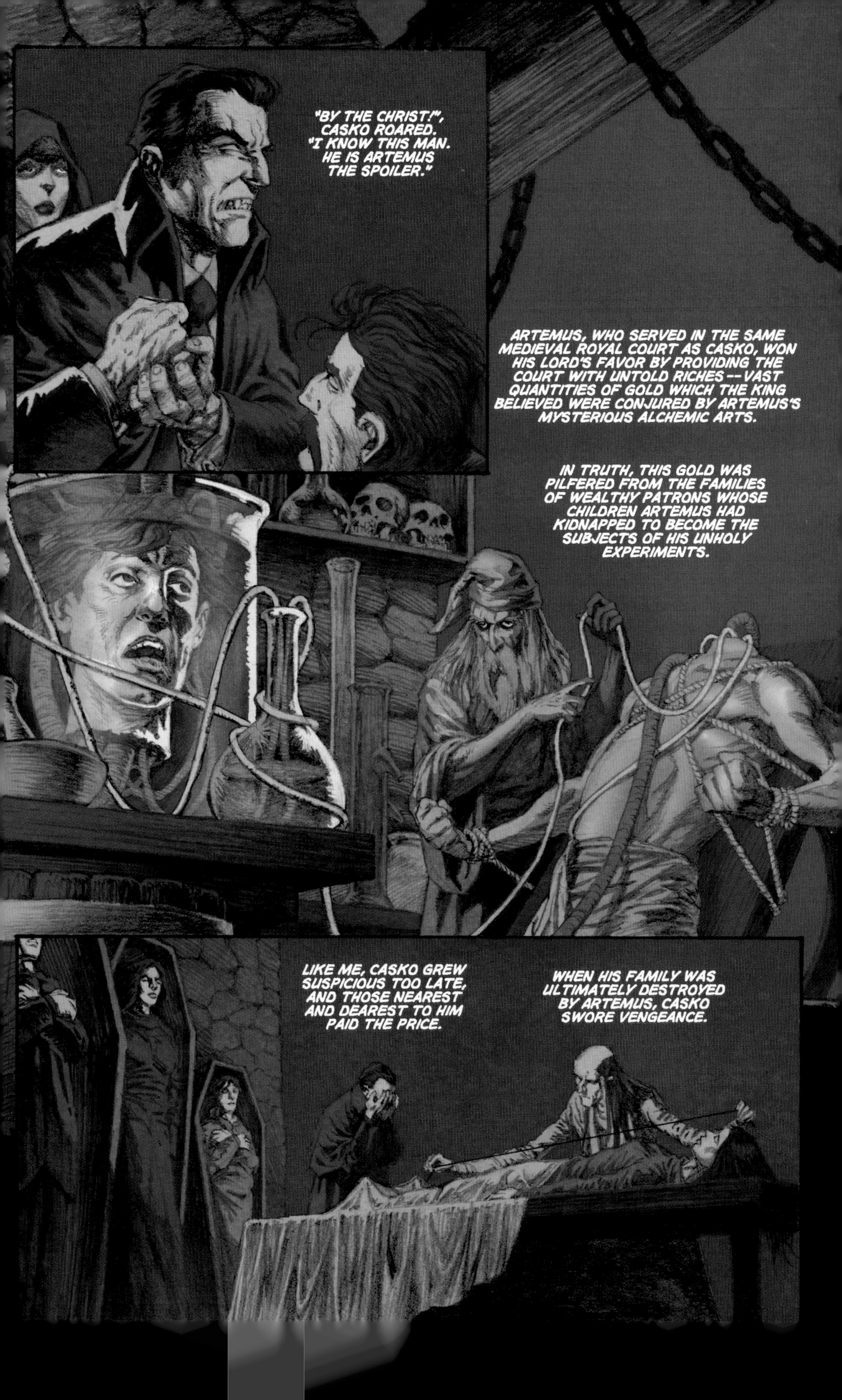
"BY THE CHRIST!", CASKO ROARED. "I KNOW THIS MAN. HE IS ARTEMUS THE SPOILER."
ARTEMUS, WHO SERVED IN THE SAME MEDIEVAL ROYAL COURT AS CASKO, WON HIS LORD'S FAVOR BY PROVIDING THE COURT WITH UNTOLD RICHES--VAST QUANTITIES OF GOLD WHICH THE KING BELIEVED WERE CONJURED BY ARTEMUS'S MYSTERIOUS ALCHEMIC ARTS.
IN TRUTH, THIS GOLD WAS PILFERED FROM THE FAMILIES OF WEALTHY PATRONS WHOSE CHILDREN ARTEMUS HAD KIDNAPPED TO BECOME THE SUBJECTS OF HIS UNHOLY EXPERIMENTS.
LIKE ME, CASKO GREW SUSPICIOUS TOO LATE, AND THOSE NEAREST AND DEAREST TO HIM PAID THE PRICE.
WHEN HIS FAMILY WAS ULTIMATELY DESTROYED BY ARTEMUS, CASKO SWORE VENGEANCE.

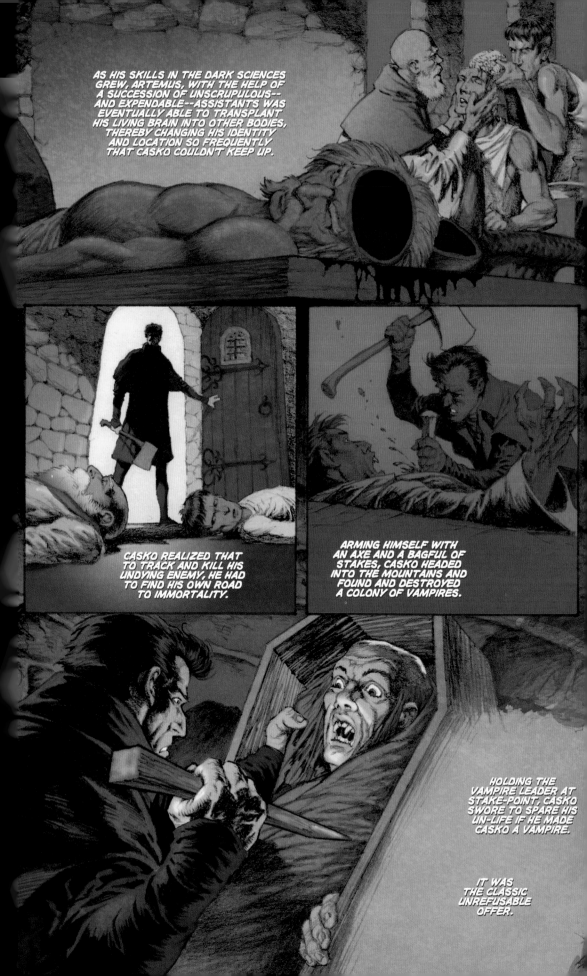

AS HIS SKILLS IN THE DARK SCIENCES GREW, ARTEMUS, WITH THE HELP OF A SUCCESSION OF UNSCRUPULOUS-- AND EXPENDABLE--ASSISTANTS WAS EVENTUALLY ABLE TO TRANSPLANT HIS LIVING BRAIN INTO OTHER BODIES, THEREBY CHANGING HIS IDENTITY AND LOCATION SO FREQUENTLY THAT CASKO COULDN'T KEEP UP.

CASKO REALIZED THAT TO TRACK AND KILL HIS UNDYING ENEMY, HE HAD TO FIND HIS OWN ROAD TO IMMORTALITY.

ARMING HIMSELF WITH AN AXE AND A BAGFUL OF STAKES, CASKO HEADED INTO THE MOUNTAINS AND FOUND AND DESTROYED A COLONY OF VAMPIRES.

HOLDING THE VAMPIRE LEADER AT STAKE-POINT, CASKO SWORE TO SPARE HIS UN-LIFE IF HE MADE CASKO A VAMPIRE.

IT WAS THE CLASSIC UNREFUSABLE OFFER.

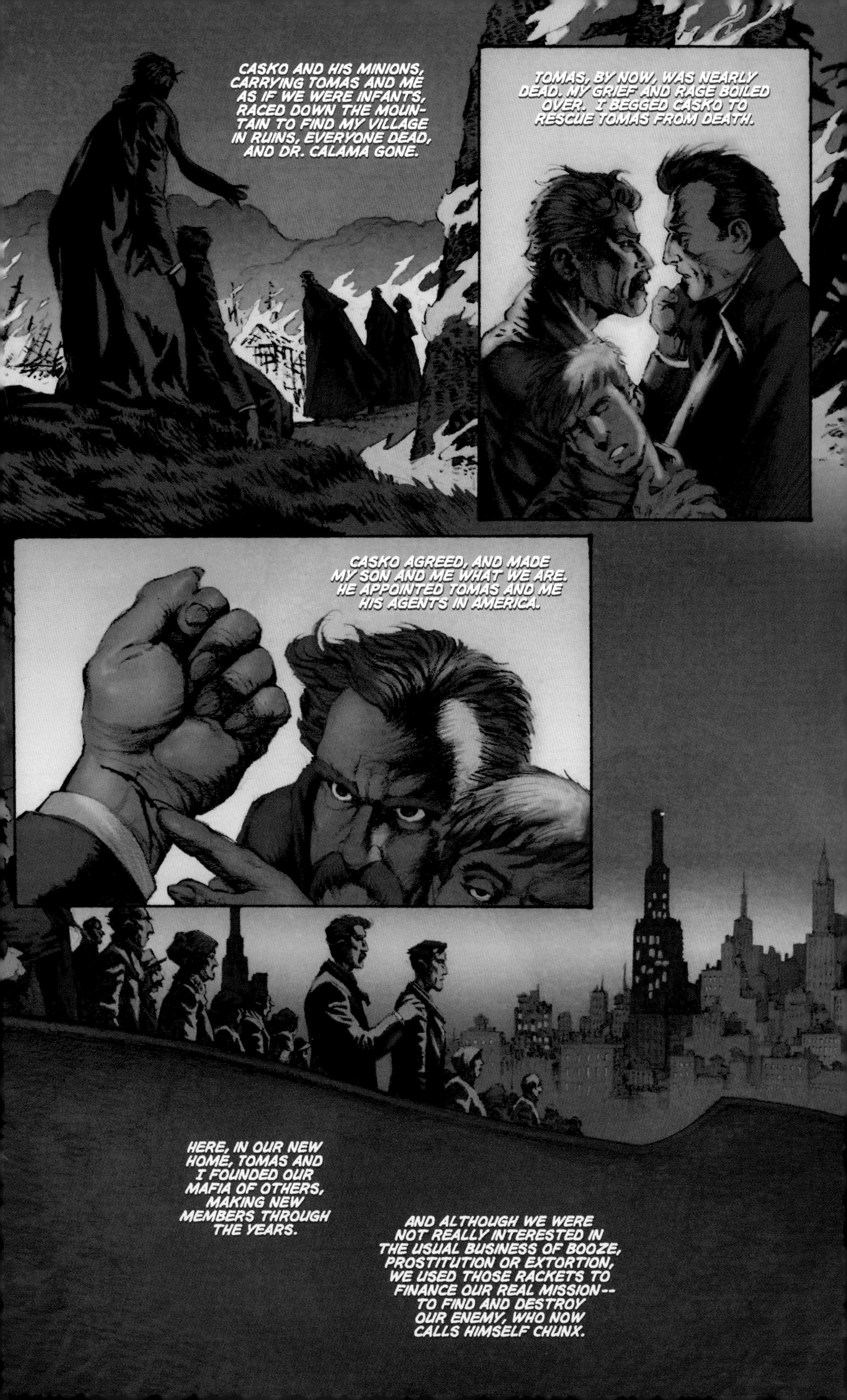
CASKO AND HIS MINIONS, CARRYING TOMAS AND ME AS IF WE WERE INFANTS, RACED DOWN THE MOUNTAIN TO FIND MY VILLAGE IN RUINS, EVERYONE DEAD, AND DR. CALAMA GONE.
TOMAS, BY NOW, WAS NEARLY DEAD. MY GRIEF AND RAGE BOILED OVER. I BEGGED CASKO TO RESCUE TOMAS FROM DEATH.
CASKO AGREED, AND MADE MY SON AND ME WHAT WE ARE. HE APPOINTED TOMAS AND ME HIS AGENTS IN AMERICA.
HERE, IN OUR NEW HOME, TOMAS AND I FOUNDED OUR MAFIA OF OTHERS, MAKING NEW MEMBERS THROUGH THE YEARS.
AND ALTHOUGH WE WERE NOT REALLY INTERESTED IN THE USUAL BUSINESS OF BOOZE, PROSTITUTION OR EXTORTION, WE USED THOSE RACKETS TO FINANCE OUR REAL MISSION-- TO FIND AND DESTROY OUR ENEMY, WHO NOW CALLS HIMSELF CHUNX.

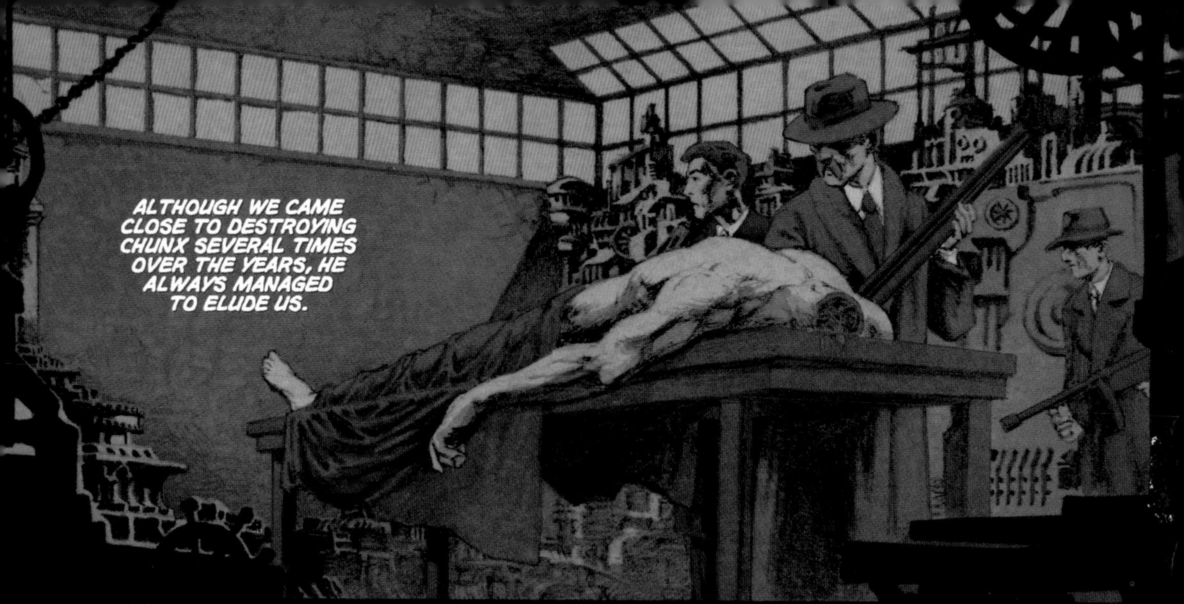
ALTHOUGH WE CAME CLOSE TO DESTROYING CHUNX SEVERAL TIMES OVER THE YEARS, HE ALWAYS MANAGED TO ELUDE US.

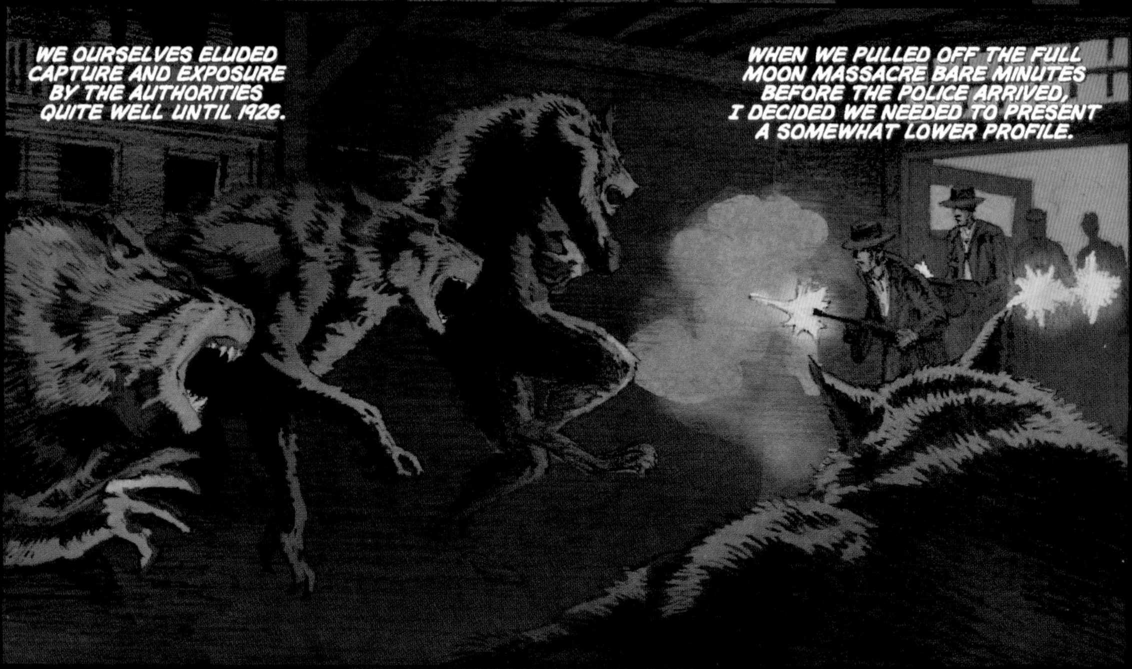
WE OURSELVES ELUDED CAPTURE AND EXPOSURE BY THE AUTHORITIES QUITE WELL UNTIL 1926.
WHEN WE PULLED OFF THE FULL MOON MASSACRE BARE MINUTES BEFORE THE POLICE ARRIVED, I DECIDED WE NEEDED TO PRESENT A SOMEWHAT LOWER PROFILE.

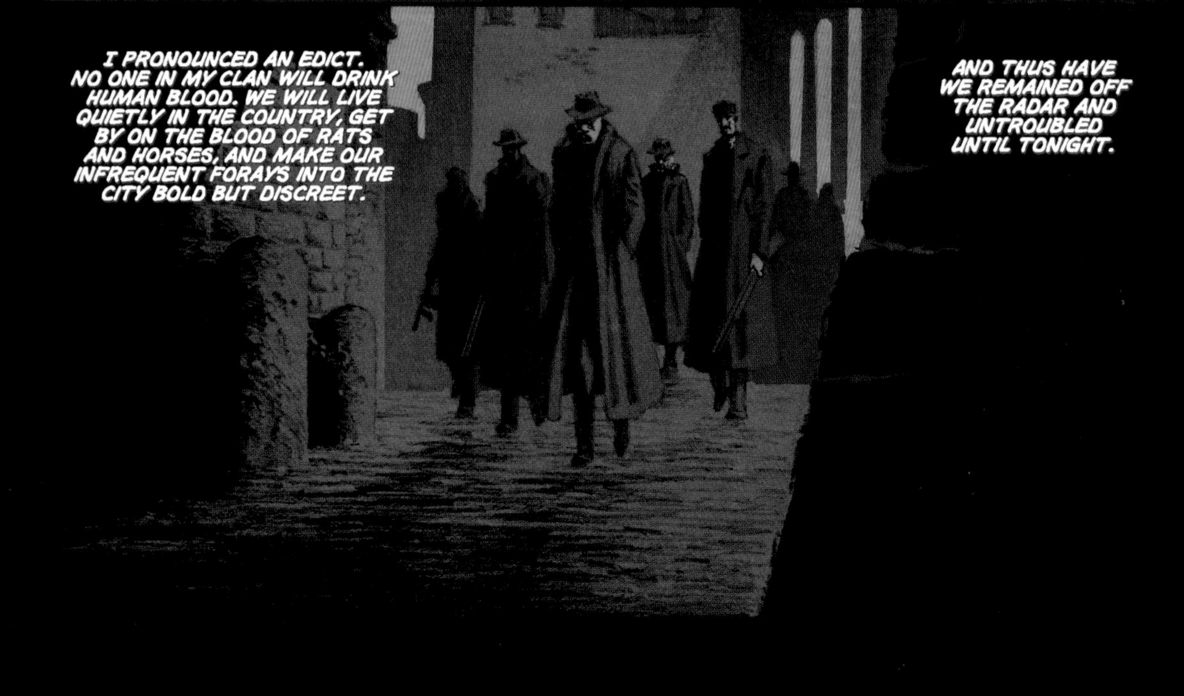
I PRONOUNCED AN EDICT. NO ONE IN MY CLAN WILL DRINK HUMAN BLOOD. WE WILL LIVE QUIETLY IN THE COUNTRY, GET BY ON THE BLOOD OF RATS AND HORSES, AND MAKE OUR INFREQUENT FORAYS INTO THE CITY BOLD BUT DISCREET.
AND THUS HAVE WE REMAINED OFF THE RADAR AND UNTROUBLED UNTIL TONIGHT.

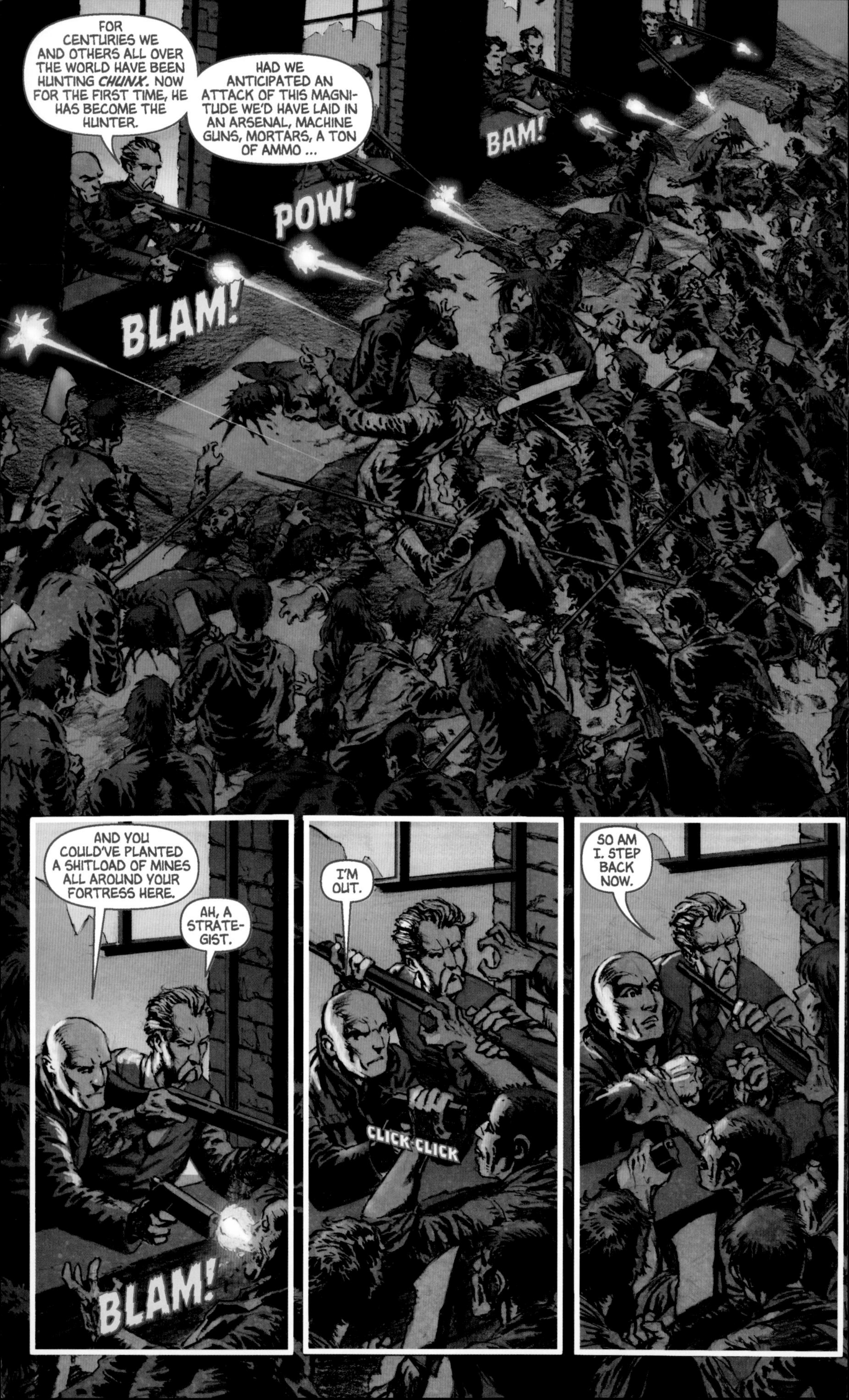
FOR CENTURIES WE AND OTHERS ALL OVER THE WORLD HAVE BEEN HUNTING *CHUNX*. NOW FOR THE FIRST TIME, HE HAS BECOME THE HUNTER.
HAD WE ANTICIPATED AN ATTACK OF THIS MAGNI-TUDE WE'D HAVE LAID IN AN ARSENAL, MACHINE GUNS, MORTARS, A TON OF AMMO ...
BAM!
POW!
BLAM!
AND YOU COULD'VE PLANTED A SHITLOAD OF MINES ALL AROUND YOUR FORTRESS HERE.
AH, A STRATE-GIST.
BLAM!
I'M OUT.
CLICK CLICK
SO AM I. STEP BACK NOW.

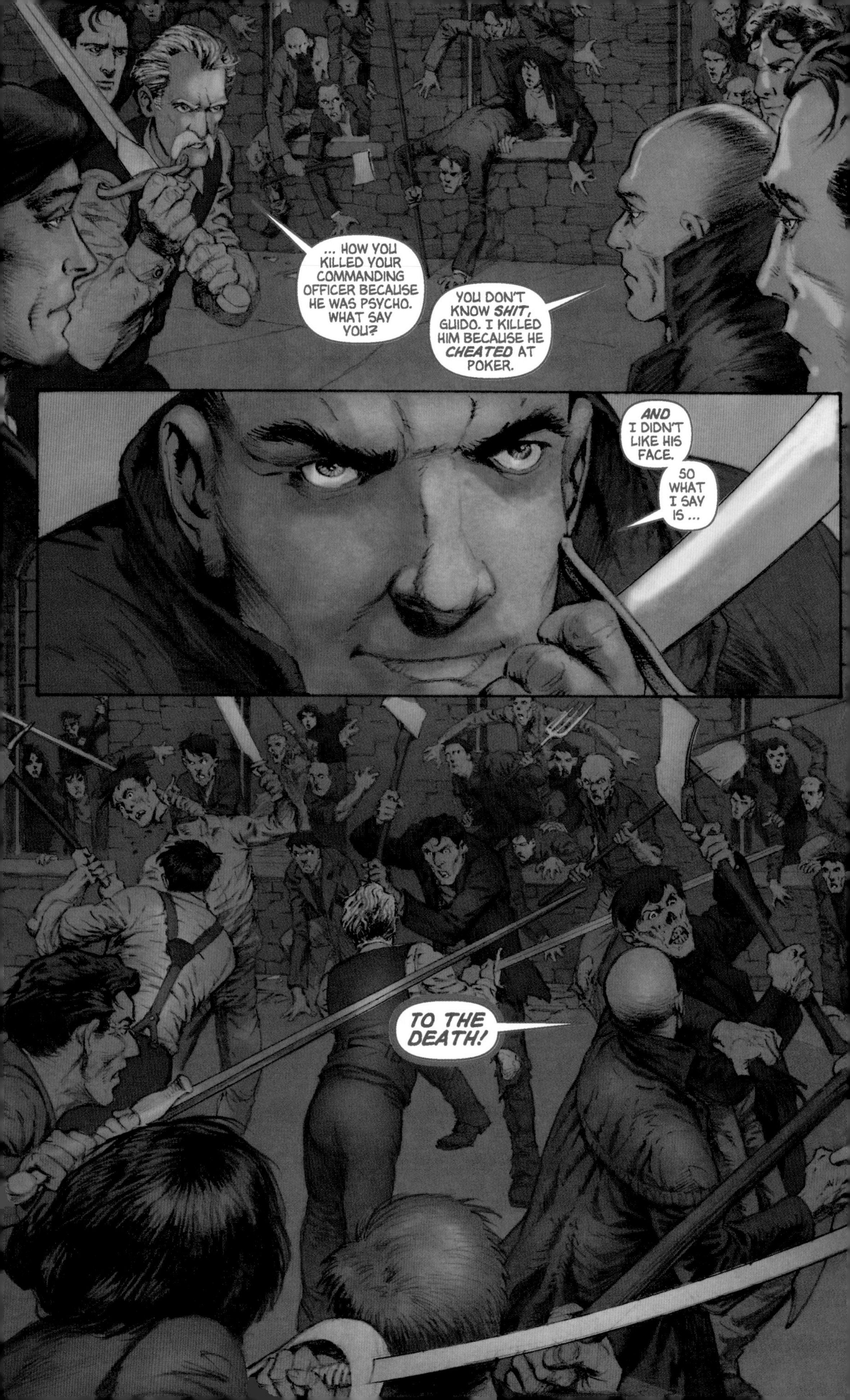

... HOW YOU KILLED YOUR COMMANDING OFFICER BECAUSE HE WAS PSYCHO. WHAT SAY YOU?
YOU DON'T KNOW *SHIT*, GUIDO. I KILLED HIM BECAUSE HE *CHEATED* AT POKER.
AND I DIDN'T LIKE HIS FACE.
SO WHAT I SAY IS ...
TO THE DEATH!

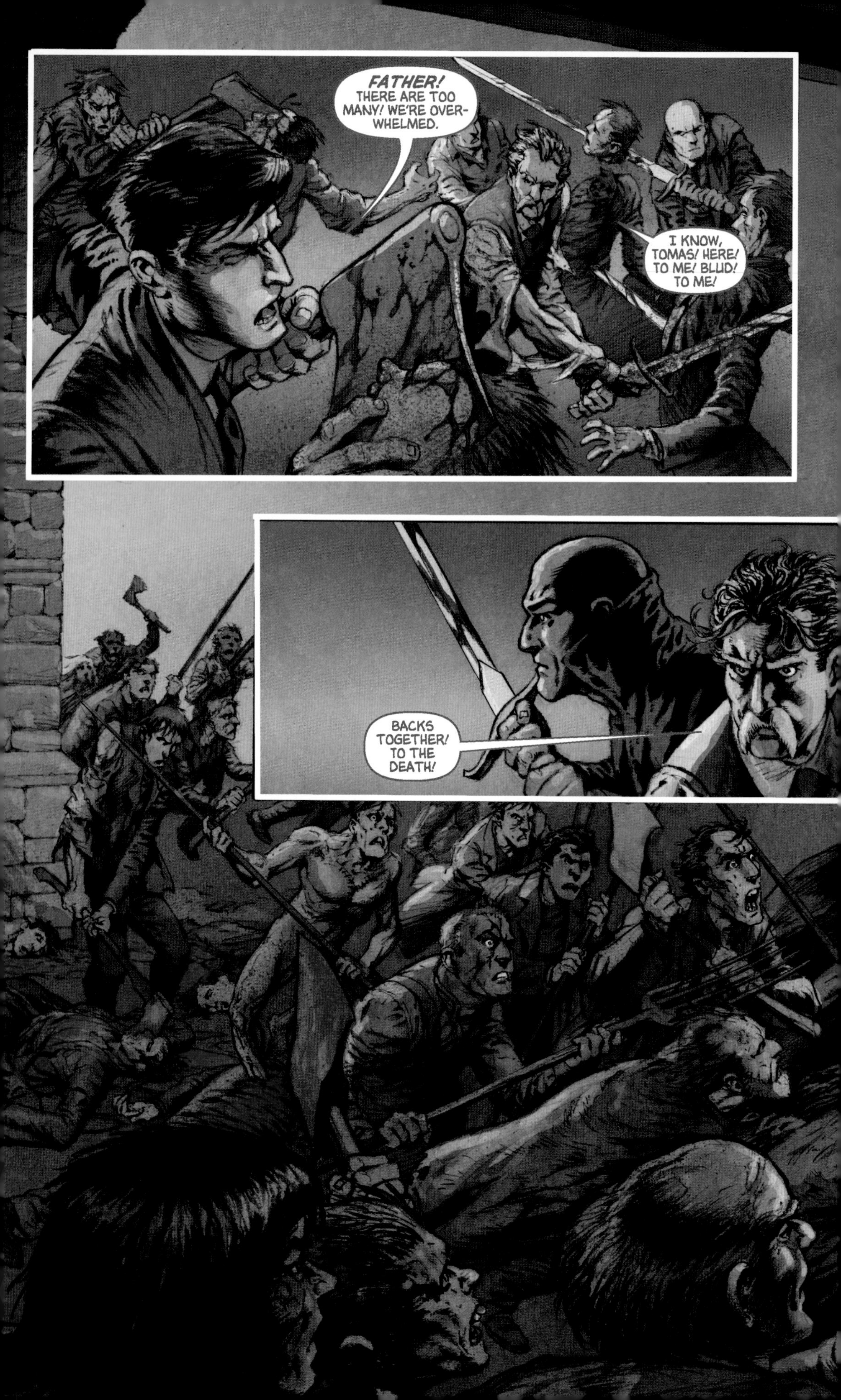
FATHER! THERE ARE TOO MANY! WE'RE OVER-WHELMED.
I KNOW, TOMAS! HERE! TO ME! BLUD! TO ME!
BACKS TOGETHER! TO THE DEATH!

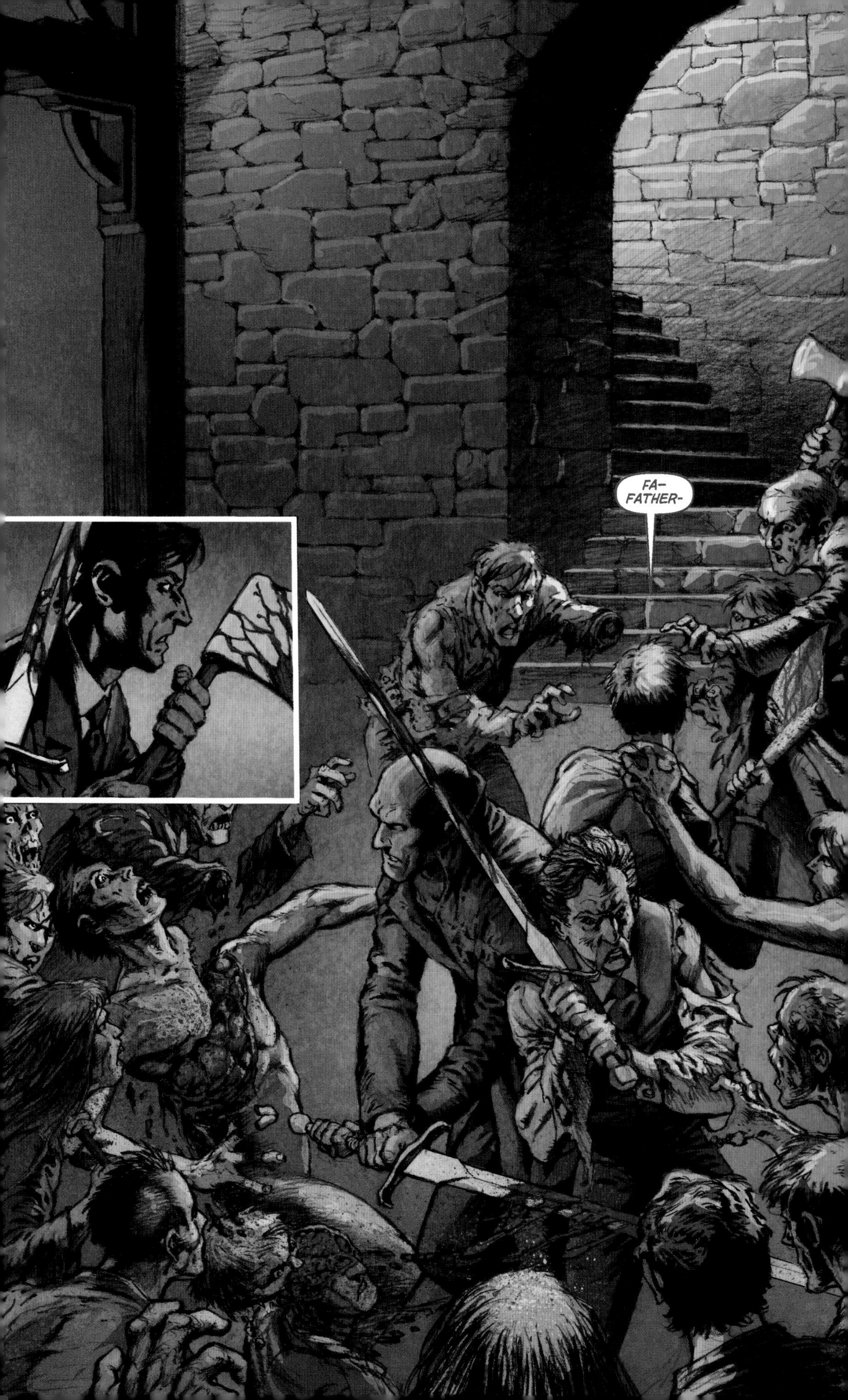
FA-
FATHER-

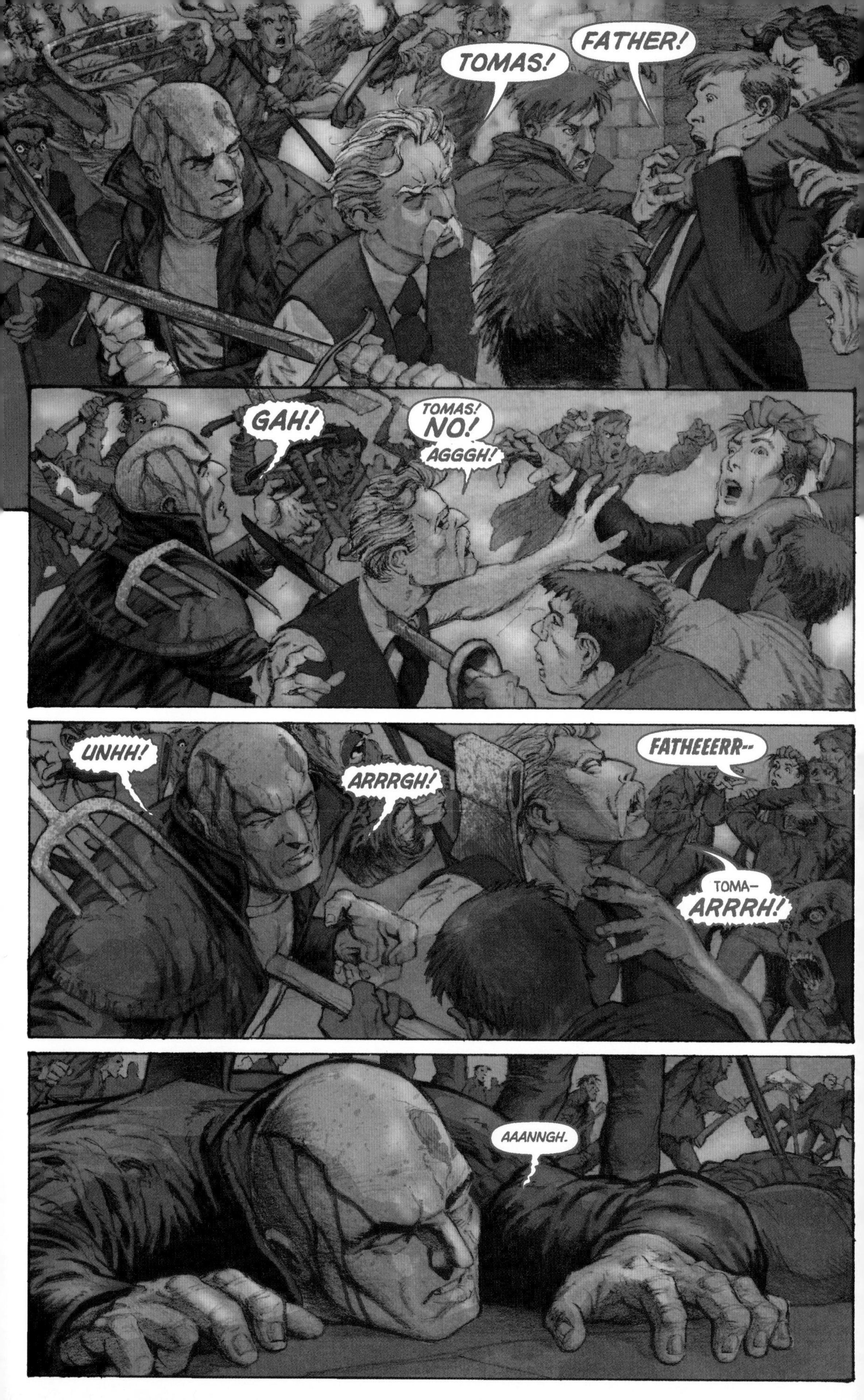
TOMAS!
FATHER!
GAH!
TOMAS! NO! AGGGH!
UNHH!
ARRRGH!
FATHEEERR--
TOMA-ARRRH!
AAANNGH.

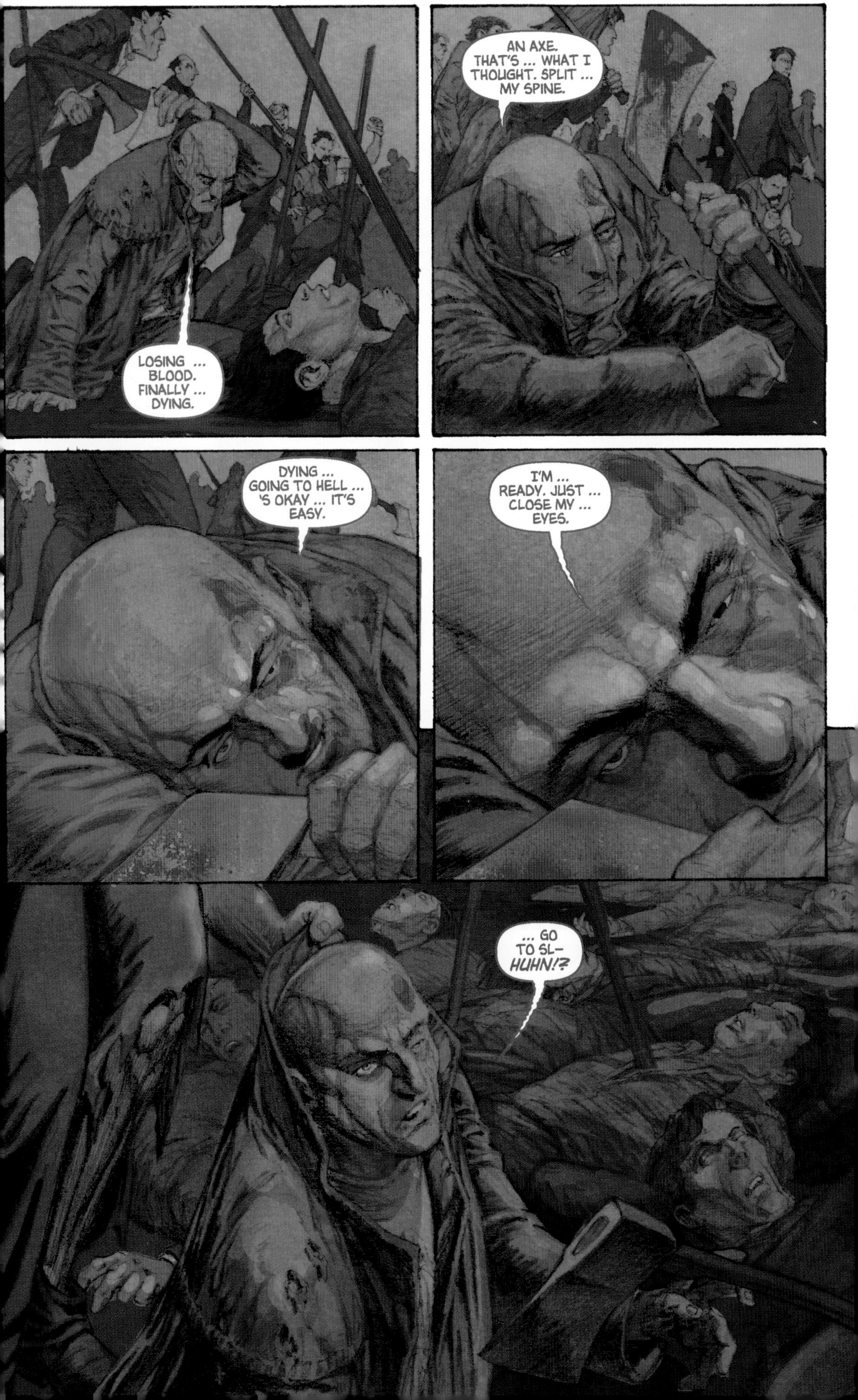
LOSING ... BLOOD. FINALLY ... DYING.
AN AXE. THAT'S ... WHAT I THOUGHT. SPLIT ... MY SPINE.
DYING ... GOING TO HELL ... 'S OKAY ... IT'S EASY.
I'M ... READY. JUST ... CLOSE MY ... EYES.
... GO TO SL-
HUHN!?

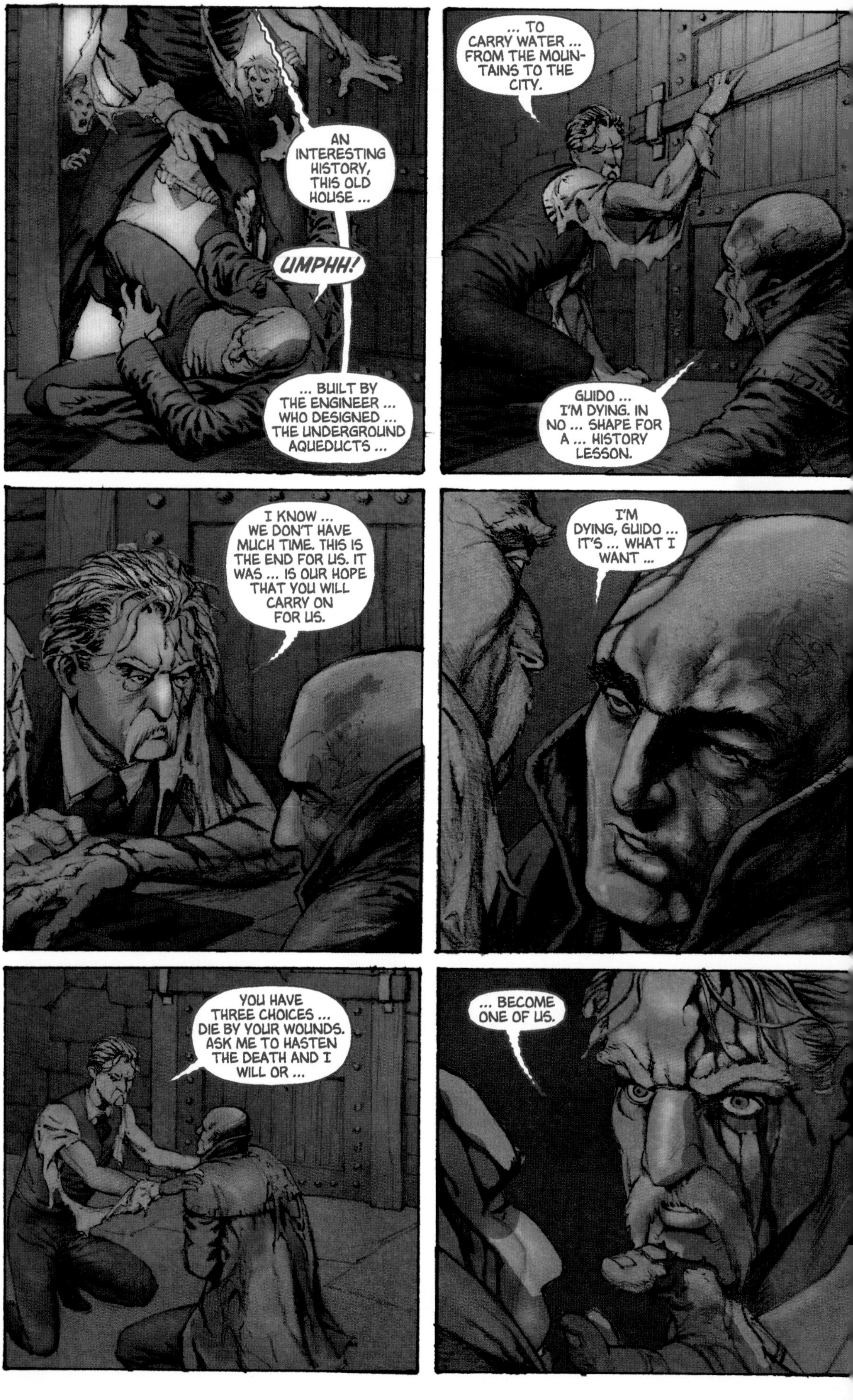
AN INTERESTING HISTORY, THIS OLD HOUSE ...
UMPHH!
... BUILT BY THE ENGINEER ... WHO DESIGNED ... THE UNDERGROUND AQUEDUCTS ...
... TO CARRY WATER ... FROM THE MOUNTAINS TO THE CITY.
GUIDO ... I'M DYING. IN NO ... SHAPE FOR A ... HISTORY LESSON.
I KNOW ... WE DON'T HAVE MUCH TIME. THIS IS THE END FOR US. IT WAS ... IS OUR HOPE THAT YOU WILL CARRY ON FOR US.
I'M DYING, GUIDO ... IT'S ... WHAT I WANT ...
YOU HAVE THREE CHOICES ... DIE BY YOUR WOUNDS. ASK ME TO HASTEN THE DEATH AND I WILL OR ...
... BECOME ONE OF US.

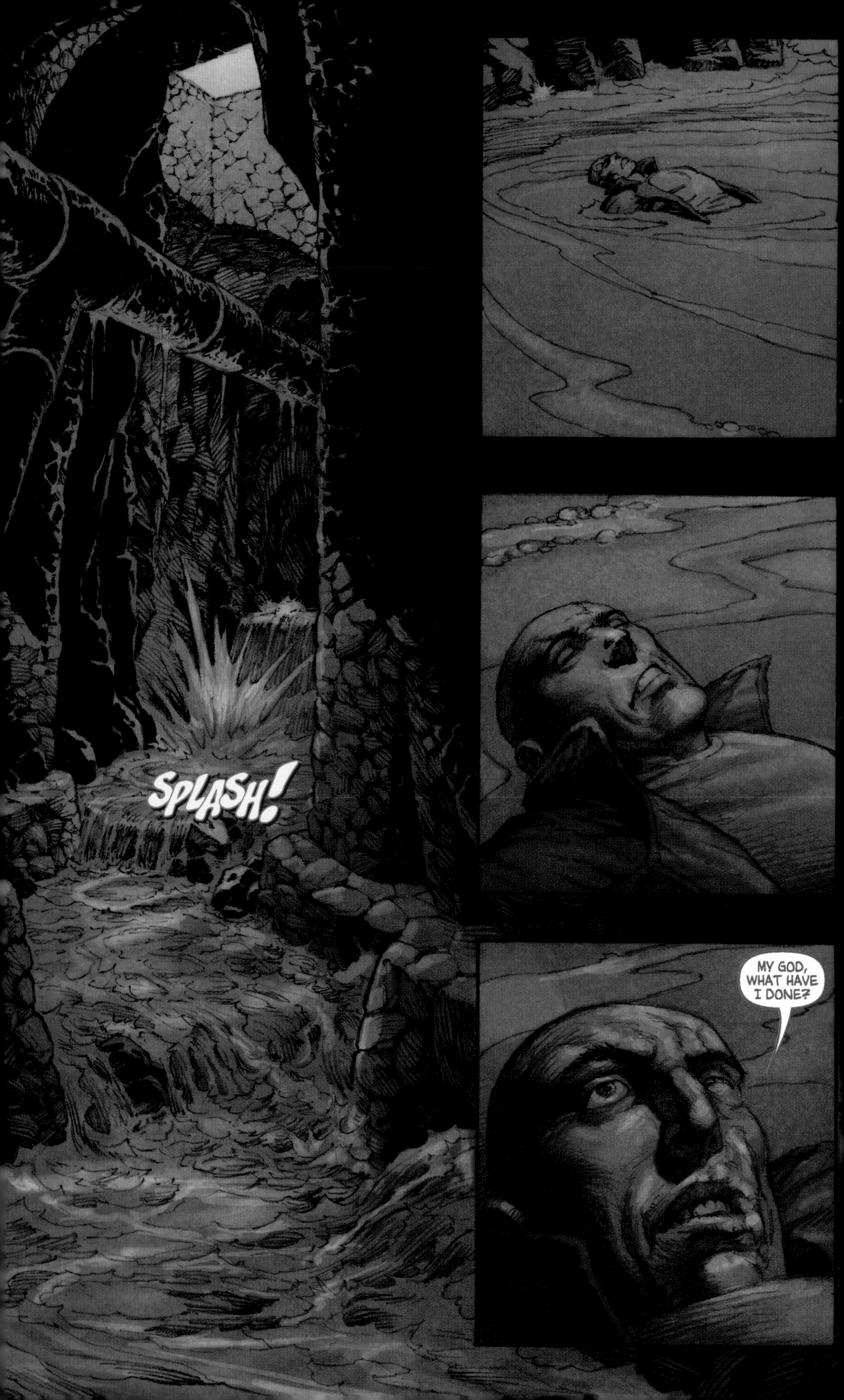
SPLASH!
MY GOD, WHAT HAVE I DONE?

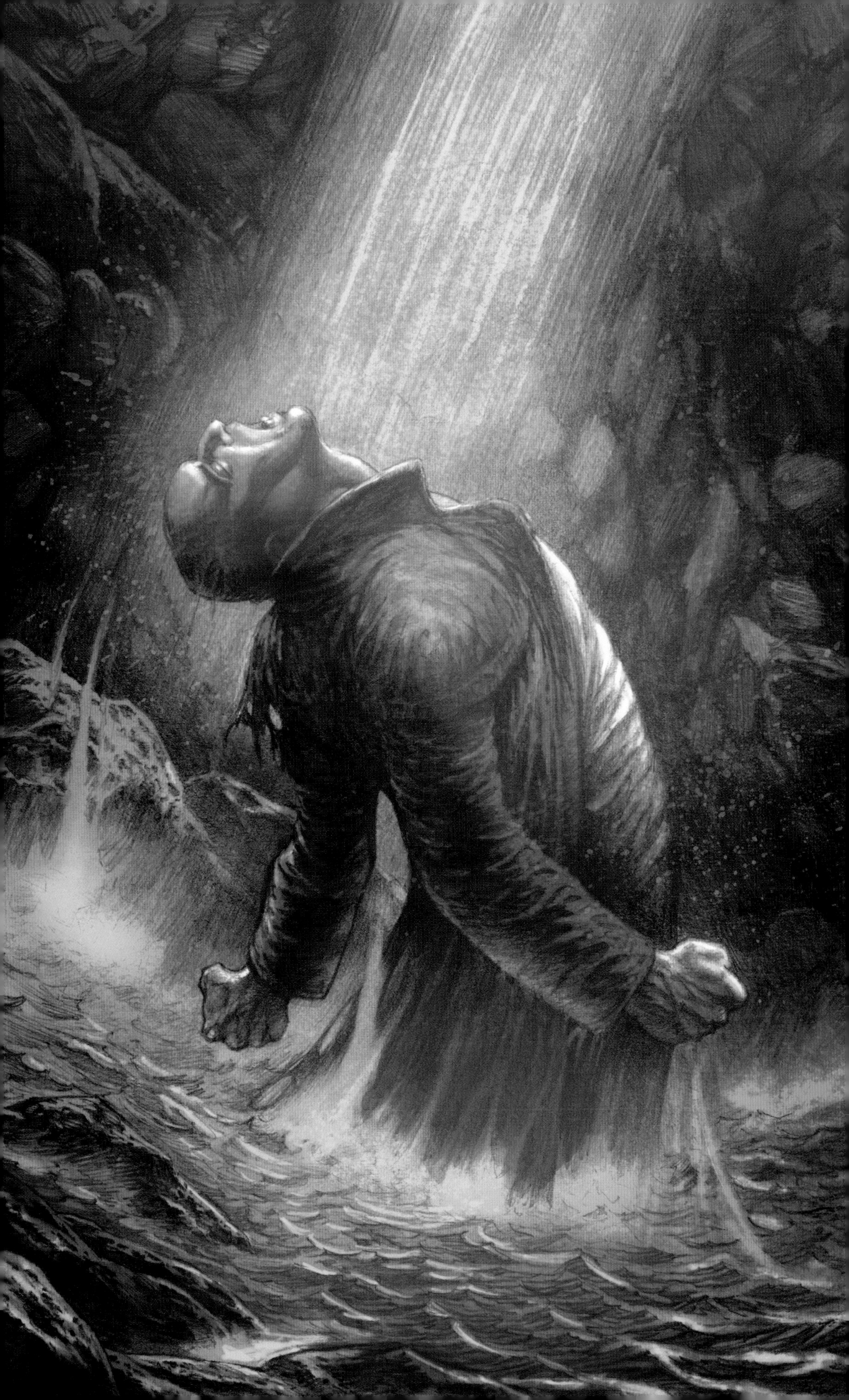

CHAPTER THREE

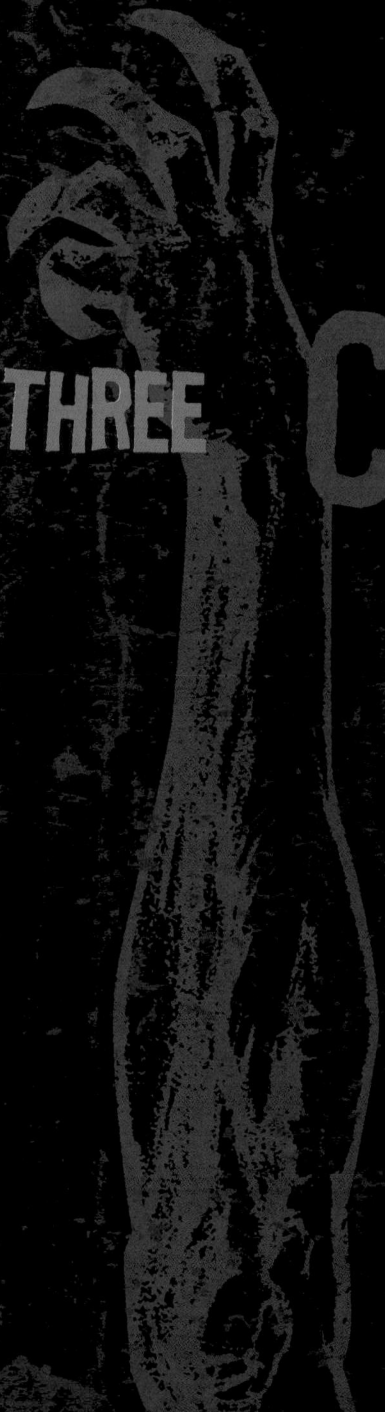

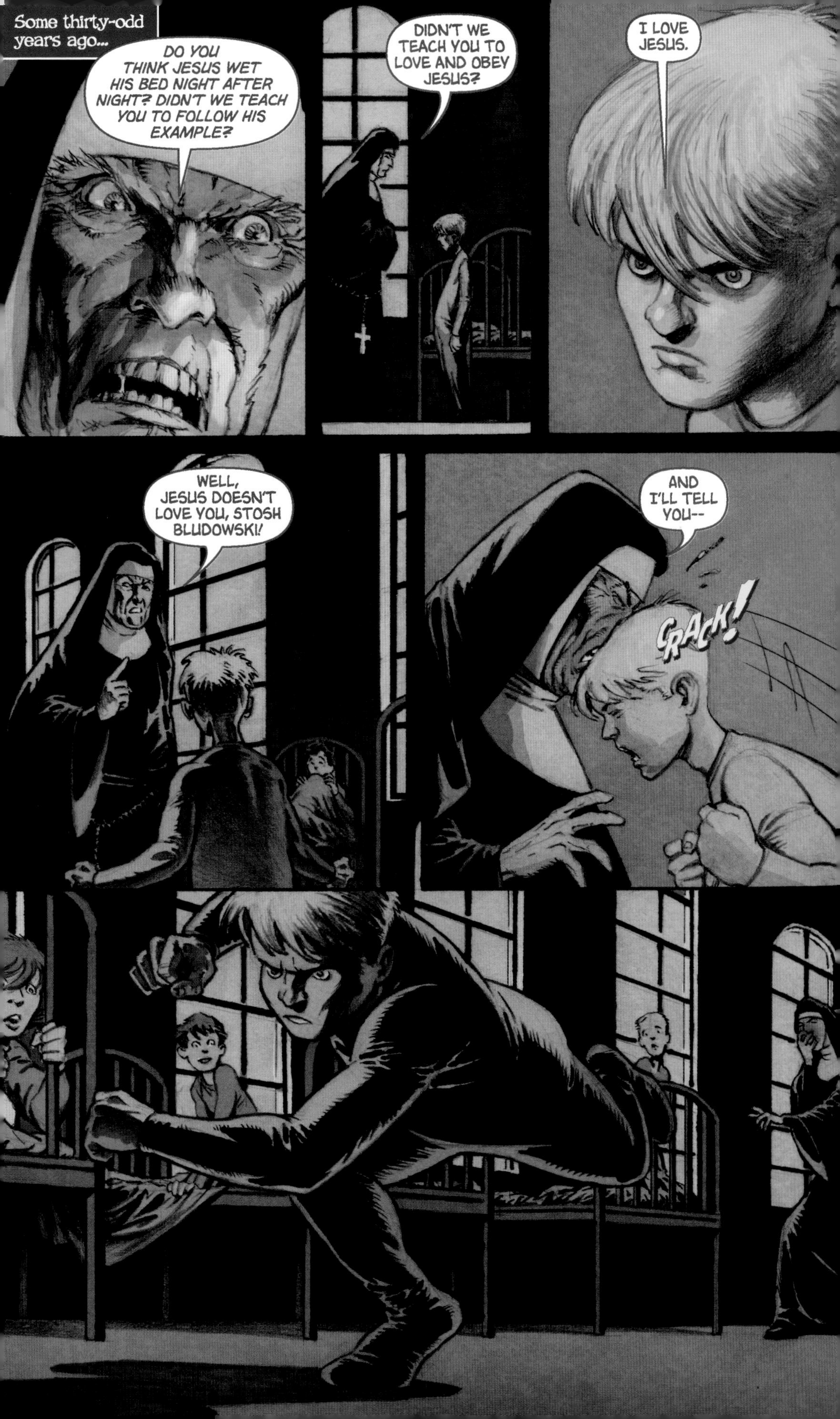

Some thirty-odd years ago...
DO YOU THINK JESUS WET HIS BED NIGHT AFTER NIGHT? DIDN'T WE TEACH YOU TO FOLLOW HIS EXAMPLE?
DIDN'T WE TEACH YOU TO LOVE AND OBEY JESUS?
I LOVE JESUS.
WELL, JESUS DOESN'T LOVE YOU, STOSH BLUDOWSKI!
AND I'LL TELL YOU--
CRACK!

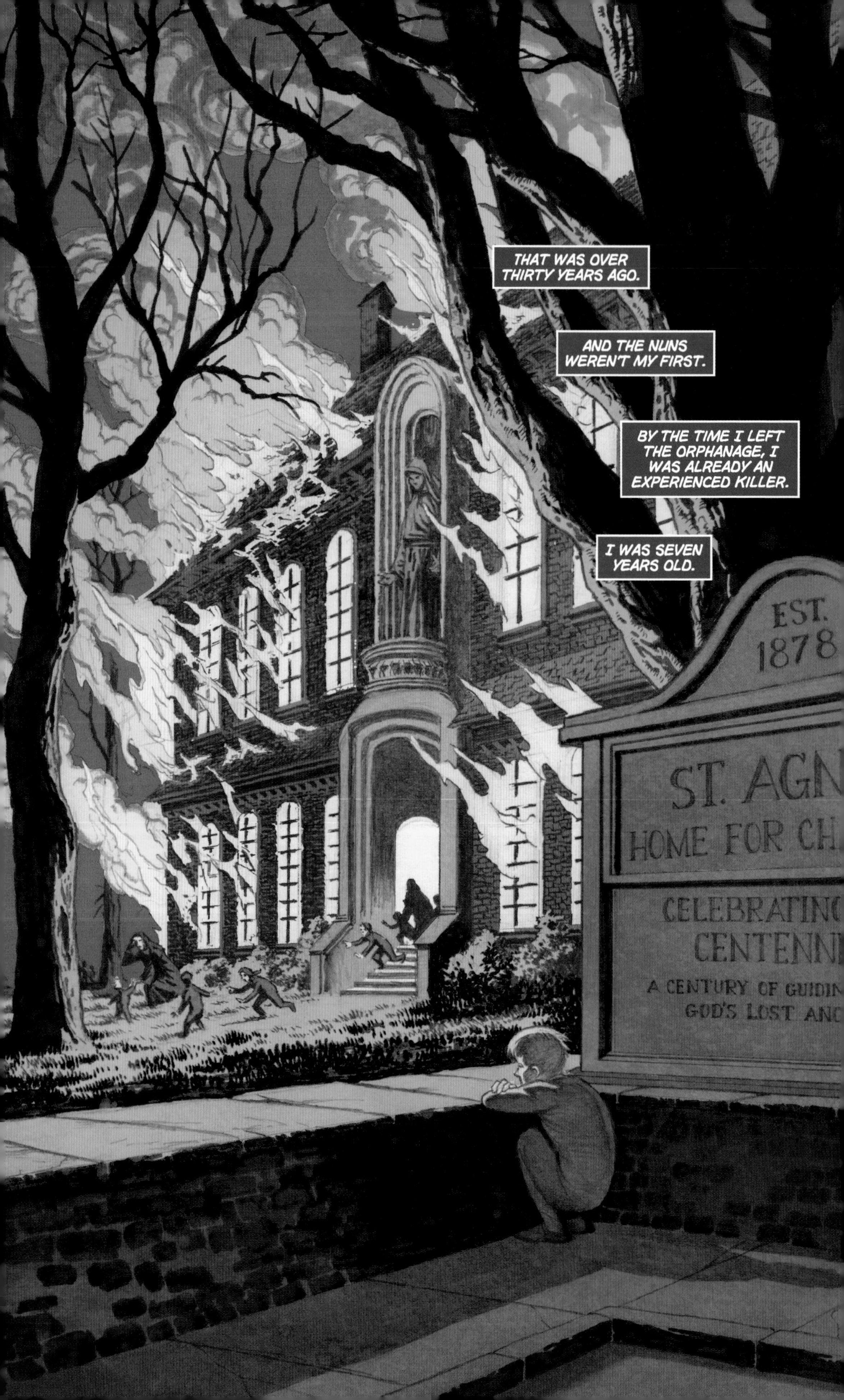
THAT WAS OVER THIRTY YEARS AGO.
AND THE NUNS WEREN'T MY FIRST.
BY THE TIME I LEFT THE ORPHANAGE, I WAS ALREADY AN EXPERIENCED KILLER.
I WAS SEVEN YEARS OLD.
EST. 1878
ST. AGN
HOME FOR CH
CELEBRATING
CENTENN
A CENTURY OF GUIDIN
GOD'S LOST AN

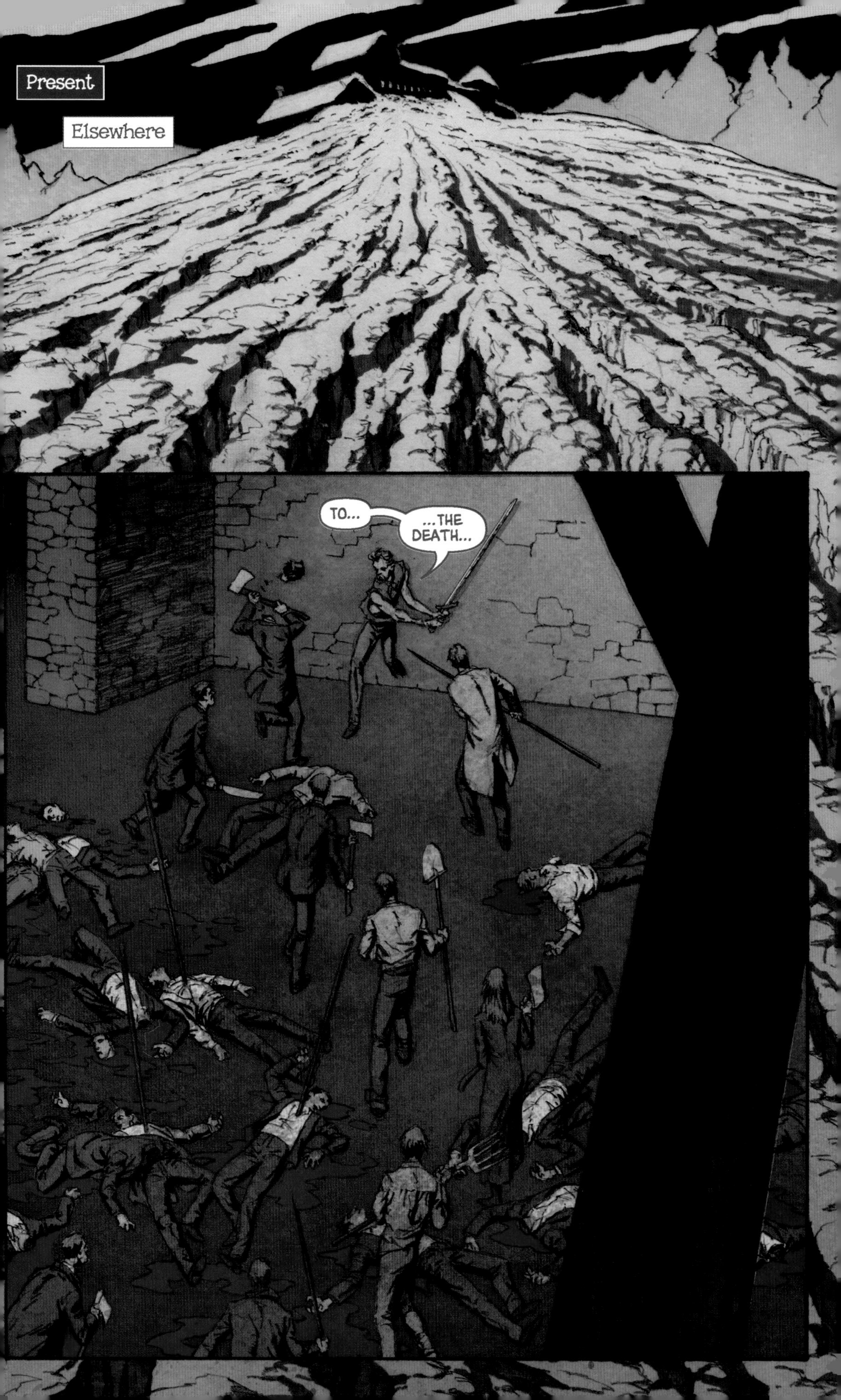
Present
Elsewhere
TO...
...THE DEATH...

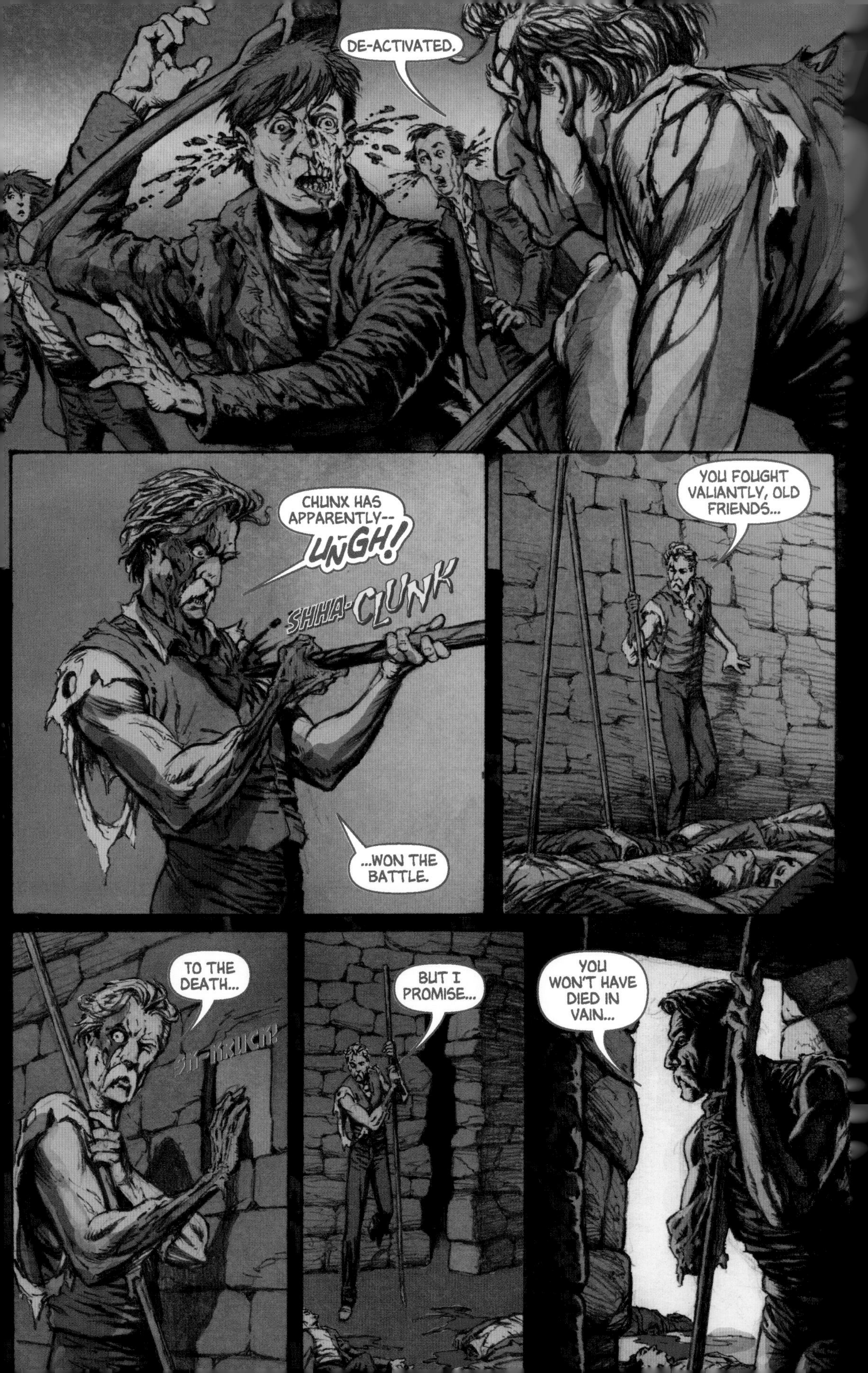
DE-ACTIVATED.
CHUNX HAS APPARENTLY--
UNGH!
SHHA-CLUNK
...WON THE BATTLE.
YOU FOUGHT VALIANTLY, OLD FRIENDS...
TO THE DEATH...
SH-KRUCK!
BUT I PROMISE...
YOU WON'T HAVE DIED IN VAIN...

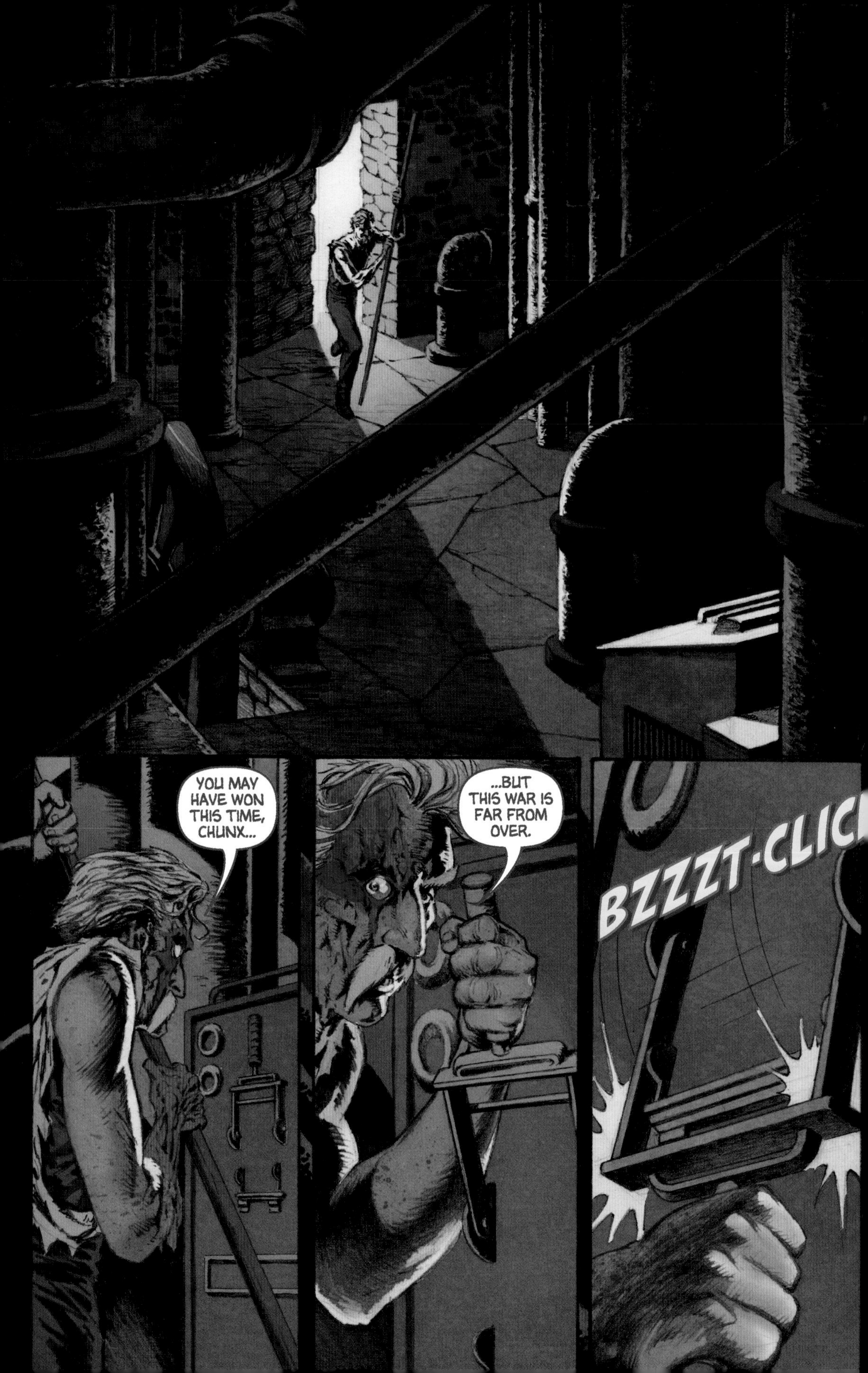
YOU MAY HAVE WON THIS TIME, CHUNX...
...BUT THIS WAR IS FAR FROM OVER.
BZZZT-CLIC

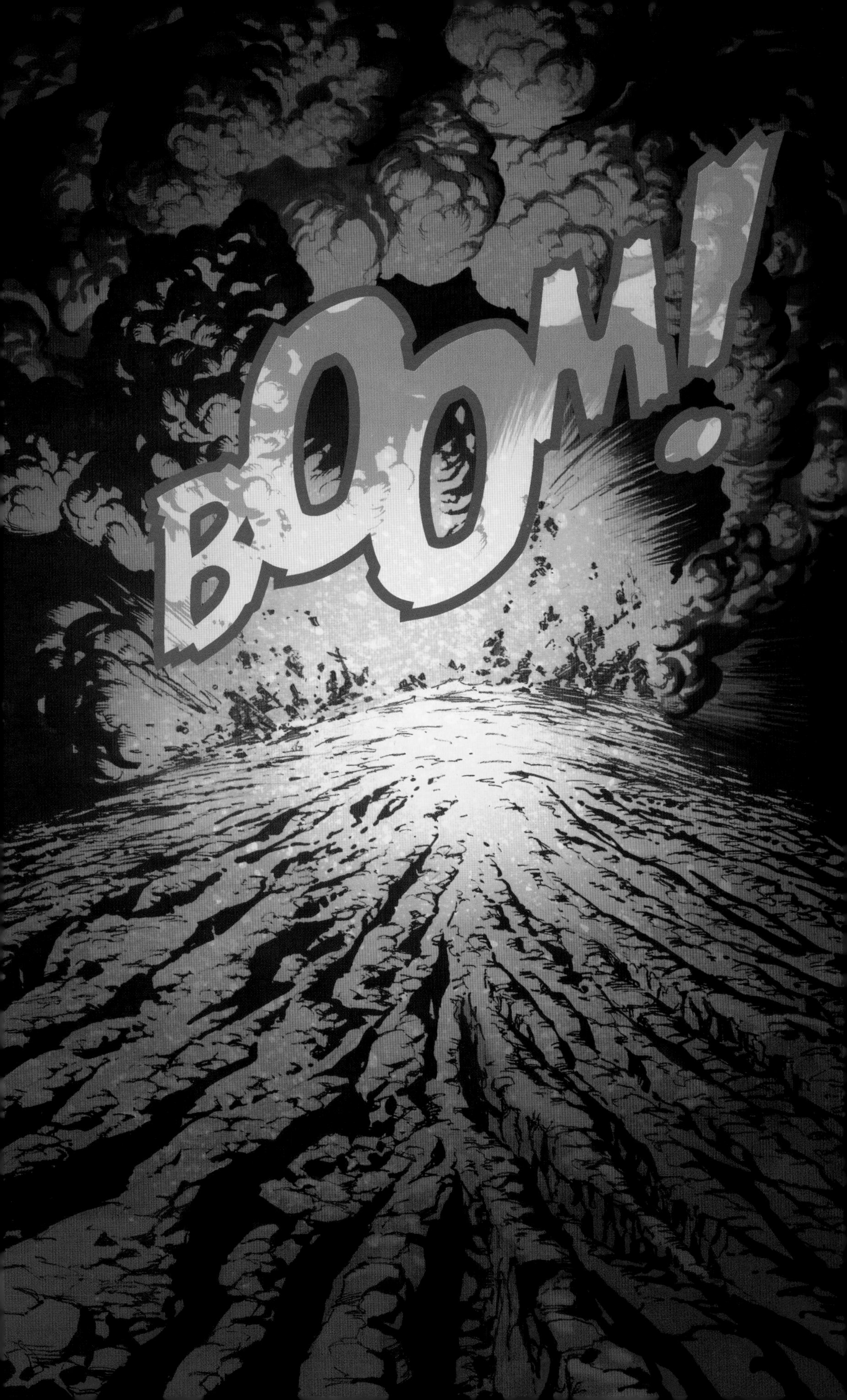
BOOM!

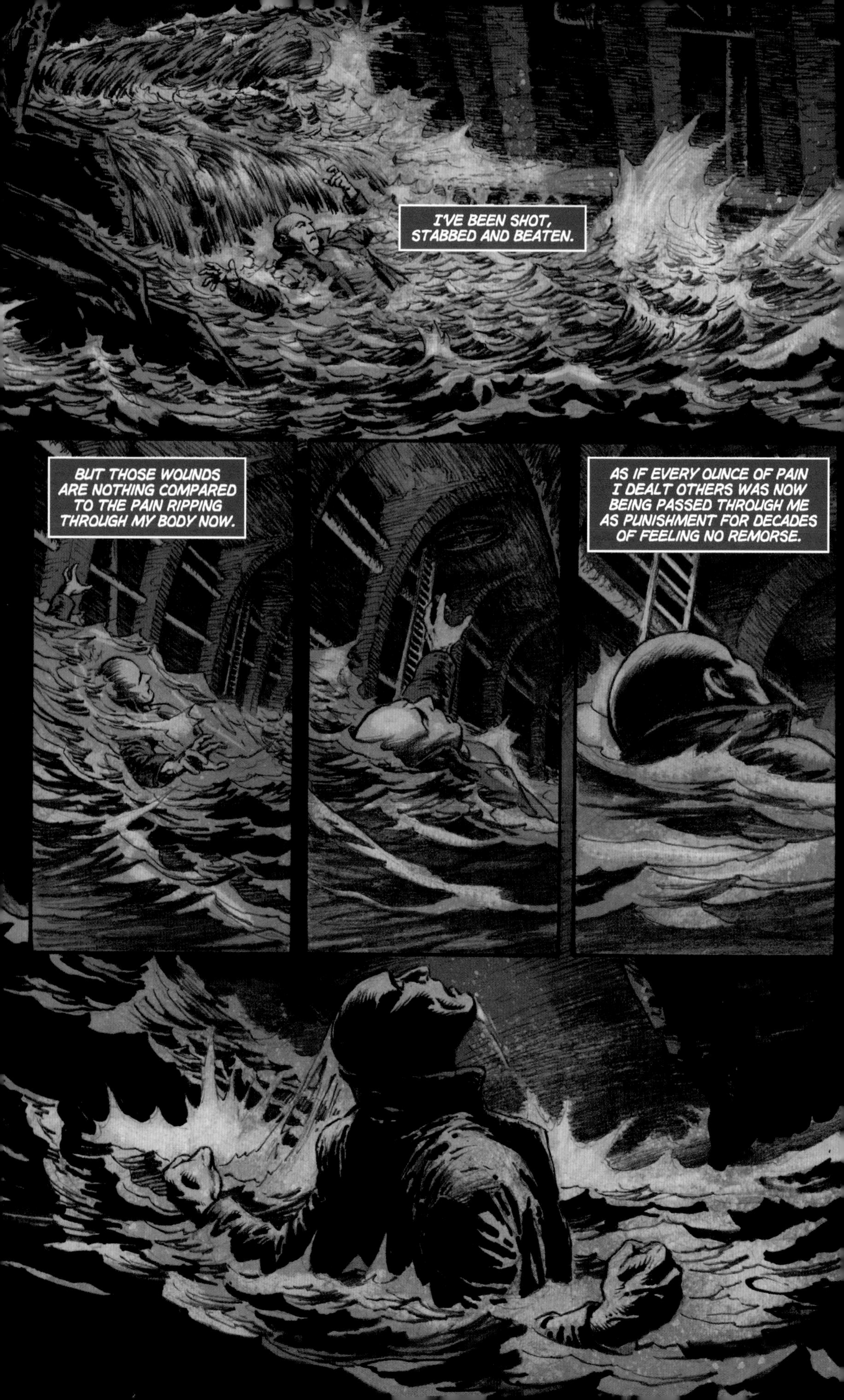
I'VE BEEN SHOT,
STABBED AND BEATEN.
BUT THOSE WOUNDS
ARE NOTHING COMPARED
TO THE PAIN RIPPING
THROUGH MY BODY NOW.
AS IF EVERY OUNCE OF PAIN
I DEALT OTHERS WAS NOW
BEING PASSED THROUGH ME
AS PUNISHMENT FOR DECADES
OF FEELING NO REMORSE.

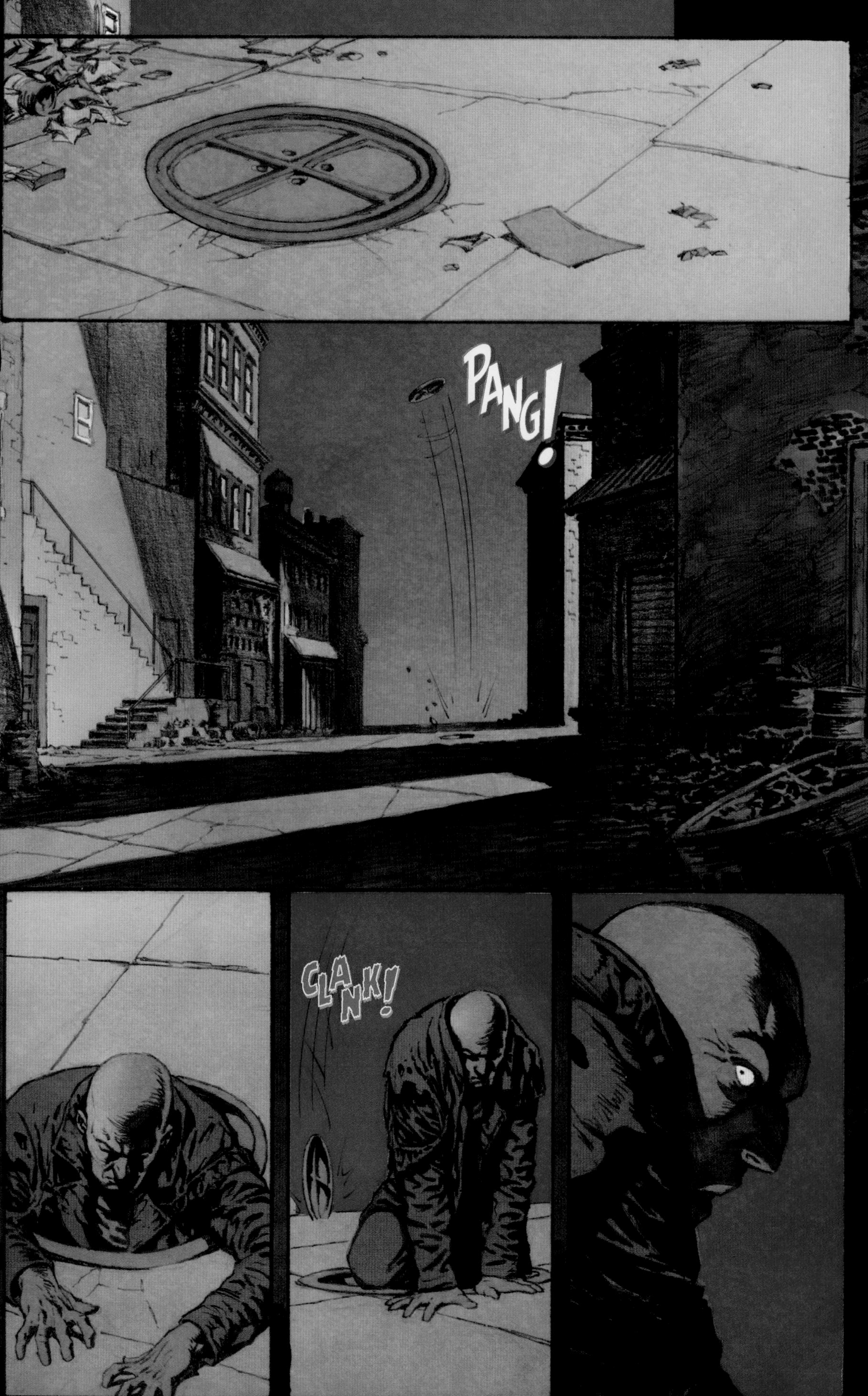
PANG!
CLANK!

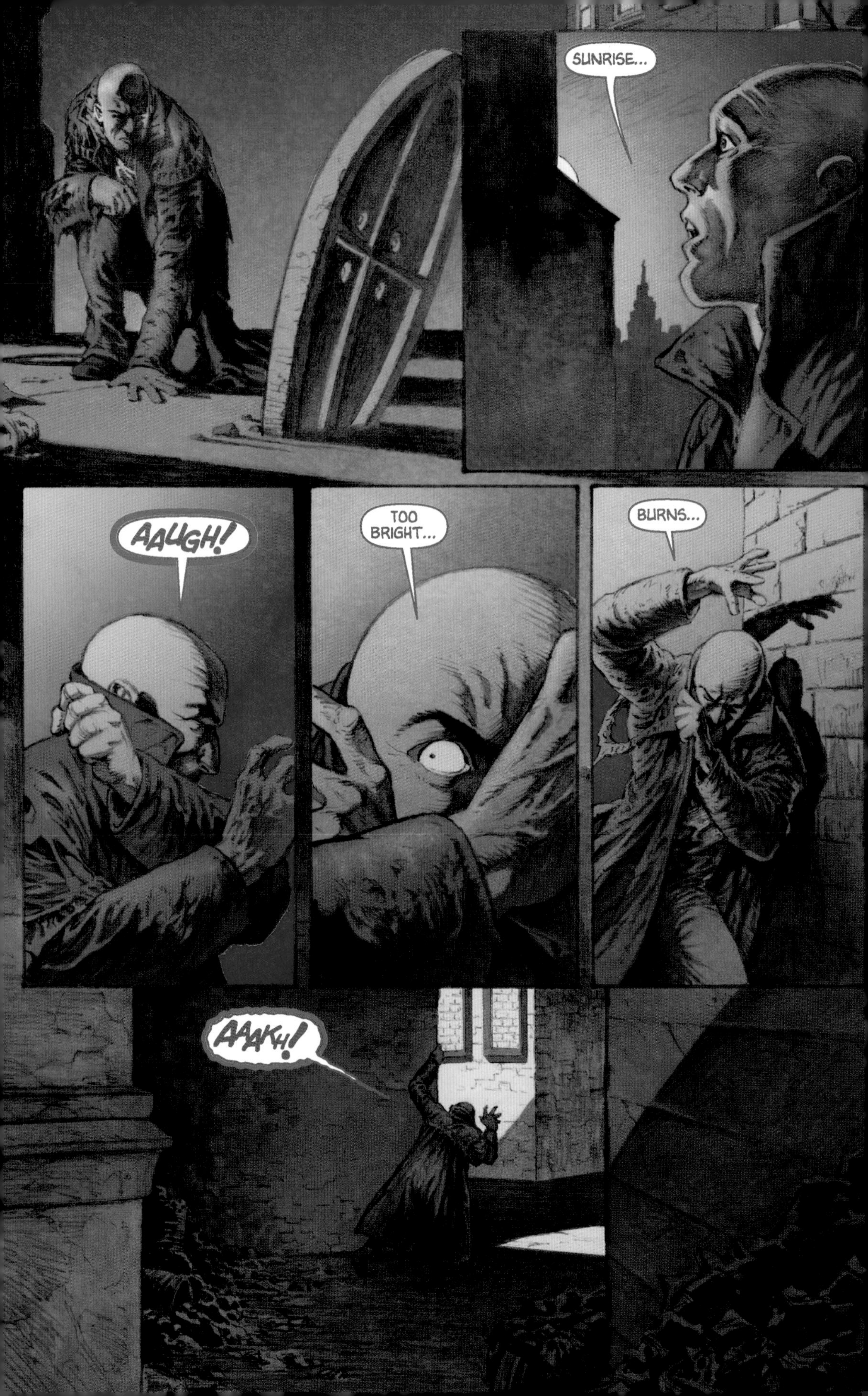
SUNRISE...
AAUGH!
TOO BRIGHT...
BURNS...
AAAKH!

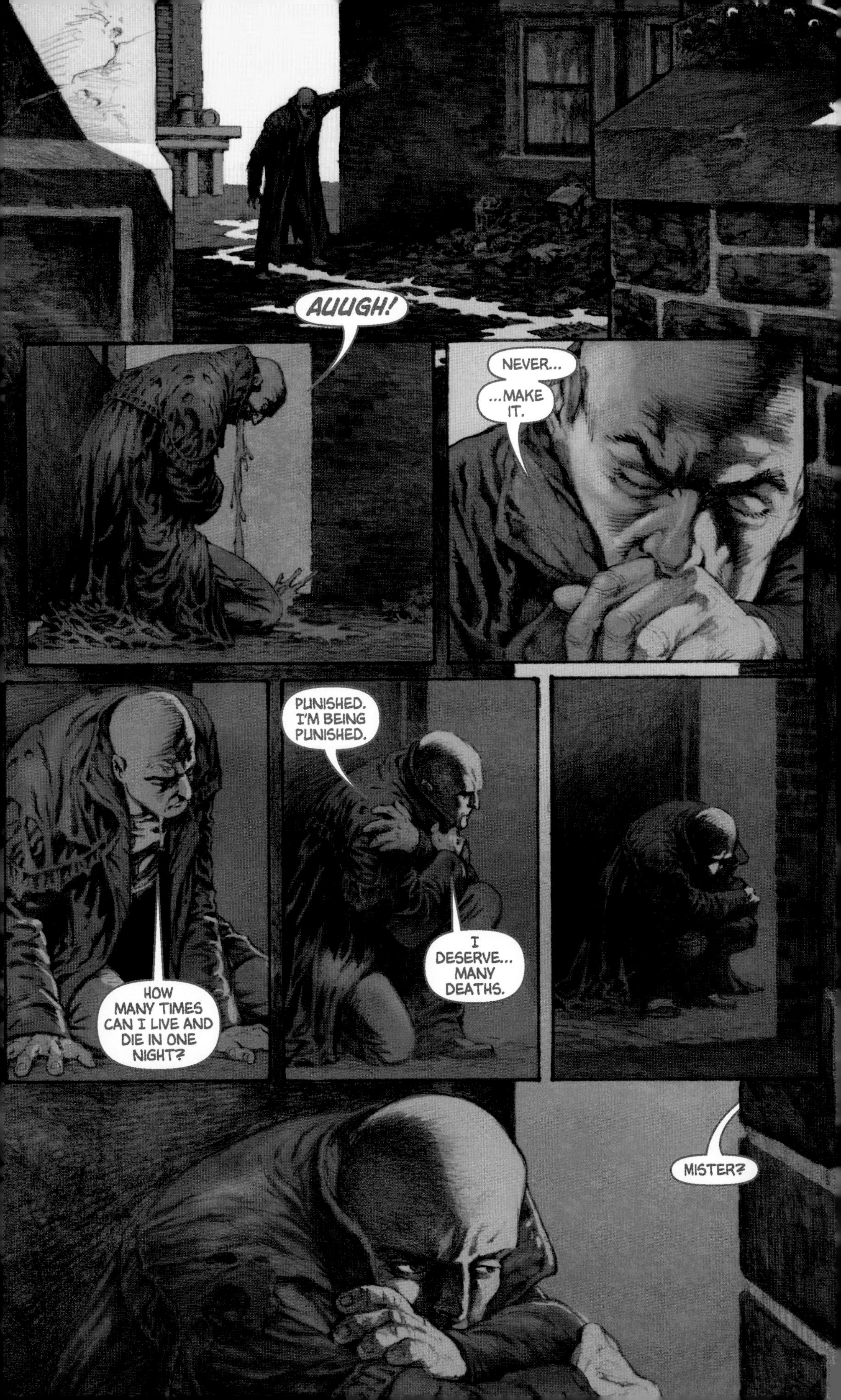
AUUGH!
NEVER...
...MAKE IT.
HOW MANY TIMES CAN I LIVE AND DIE IN ONE NIGHT?
PUNISHED. I'M BEING PUNISHED.
I DESERVE... MANY DEATHS.
MISTER?

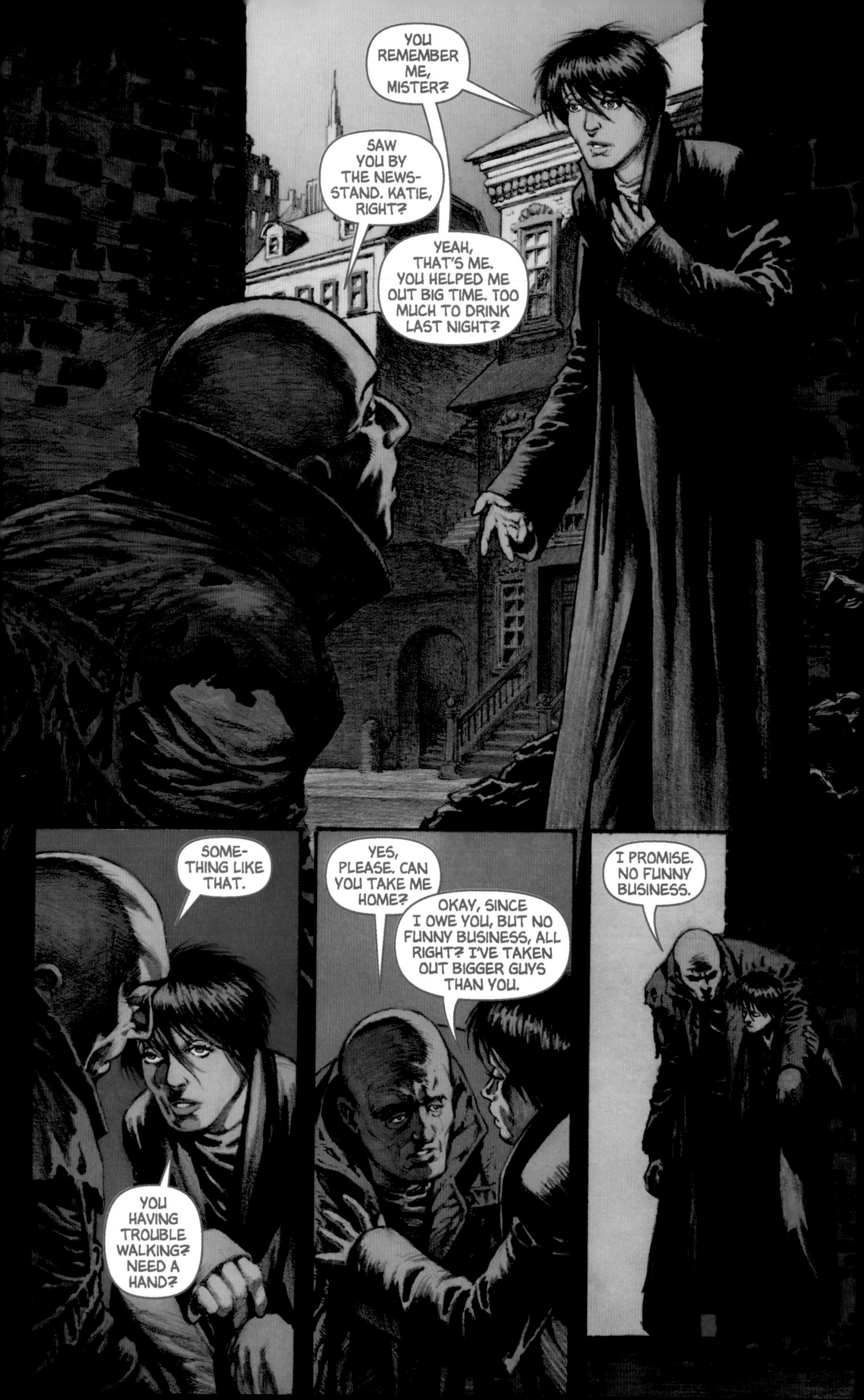

YOU REMEMBER ME, MISTER?
SAW YOU BY THE NEWS-STAND. KATIE, RIGHT?
YEAH, THAT'S ME. YOU HELPED ME OUT BIG TIME. TOO MUCH TO DRINK LAST NIGHT?
SOME-THING LIKE THAT.
YOU HAVING TROUBLE WALKING? NEED A HAND?
YES, PLEASE. CAN YOU TAKE ME HOME?
OKAY, SINCE I OWE YOU, BUT NO FUNNY BUSINESS, ALL RIGHT? I'VE TAKEN OUT BIGGER GUYS THAN YOU.
I PROMISE. NO FUNNY BUSINESS.

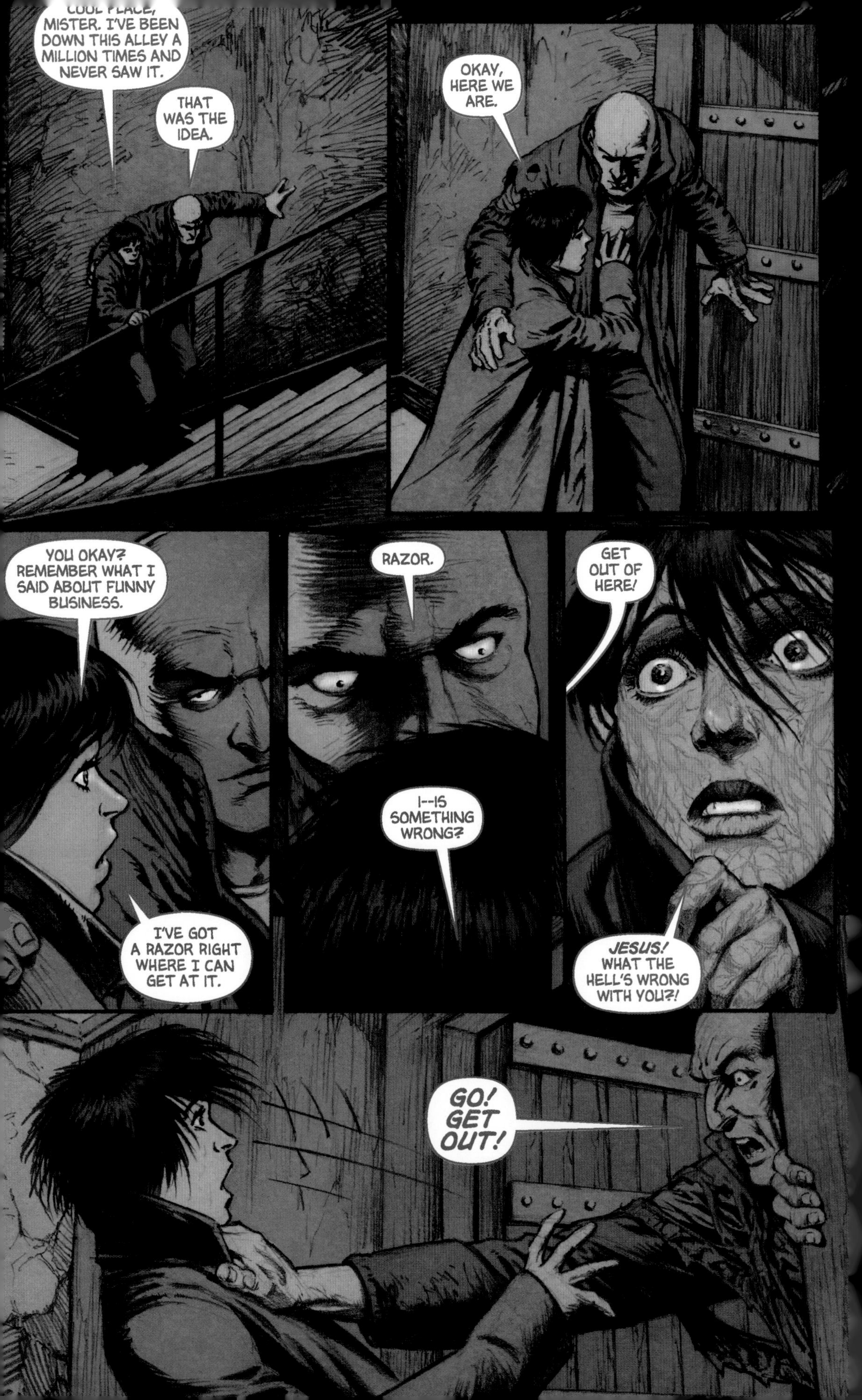
MISTER. I'VE BEEN DOWN THIS ALLEY A MILLION TIMES AND NEVER SAW IT.
THAT WAS THE IDEA.
OKAY, HERE WE ARE.
YOU OKAY? REMEMBER WHAT I SAID ABOUT FUNNY BUSINESS.
I'VE GOT A RAZOR RIGHT WHERE I CAN GET AT IT.
RAZOR.
I--IS SOMETHING WRONG?
GET OUT OF HERE!
JESUS! WHAT THE HELL'S WRONG WITH YOU?!
GO! GET OUT!

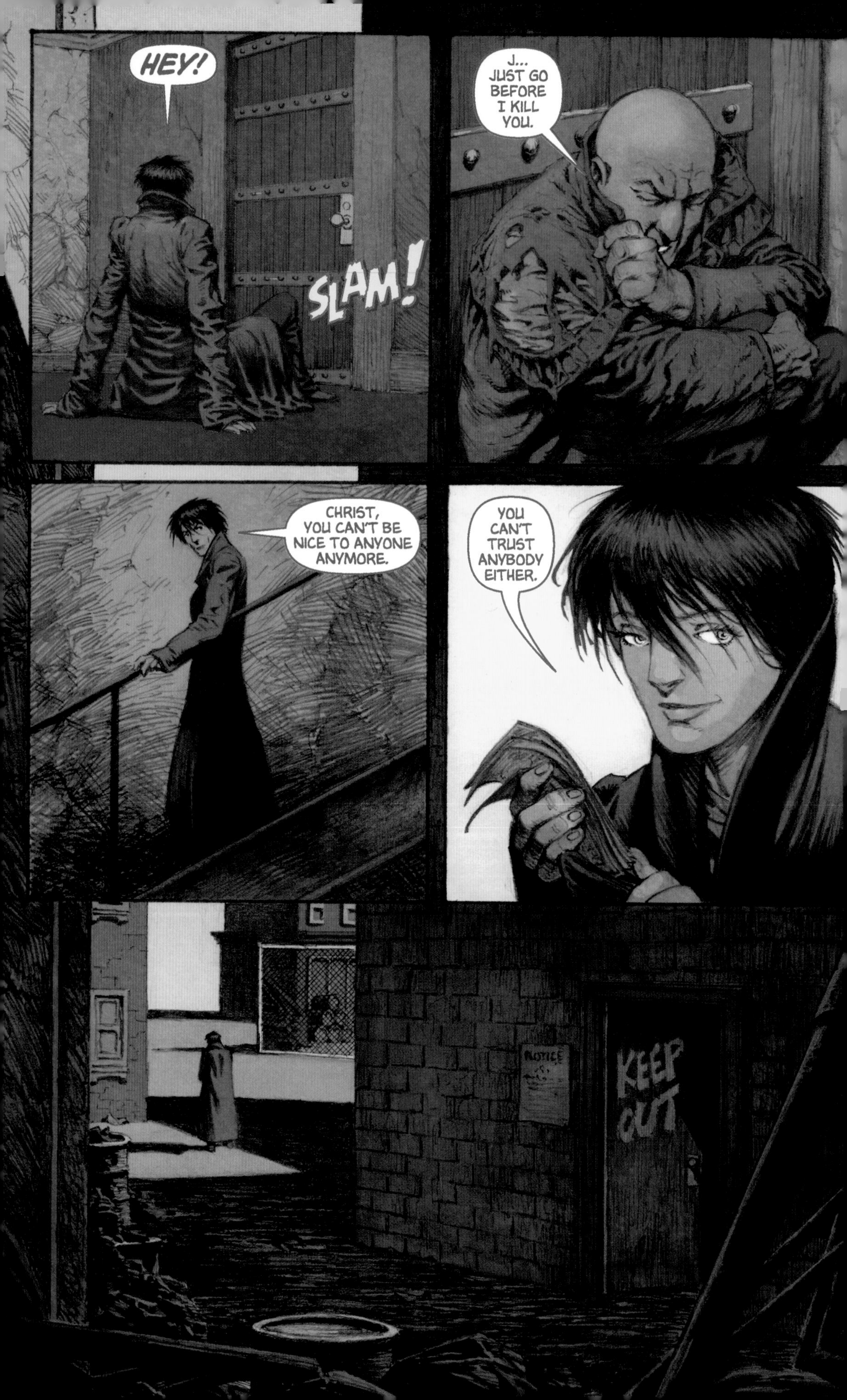
HEY!
SLAM!
J... JUST GO BEFORE I KILL YOU.
CHRIST, YOU CAN'T BE NICE TO ANYONE ANYMORE.
YOU CAN'T TRUST ANYBODY EITHER.
KEEP OUT

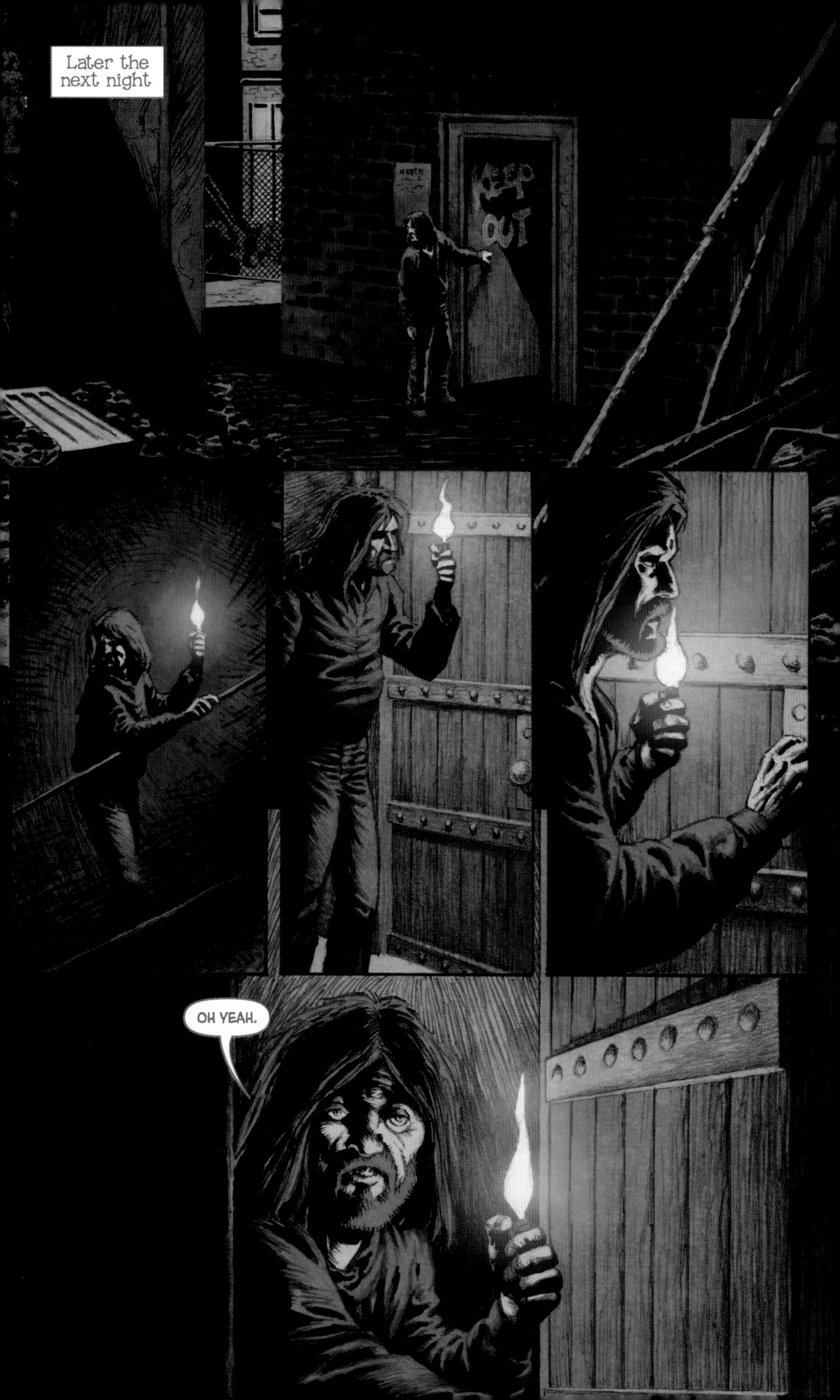
Later the next night
KEEP OUT
OH YEAH.

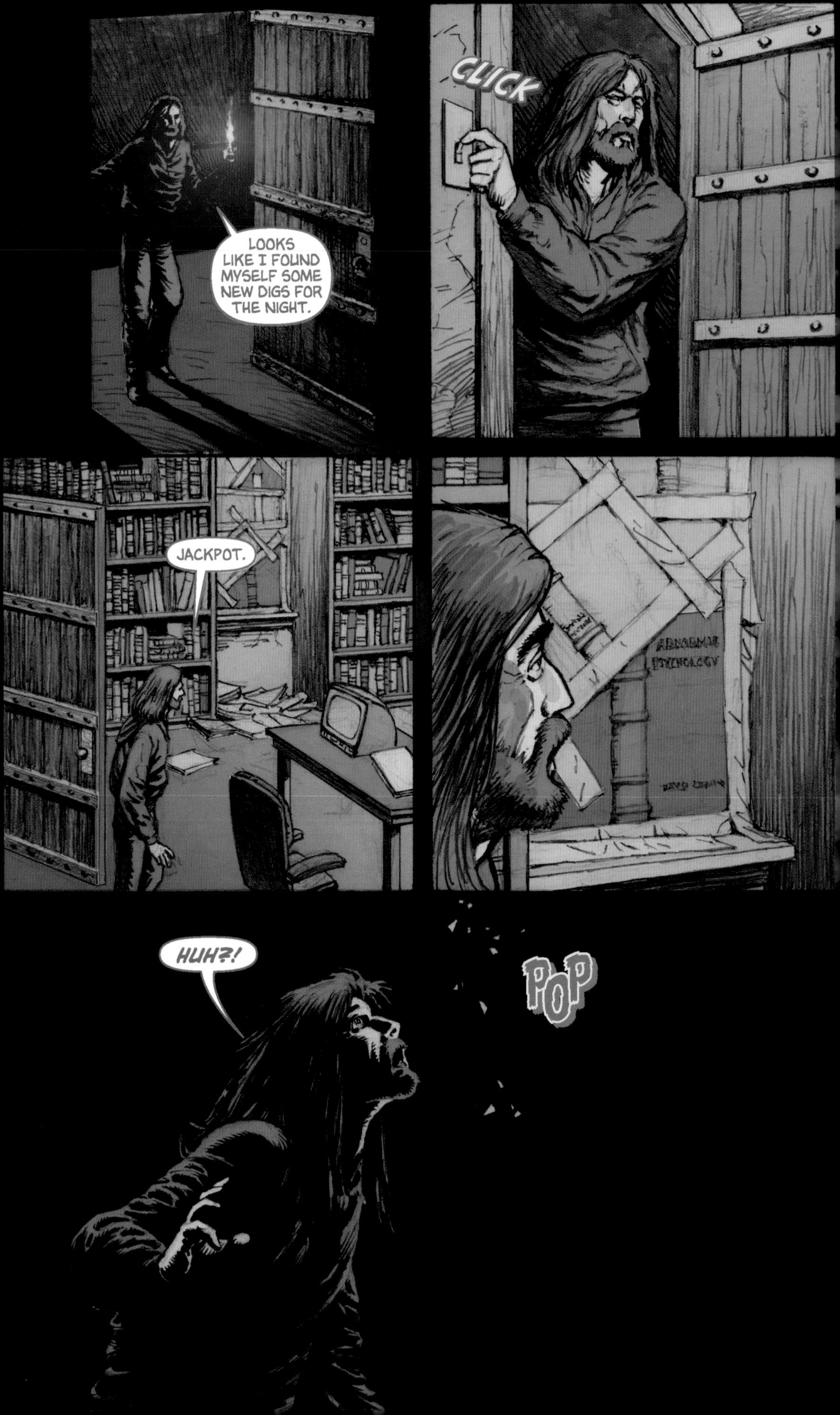
LOOKS LIKE I FOUND MYSELF SOME NEW DIGS FOR THE NIGHT.
CLICK
JACKPOT.
ABNORMAL PSYCHOLOGY
HUH?!
POP

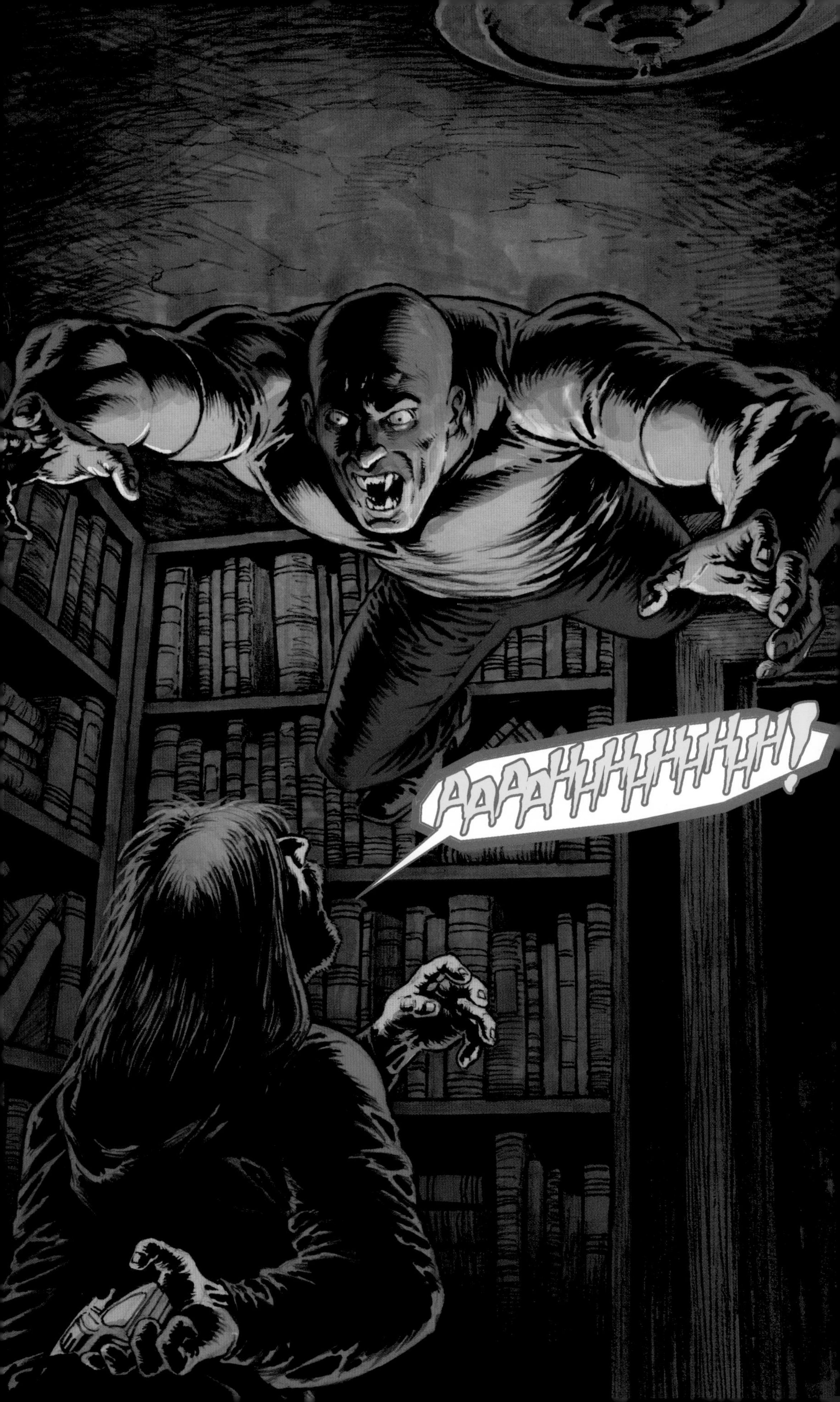
AAAAHHHHHHHHH!

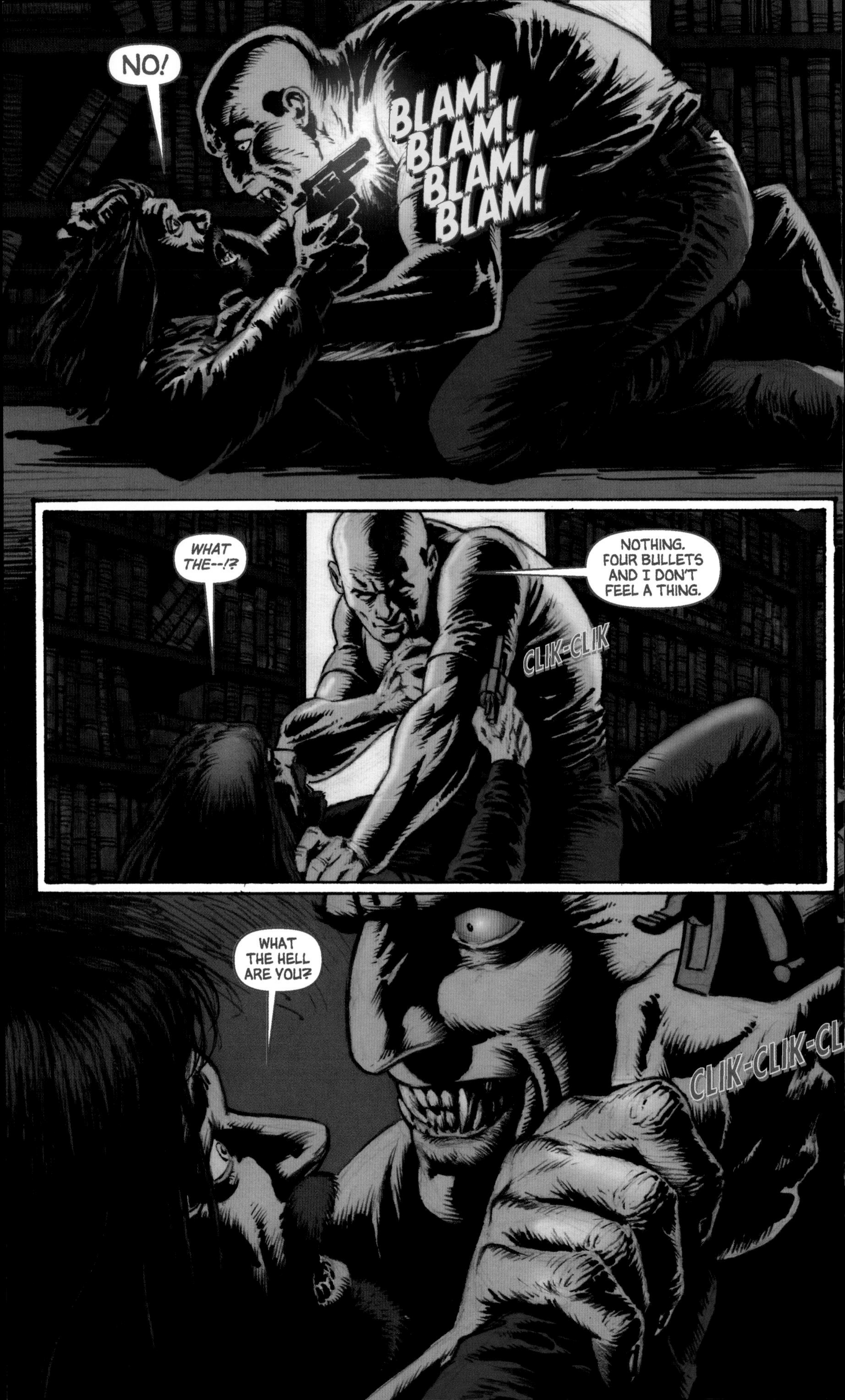
NO!
BLAM! BLAM! BLAM! BLAM!
WHAT THE--!?
NOTHING. FOUR BULLETS AND I DON'T FEEL A THING.
CLIK-CLIK
WHAT THE HELL ARE YOU?
CLIK-CLIK-CL

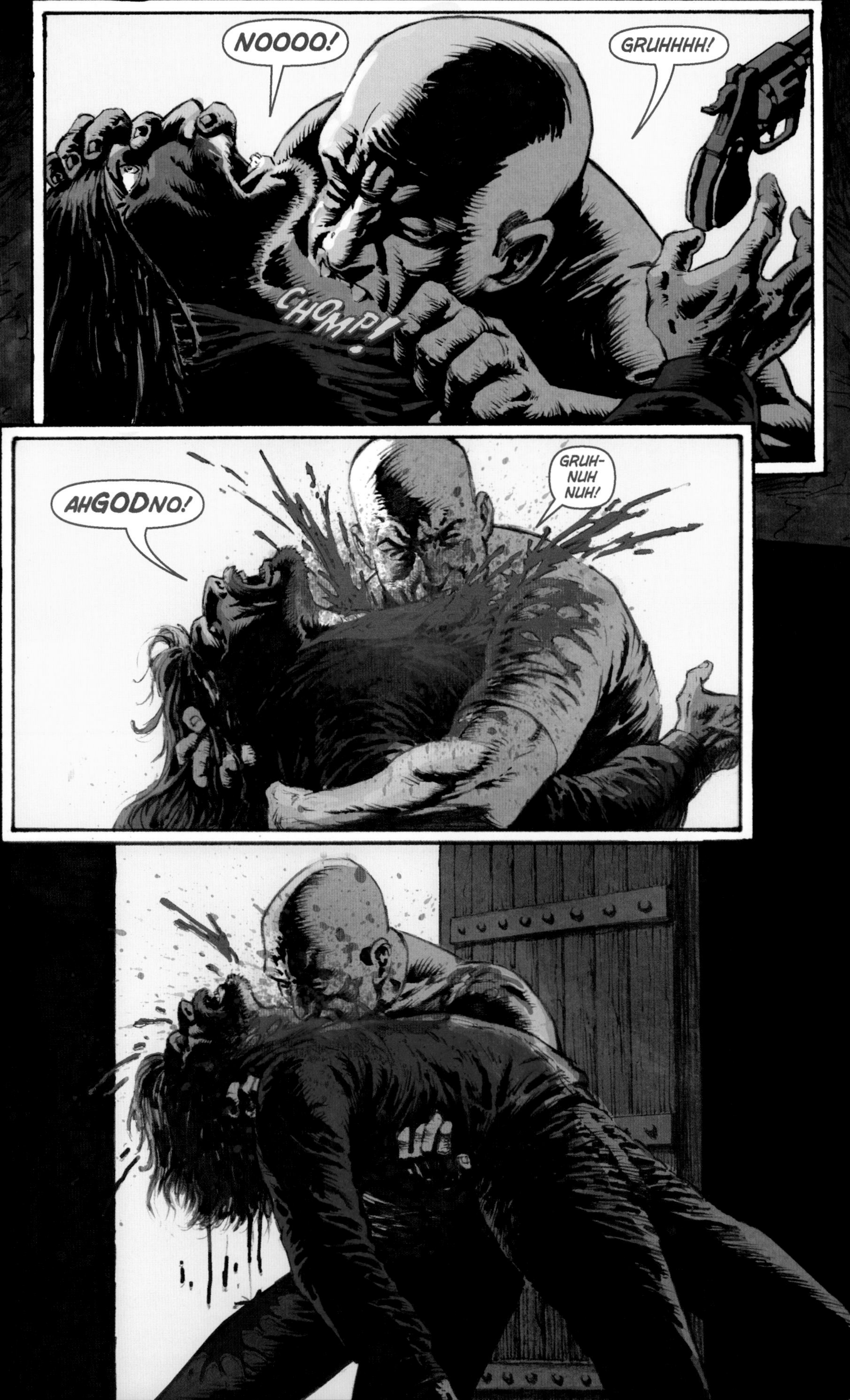
NOOOO!
GRUHHHH!
CHOMP!
AHGODNO!
GRUH-
NUH
NUH!

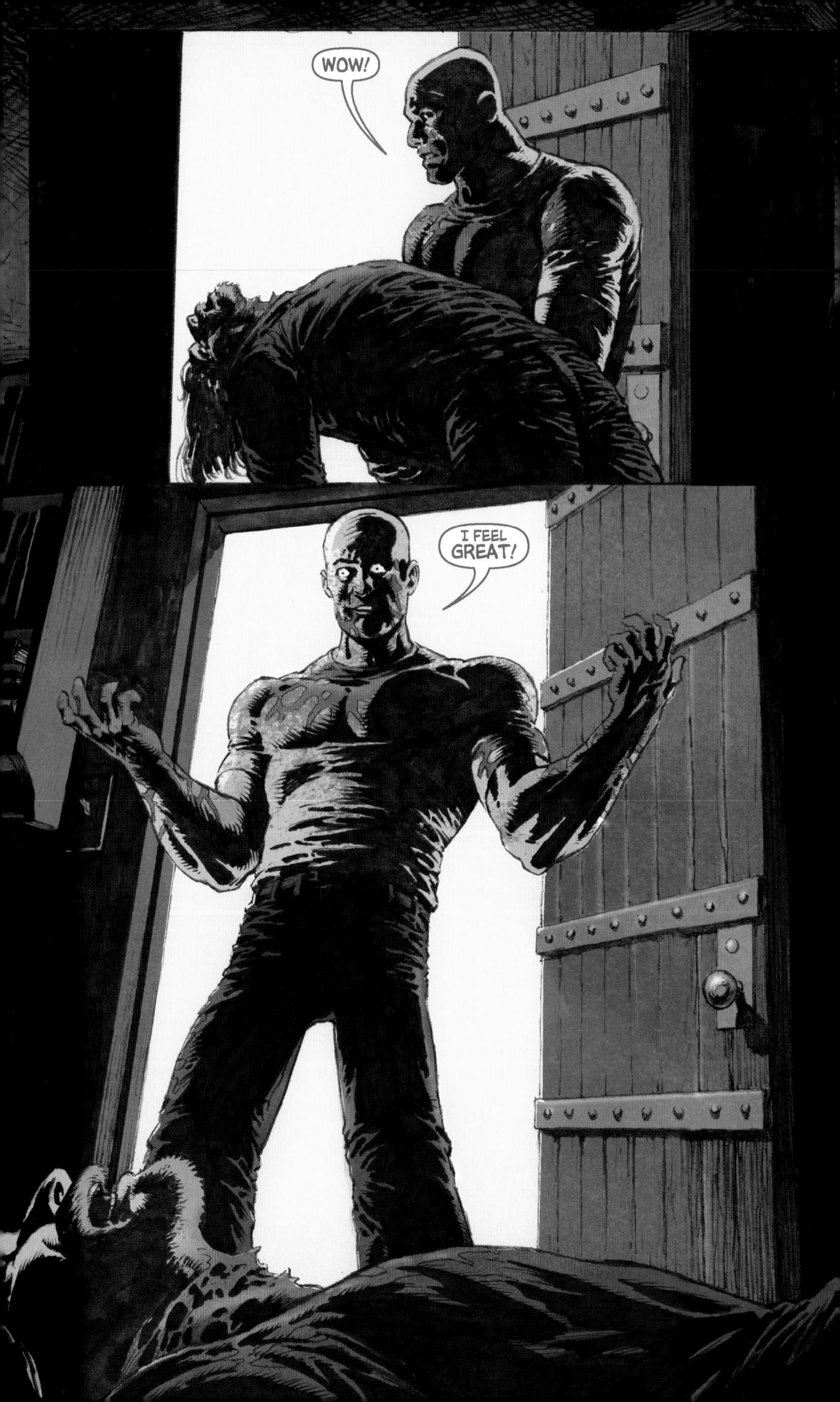
WOW!
I FEEL GREAT!

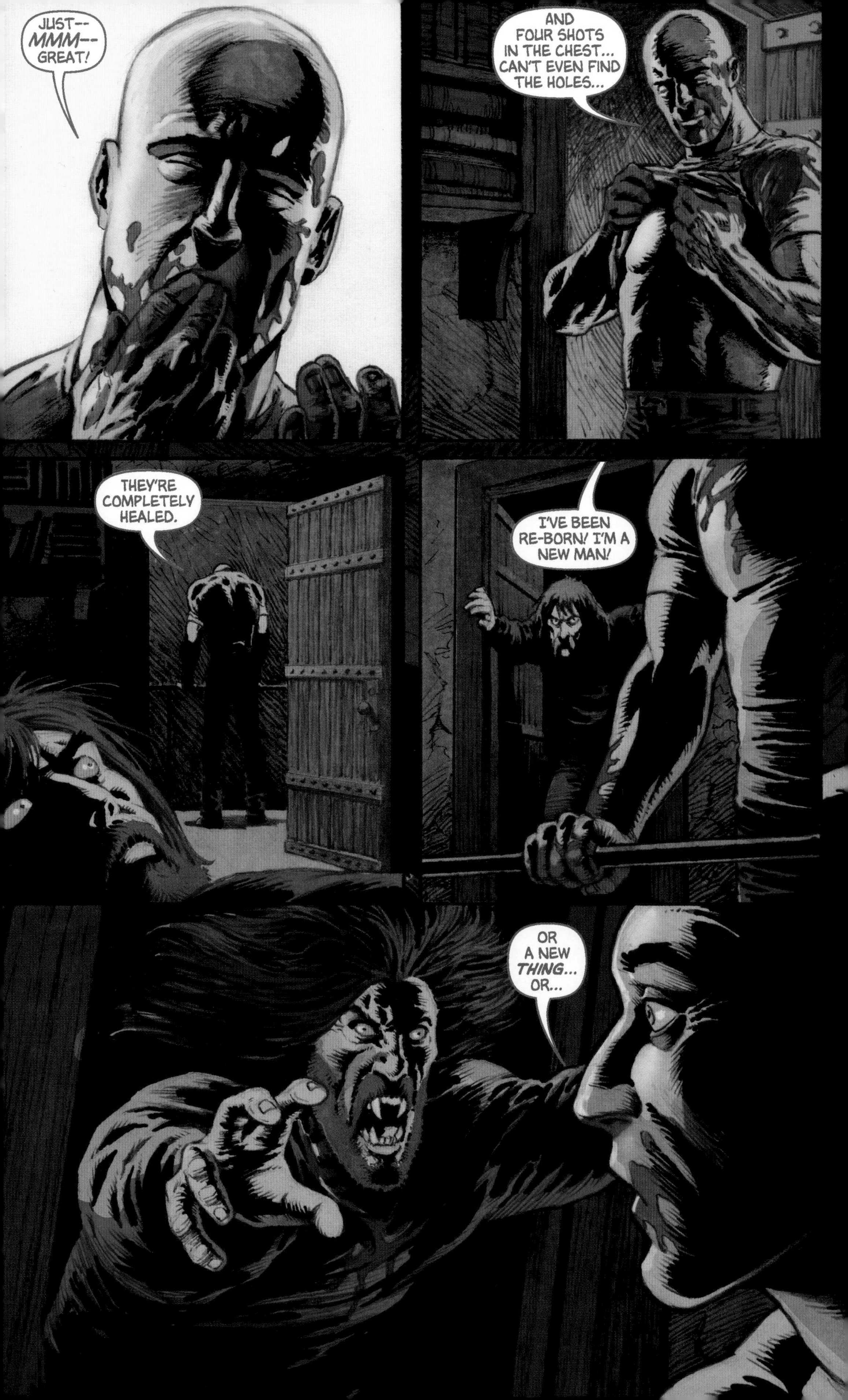
JUST-- MMM-- GREAT!
AND FOUR SHOTS IN THE CHEST... CAN'T EVEN FIND THE HOLES...
THEY'RE COMPLETELY HEALED.
I'VE BEEN RE-BORN! I'M A NEW MAN!
OR A NEW THING... OR...

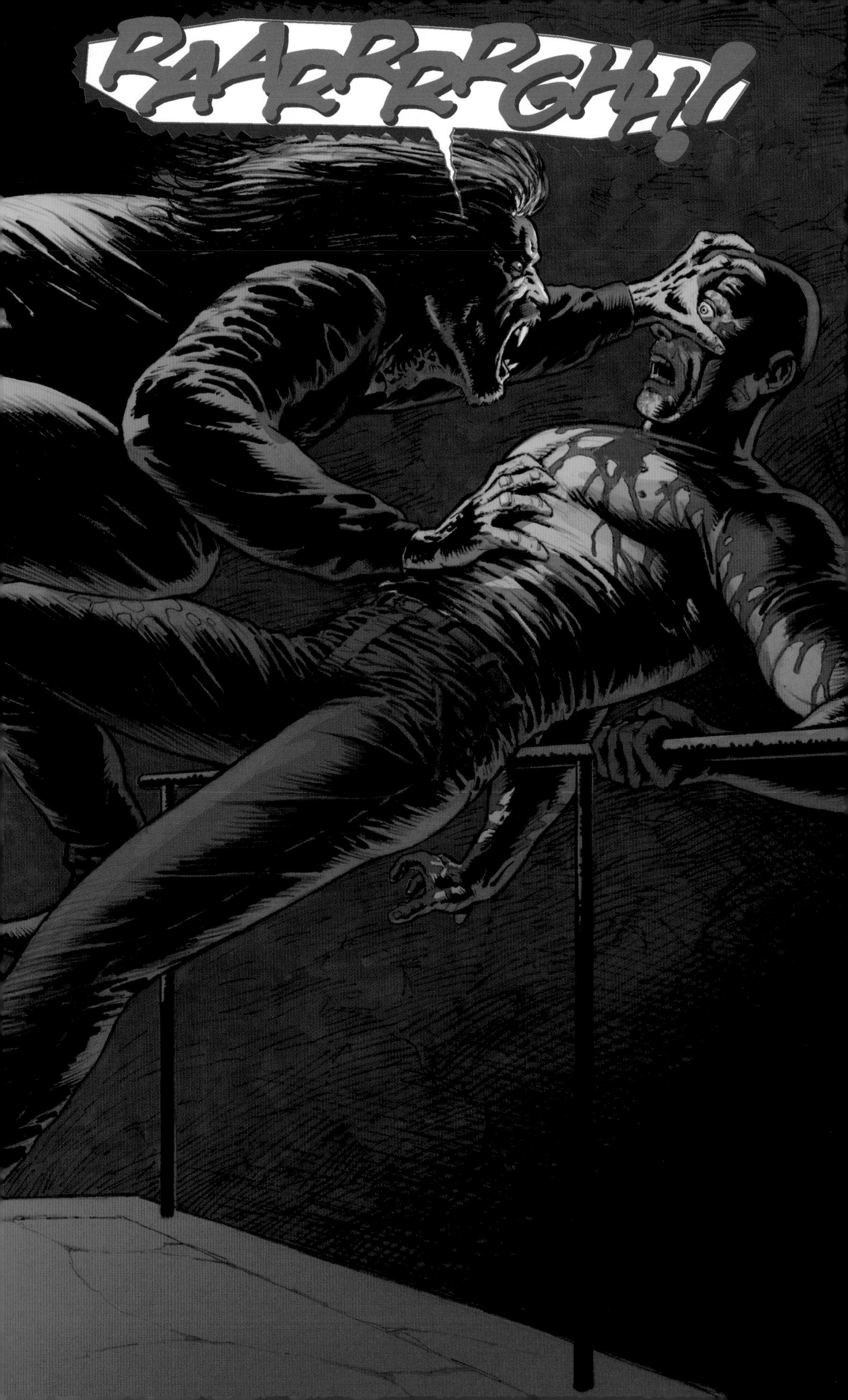
RAARRRGHH!!

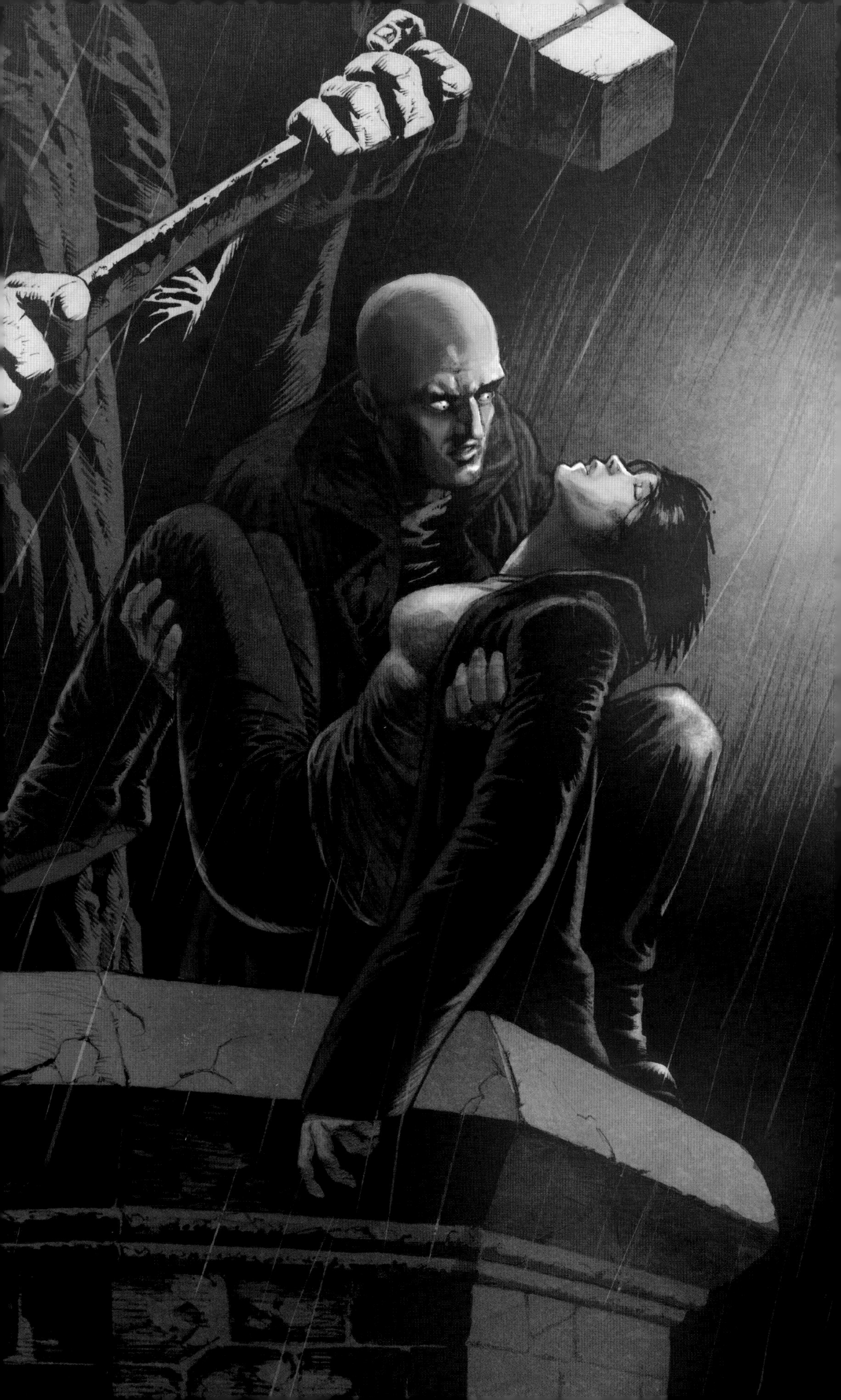

CHAPTER FOUR

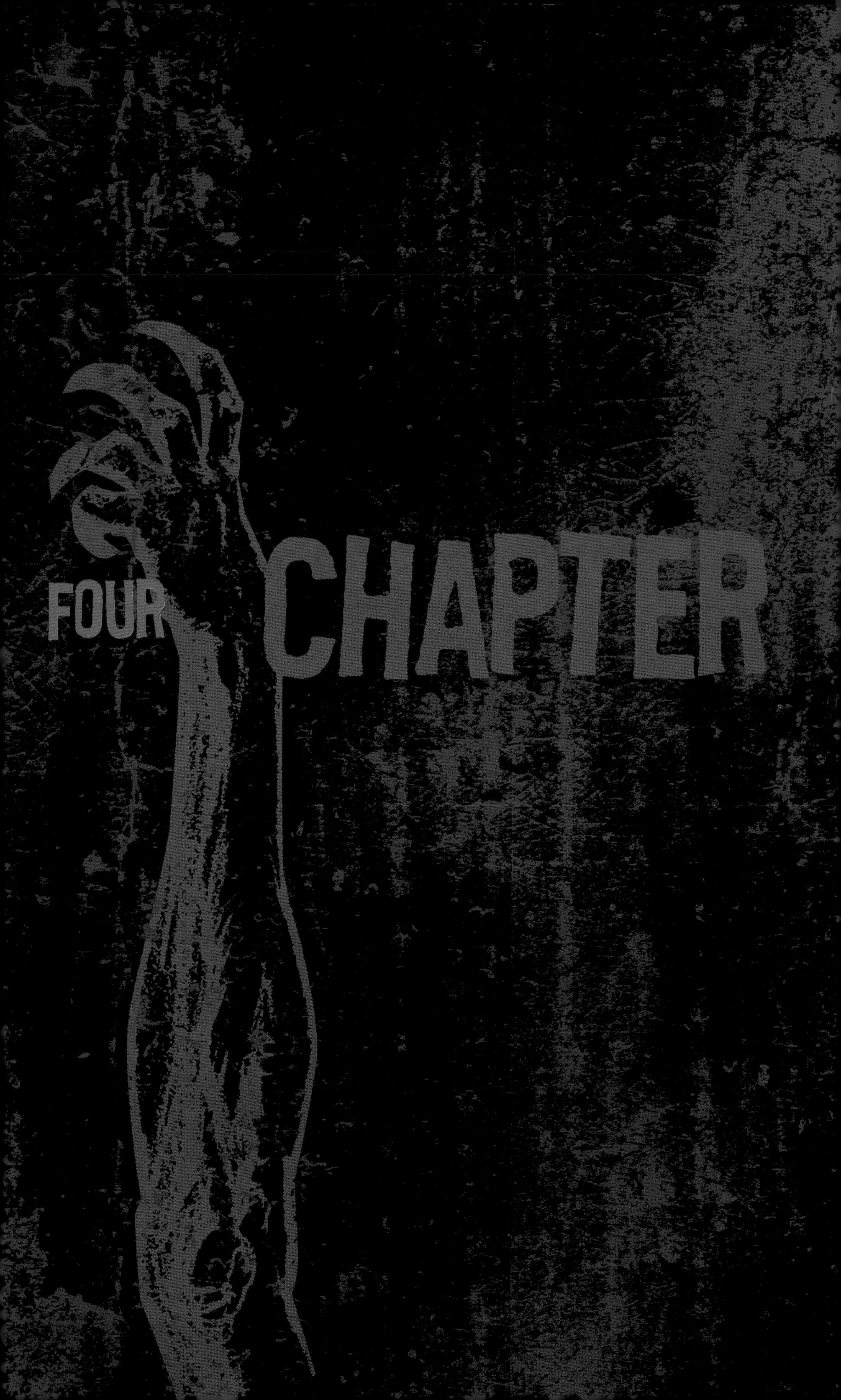

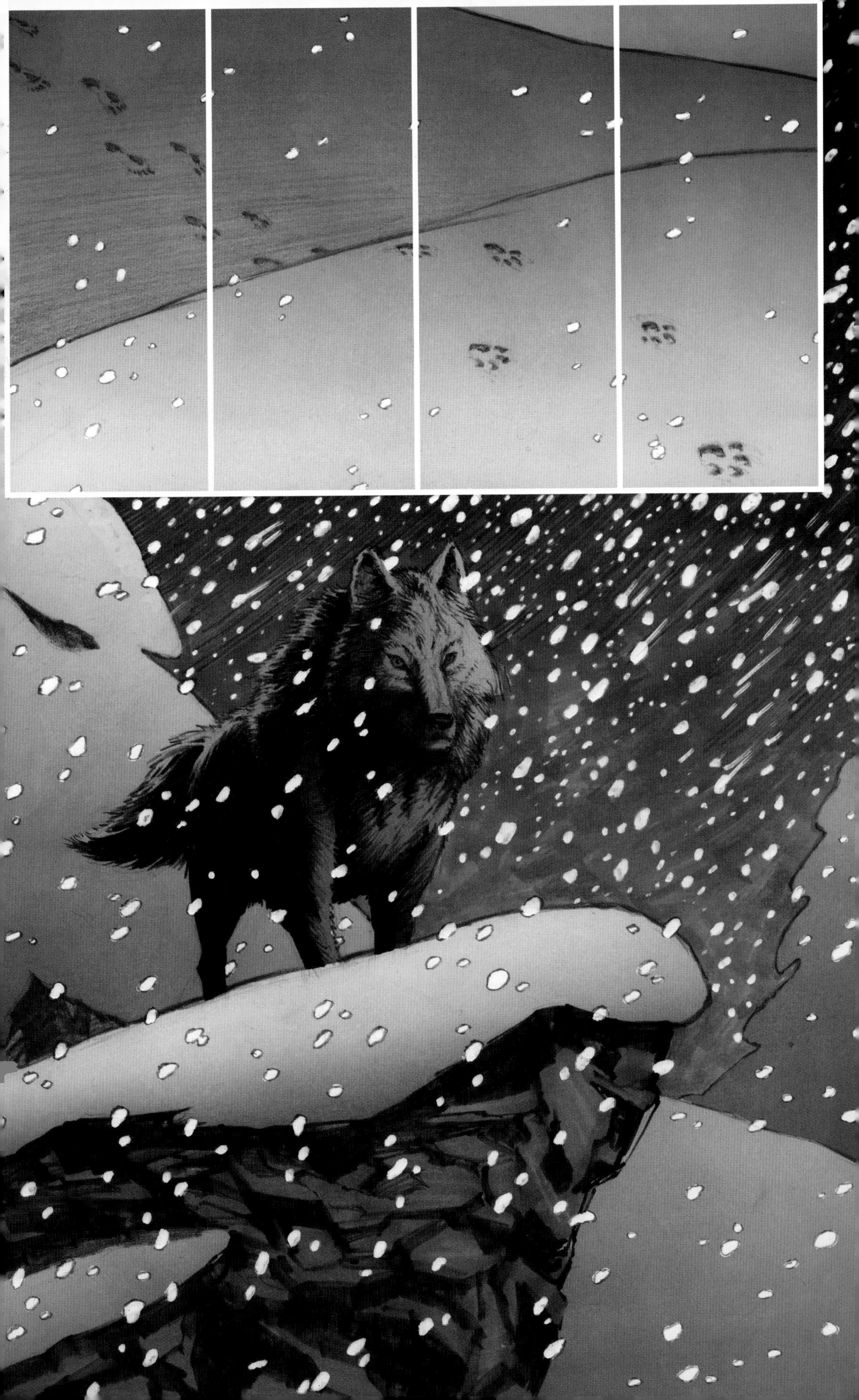

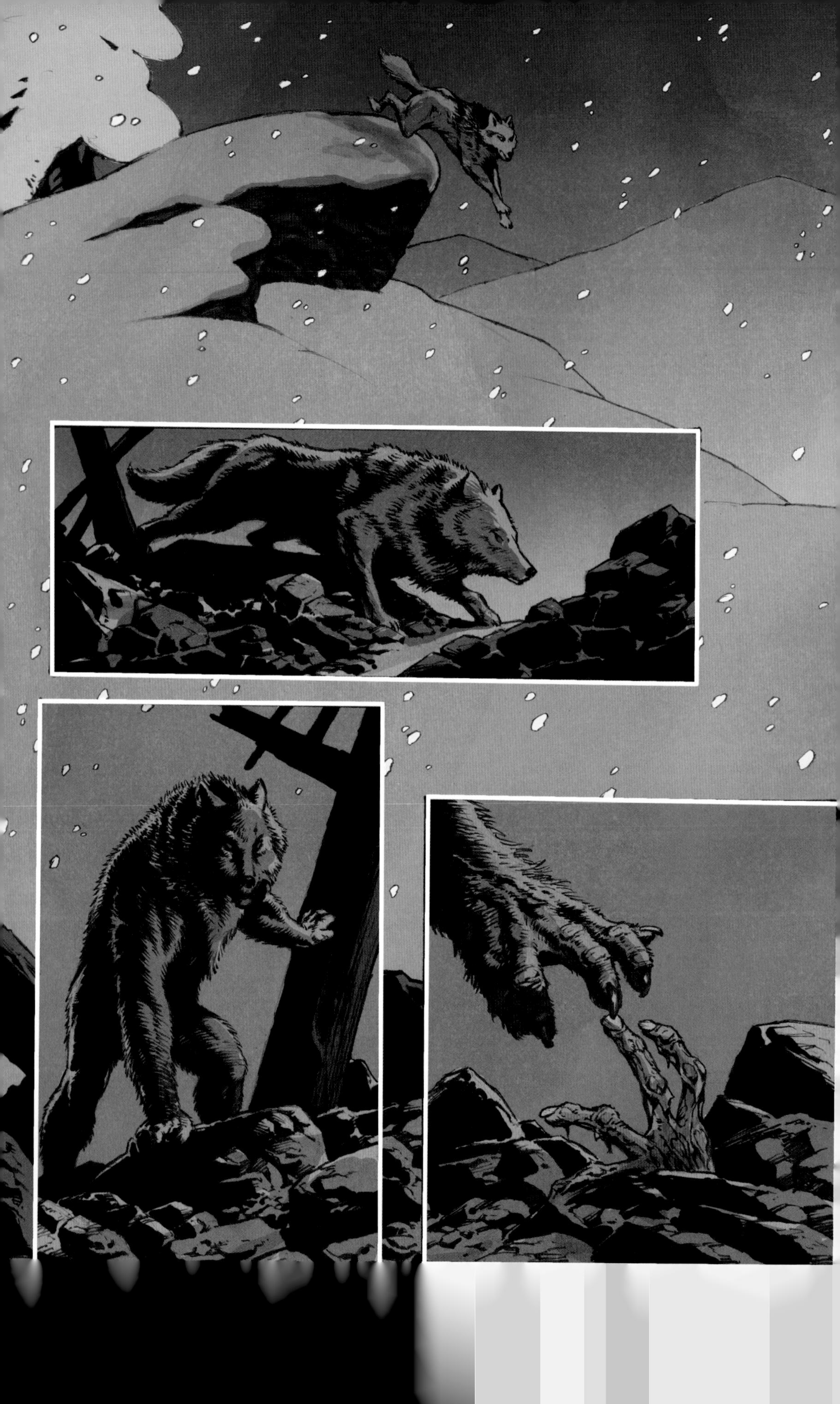

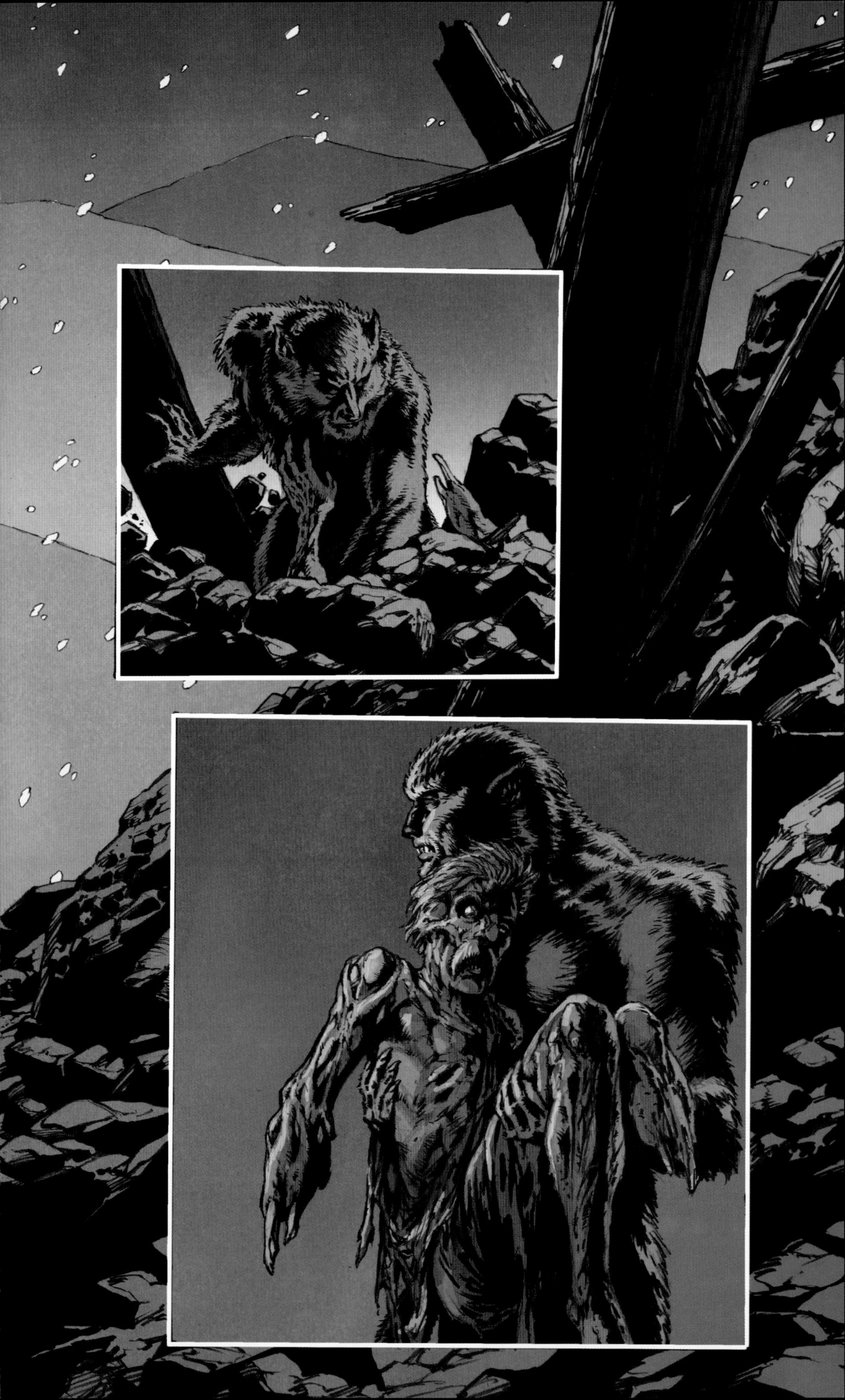

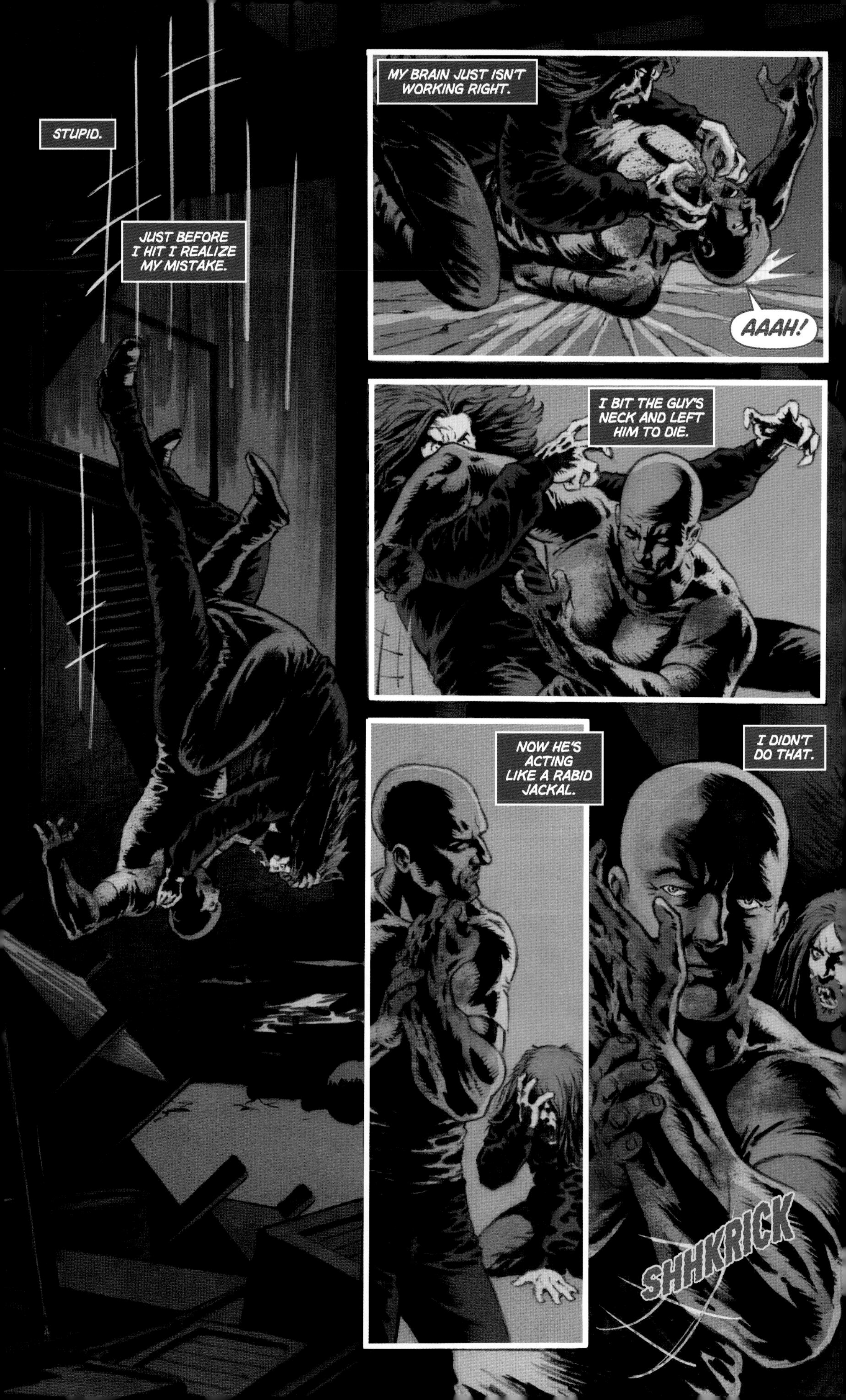
STUPID.
JUST BEFORE I HIT I REALIZE MY MISTAKE.
MY BRAIN JUST ISN'T WORKING RIGHT.
AAAH!
I BIT THE GUY'S NECK AND LEFT HIM TO DIE.
NOW HE'S ACTING LIKE A RABID JACKAL.
I DIDN'T DO THAT.
SHHKRICK

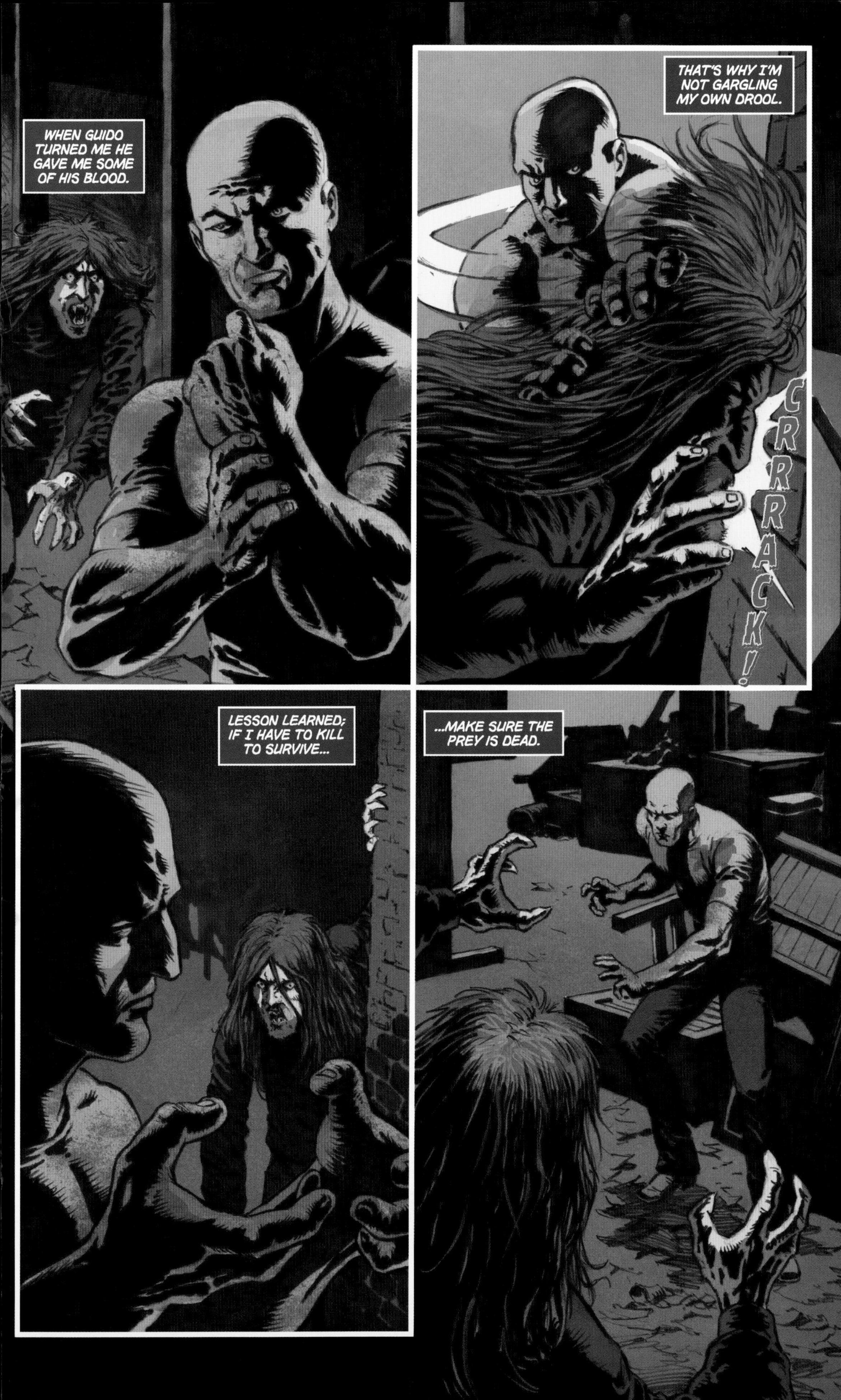
WHEN GUIDO TURNED ME HE GAVE ME SOME OF HIS BLOOD.
THAT'S WHY I'M NOT GARGLING MY OWN DROOL.
CRRRRACK!
LESSON LEARNED; IF I HAVE TO KILL TO SURVIVE...
...MAKE SURE THE PREY IS DEAD.

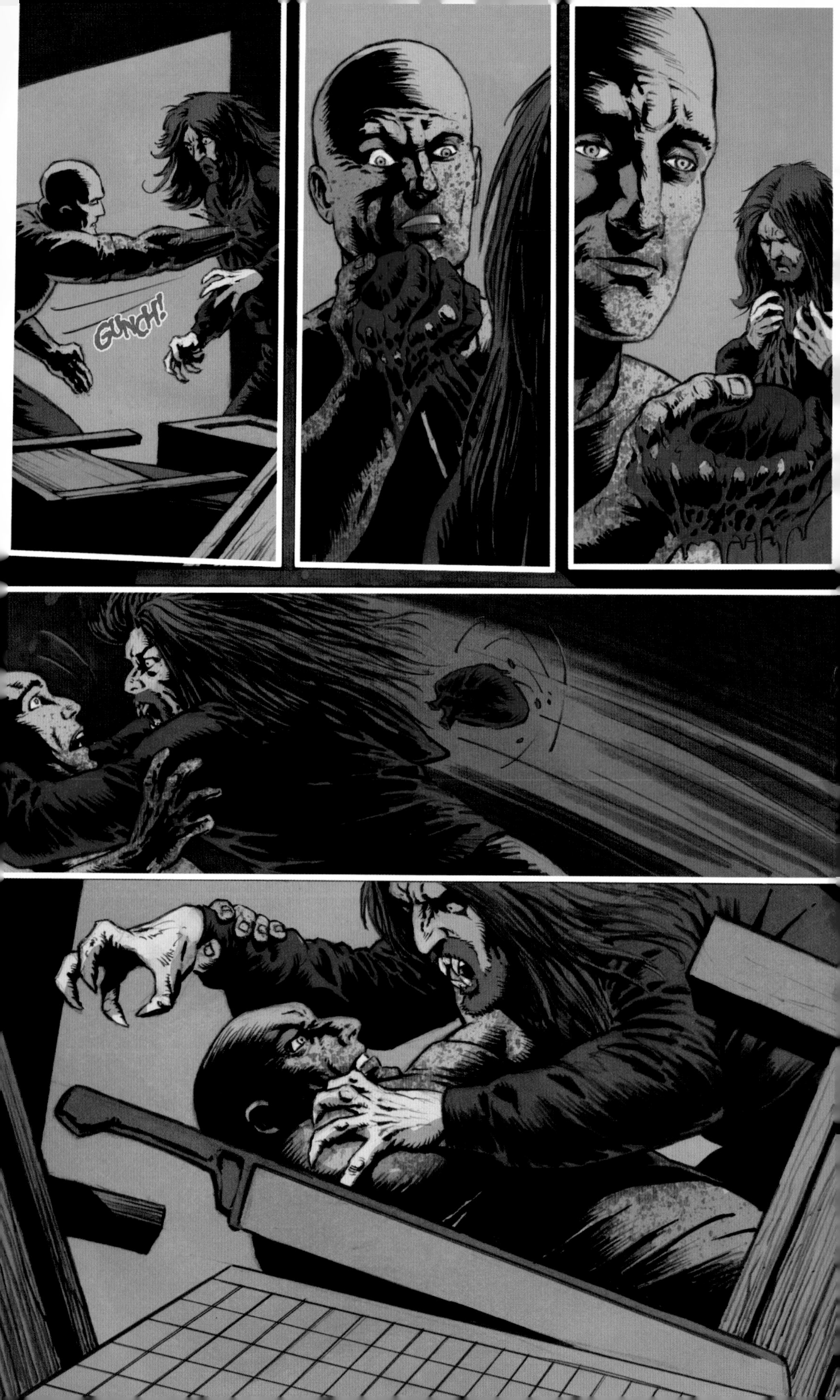
GUNCH!

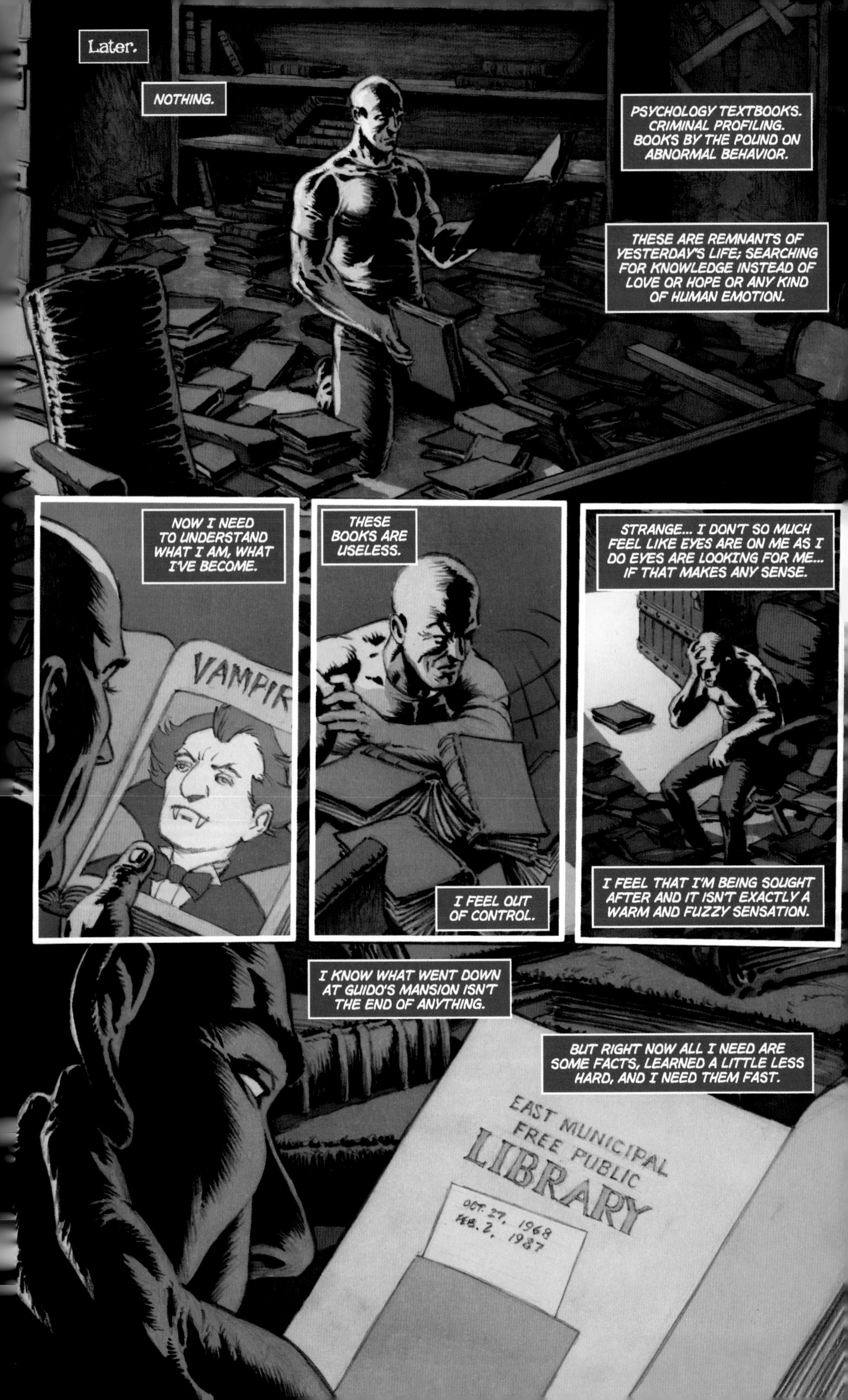
Later.
NOTHING.
PSYCHOLOGY TEXTBOOKS. CRIMINAL PROFILING. BOOKS BY THE POUND ON ABNORMAL BEHAVIOR.
THESE ARE REMNANTS OF YESTERDAY'S LIFE; SEARCHING FOR KNOWLEDGE INSTEAD OF LOVE OR HOPE OR ANY KIND OF HUMAN EMOTION.
NOW I NEED TO UNDERSTAND WHAT I AM, WHAT I'VE BECOME.
VAMPIR
THESE BOOKS ARE USELESS.
I FEEL OUT OF CONTROL.
STRANGE... I DON'T SO MUCH FEEL LIKE EYES ARE ON ME AS I DO EYES ARE LOOKING FOR ME... IF THAT MAKES ANY SENSE.
I FEEL THAT I'M BEING SOUGHT AFTER AND IT ISN'T EXACTLY A WARM AND FUZZY SENSATION.
I KNOW WHAT WENT DOWN AT GUIDO'S MANSION ISN'T THE END OF ANYTHING.
BUT RIGHT NOW ALL I NEED ARE SOME FACTS, LEARNED A LITTLE LESS HARD, AND I NEED THEM FAST.
EAST MUNICIPAL FREE PUBLIC LIBRARY
OCT. 27, 1968
FEB. 2, 1987

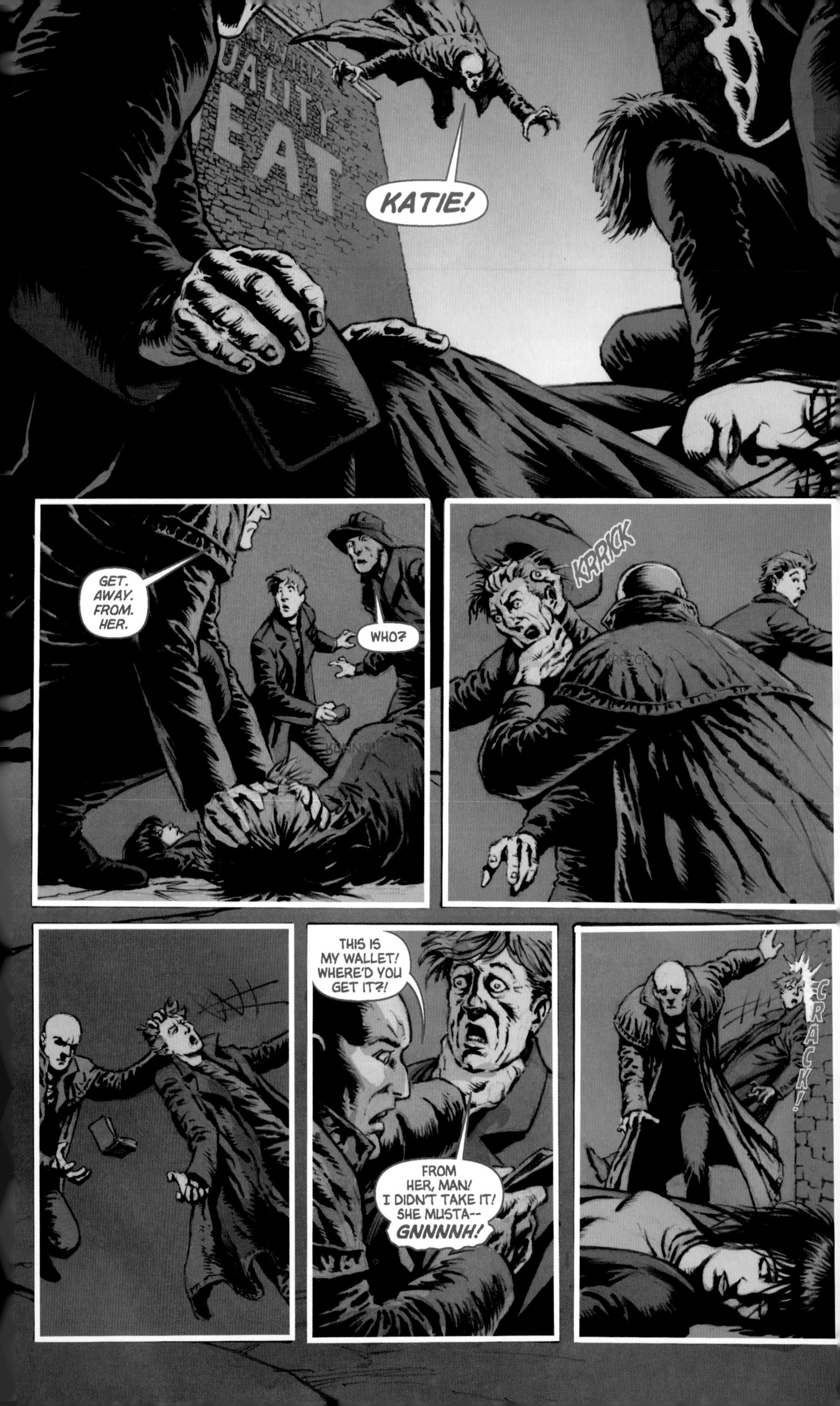
KATIE!
GET. AWAY. FROM. HER.
WHO?
KRRKCK
THIS IS MY WALLET! WHERE'D YOU GET IT?!
FROM HER, MAN! I DIDN'T TAKE IT! SHE MUSTA-- GNNNNH!
CRACK!

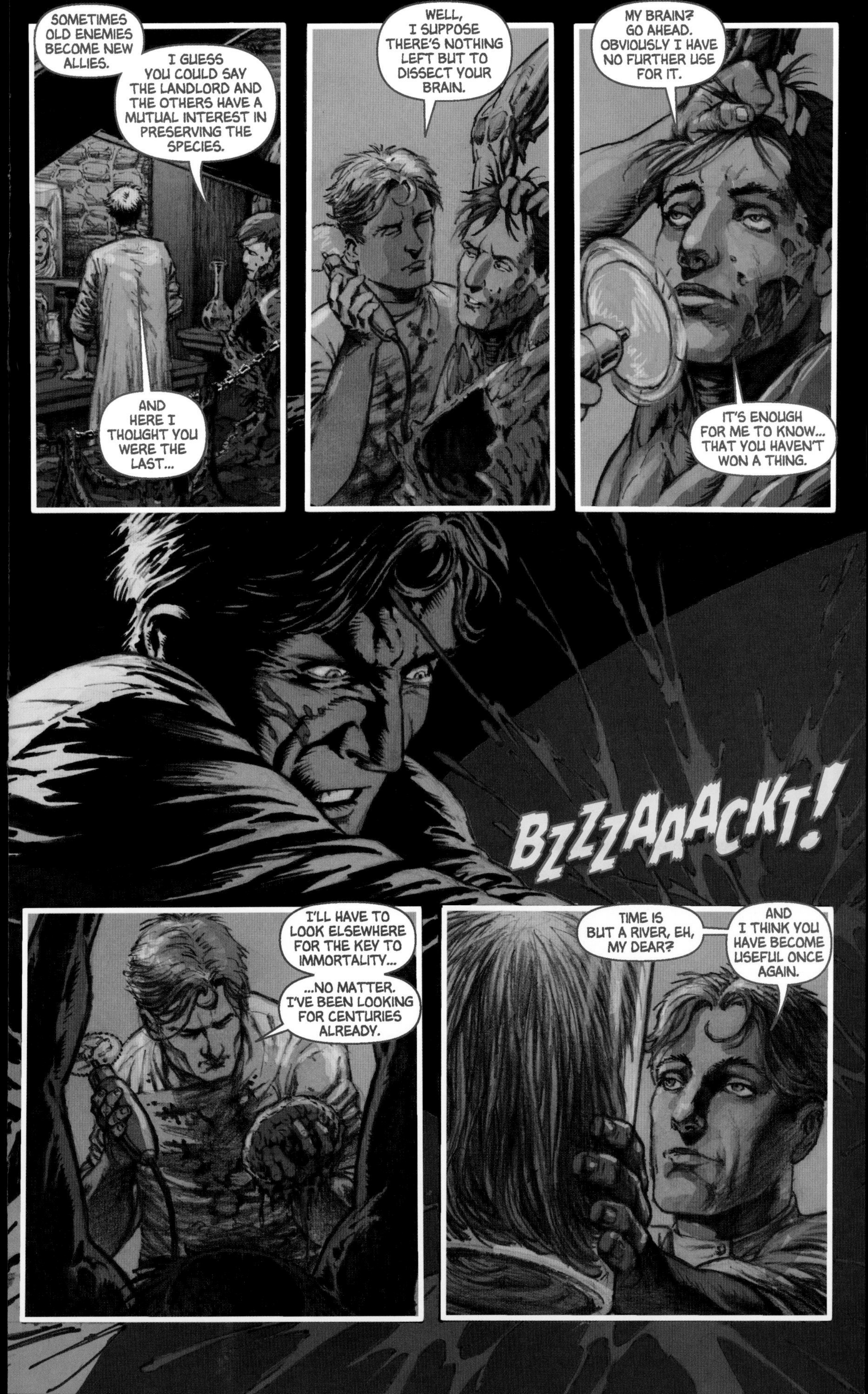
SOMETIMES OLD ENEMIES BECOME NEW ALLIES.
I GUESS YOU COULD SAY THE LANDLORD AND THE OTHERS HAVE A MUTUAL INTEREST IN PRESERVING THE SPECIES.
AND HERE I THOUGHT YOU WERE THE LAST...
WELL, I SUPPOSE THERE'S NOTHING LEFT BUT TO DISSECT YOUR BRAIN.
MY BRAIN? GO AHEAD. OBVIOUSLY I HAVE NO FURTHER USE FOR IT.
IT'S ENOUGH FOR ME TO KNOW... THAT YOU HAVEN'T WON A THING.
BZZZAAACKT!
I'LL HAVE TO LOOK ELSEWHERE FOR THE KEY TO IMMORTALITY...
...NO MATTER. I'VE BEEN LOOKING FOR CENTURIES ALREADY.
TIME IS BUT A RIVER, EH, MY DEAR?
AND I THINK YOU HAVE BECOME USEFUL ONCE AGAIN.

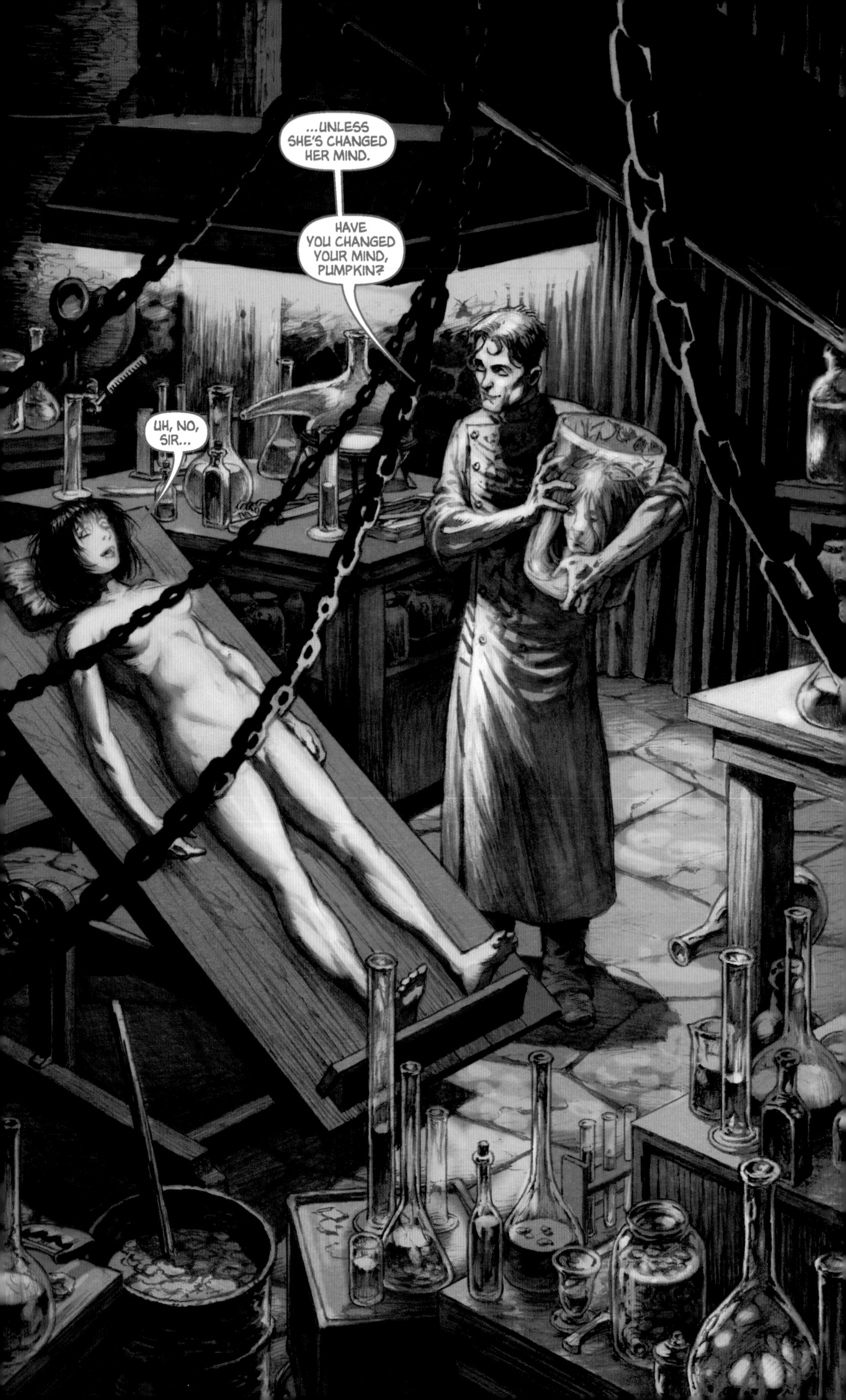
...UNLESS SHE'S CHANGED HER MIND.
HAVE YOU CHANGED YOUR MIND, PUMPKIN?
UH, NO, SIR...

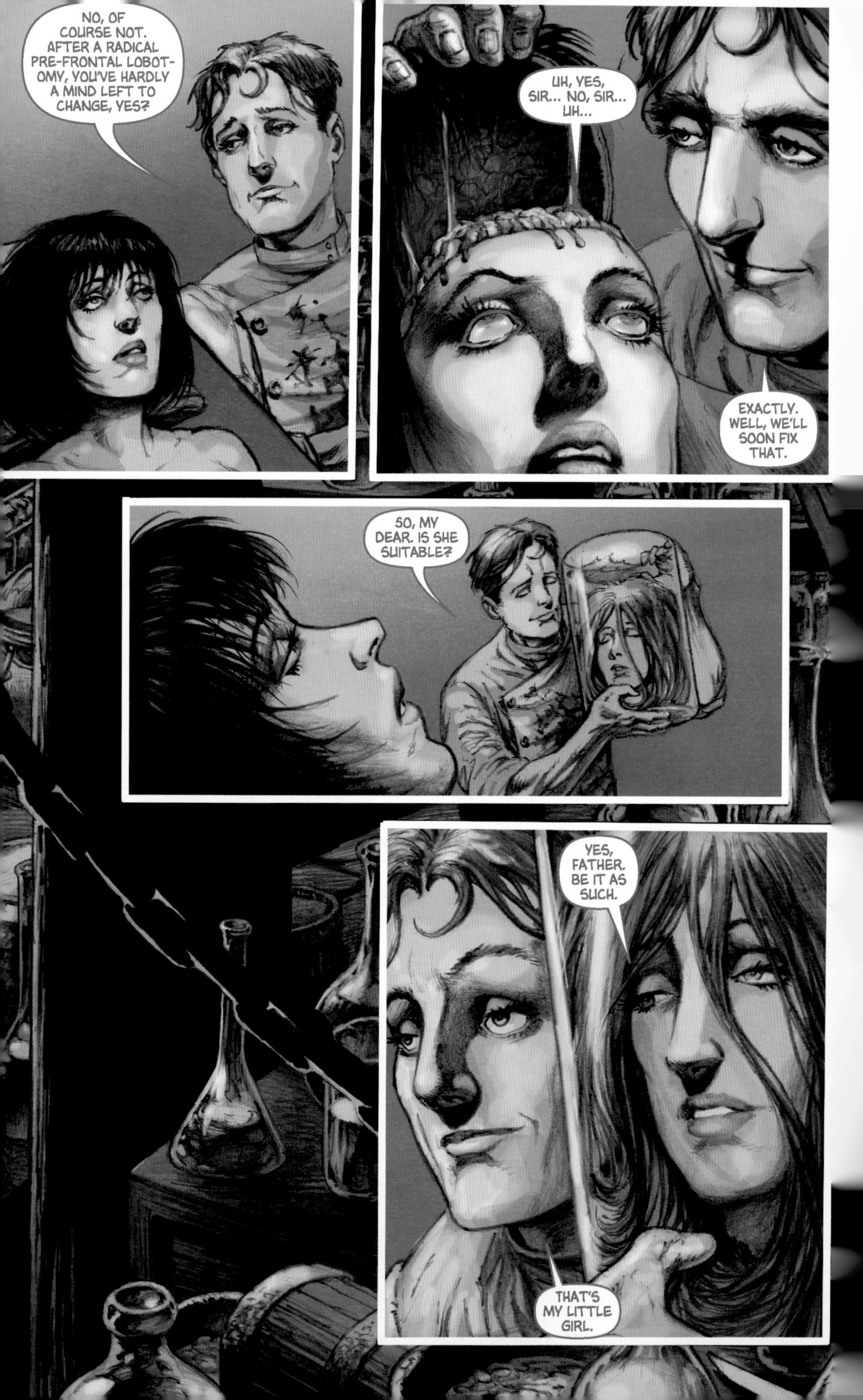
NO, OF COURSE NOT. AFTER A RADICAL PRE-FRONTAL LOBOT-OMY, YOU'VE HARDLY A MIND LEFT TO CHANGE, YES?
UH, YES, SIR... NO, SIR... UH...
EXACTLY. WELL, WE'LL SOON FIX THAT.
SO, MY DEAR. IS SHE SUITABLE?
YES, FATHER. BE IT AS SUCH.
THAT'S MY LITTLE GIRL.

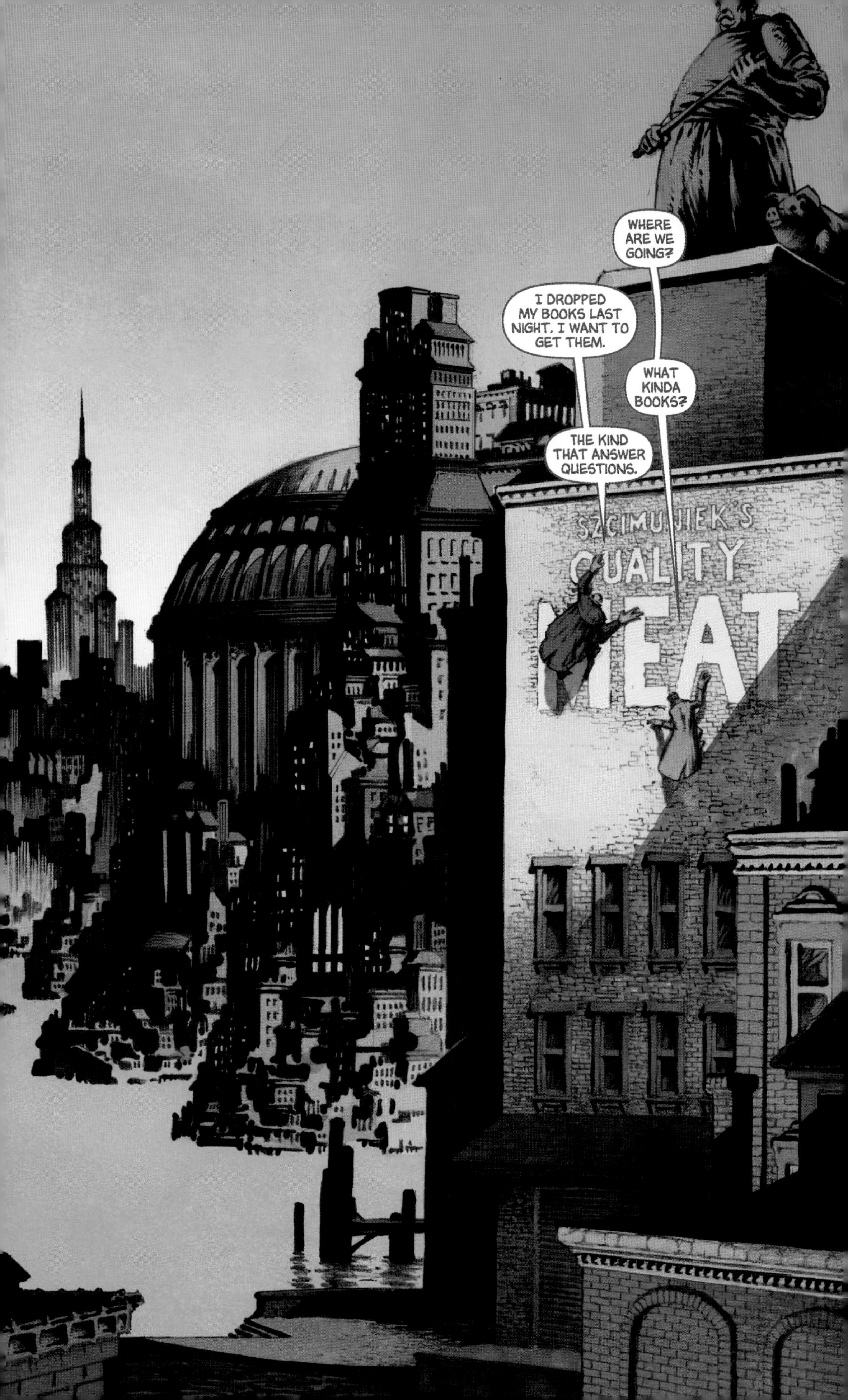
WHERE ARE WE GOING?
I DROPPED MY BOOKS LAST NIGHT. I WANT TO GET THEM.
WHAT KINDA BOOKS?
THE KIND THAT ANSWER QUESTIONS.
QUALITY

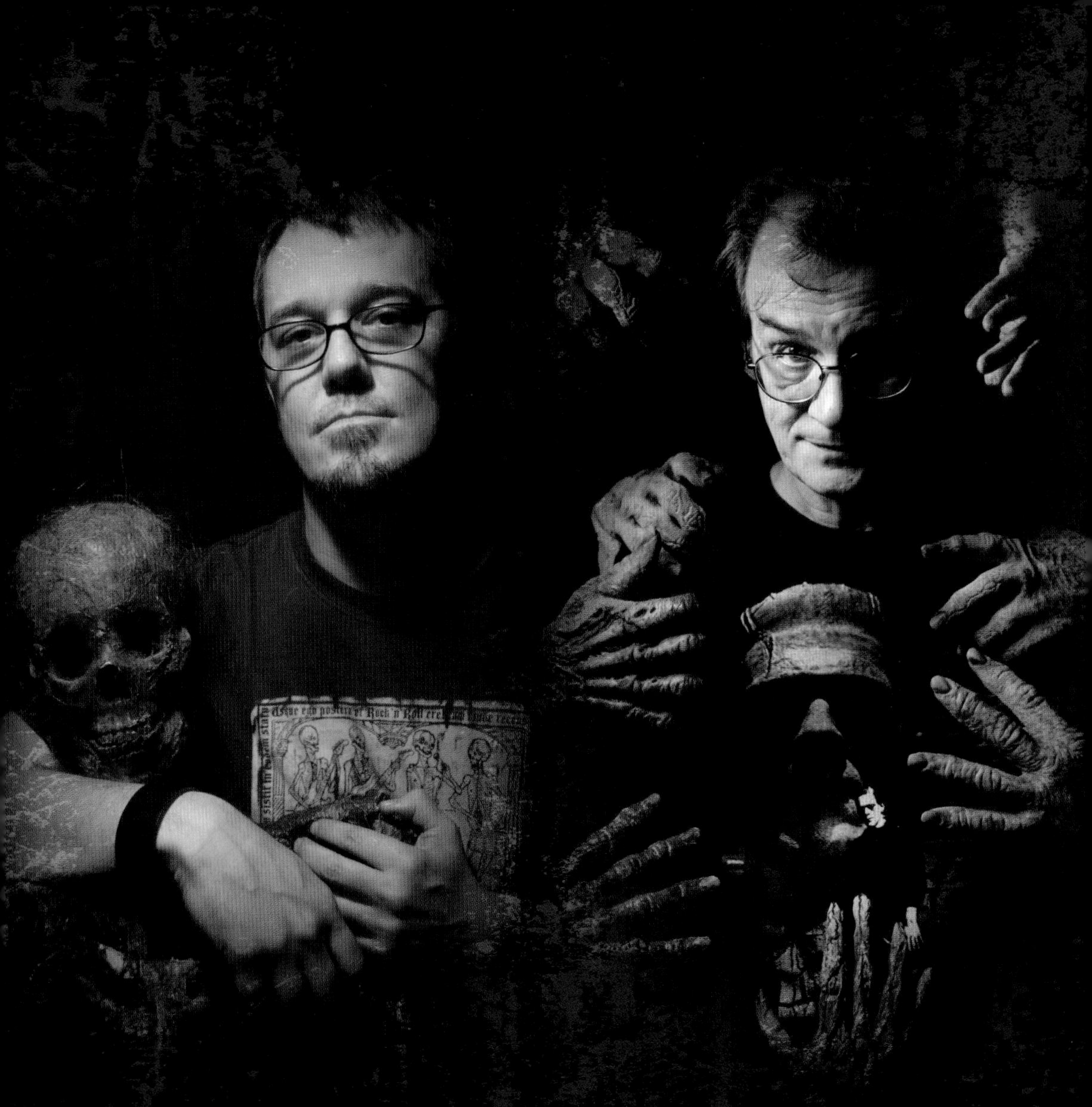

STEVE NILES has been writing, editing, and publishing horror stories in various forms for so long it's scary. He was recently named by *Fangoria* magazine as one of its "thirteen rising talents who promise to keep us terrified for the next twentyfive years." His hit graphic novel *30 Days of Night* helped resurrect the genre of horror comics in 2002, and Sam Raimi's long-anticipated film adaptation of that story was released to rave reviews in 2007. Steve spends his days and nights (and weekends, and what should be his sleepy-time) writing comics, screenplays, prose stories, and more comics. He lives in Los Angeles in a dark cave filled with turtles, cats, and other critters of the night.

BERNIE WRIGHTSON has been creating horror art for more than thirty years. Best known for co-creating (with writer Len Wein) the classic comic character Swamp Thing, and for definitively illustrating Mary Shelley's *Frankenstein*, Bernie has also worked with author Stephen King on illustrated versions of *The Stand, Cycle of the Werewolf*, and *The Dark Tower V.* After spending years working as a conceptual artist for films and television (including work on *Ghostbusters*, *Spider-man*, and George Romero's *Land of the Dead*), Bernie recently returned to his favorite medium and is again bringing the fun of flesh-dripping, brain-eating horror to comics. Bernie lives in Los Angeles with his adorable wife Liz.

Photographs by Tim Bradstreet

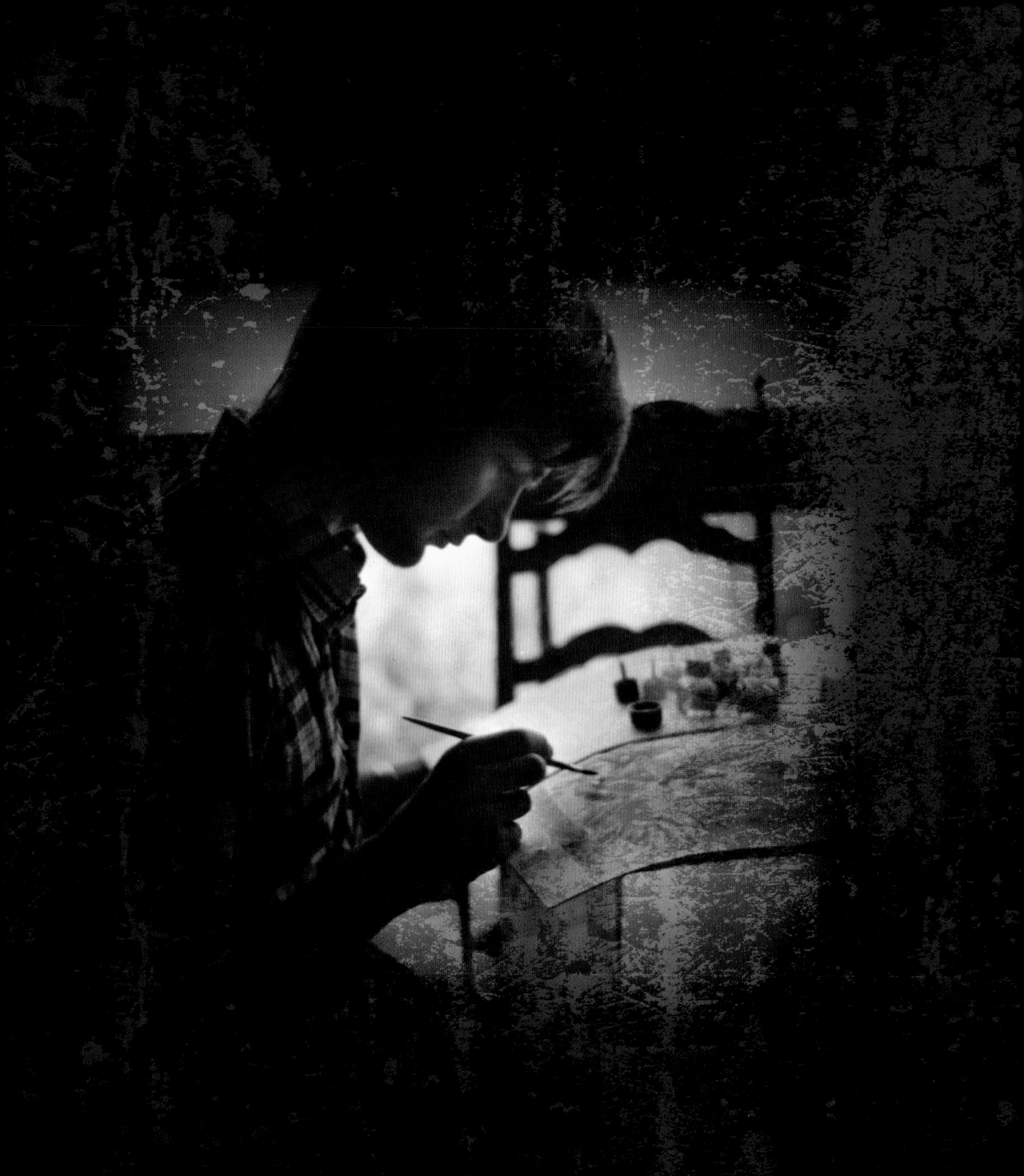

JOSÉ VILLARRUBIA discovered the work of Bernie Wrightson at age fourteen, when, while attending a meeting of the mythic Club Dhin, Spain's first association of comics professionals, he was shown the story "The Last Hunters" reprinted in the fanzine "*El Golem*" as an example of great comics art. From that moment on he followed Bernie's work fanatically. He later ordered "*The Monsters Color-the-Creature Book*" and attacked it with gusto. In 1992, he finally got to meet his hero in person when he curated the exhibit: Sequential Art, Art of the Comic-Book, at Maryland Art Place, in Bernie's hometown, Baltimore. Fourteen years later José finally got to work with Bernie in the book you are holding in your hands, and it goes without saying that for José this is a dream come true. While waiting to work with Bernie, José became a fine art painter, photographer, and digital artist as well as a professor at the Maryland Institute College of Art, where he teaches today. He has colored many comic books and has illustrated two books by author Alan Moore.

Photograph by Luz J. Momediano

BERNIE WRIGHTSON'S
CITY OF OTHERS SKETCHBOOK

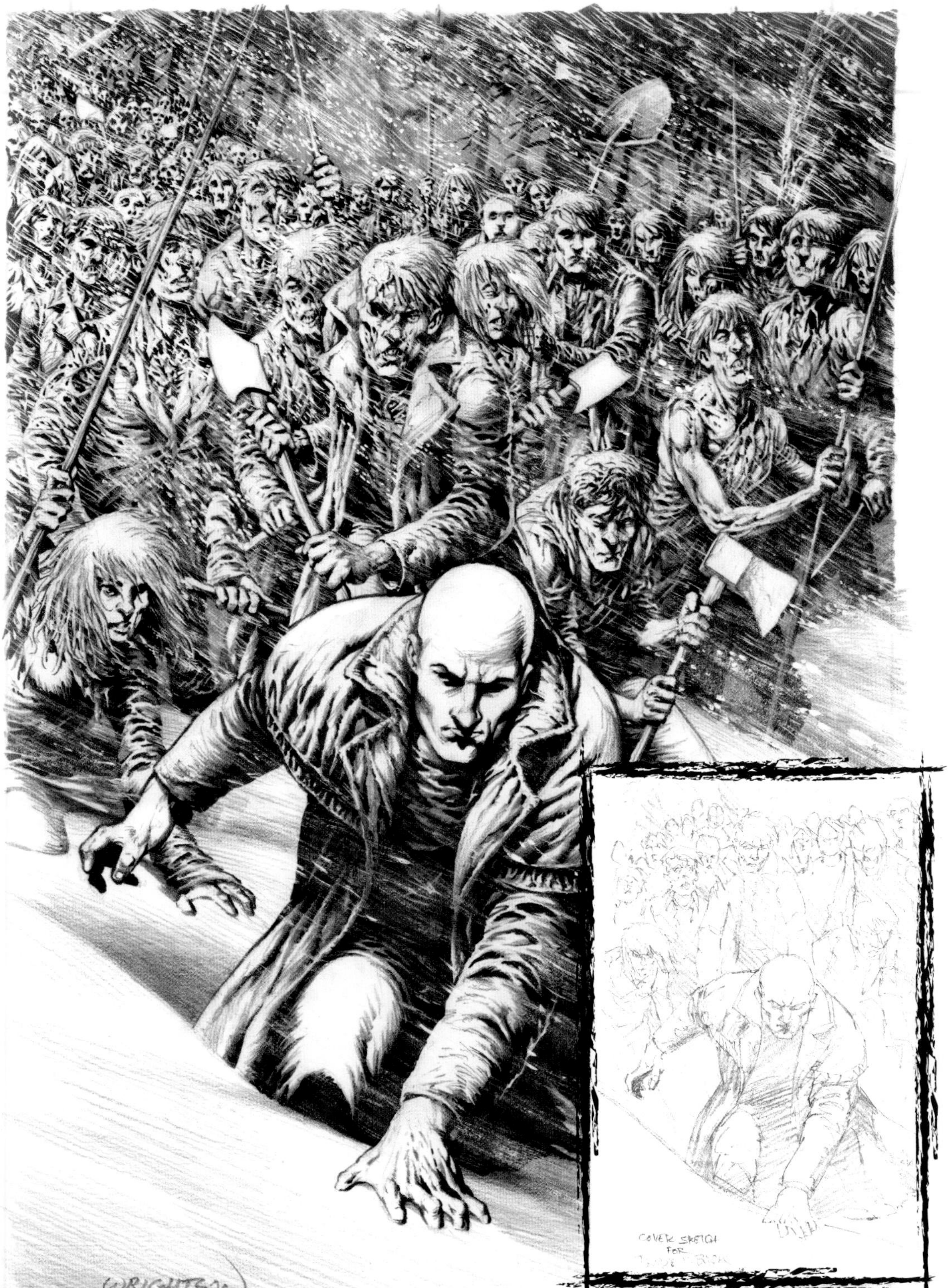
WRIGHTSON
COVER SKETCH
FOR

Above: The finished pencils for the cover of this book.

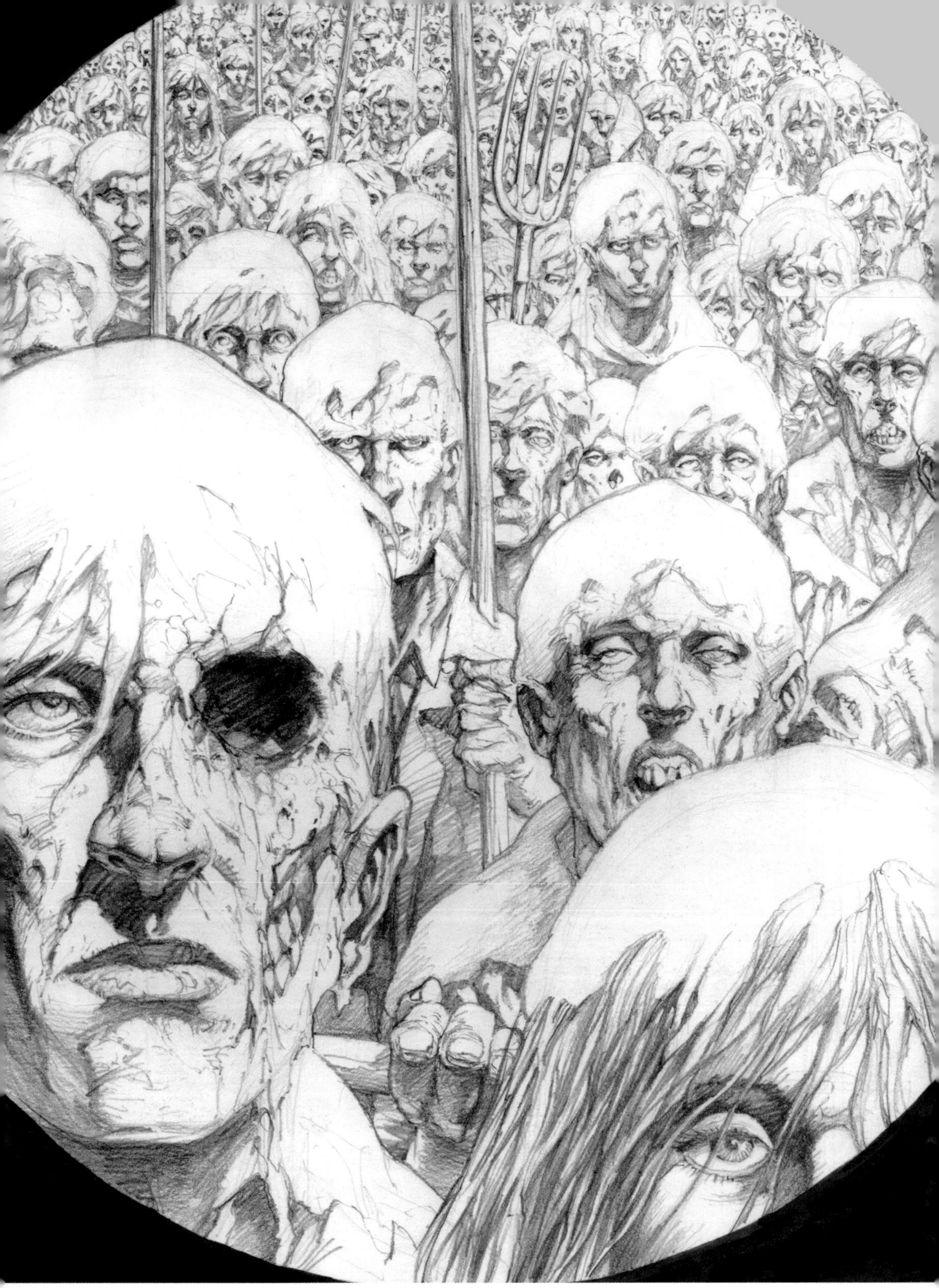

Above: Bernie's finished line art for the descending zombie horde from issue #2.

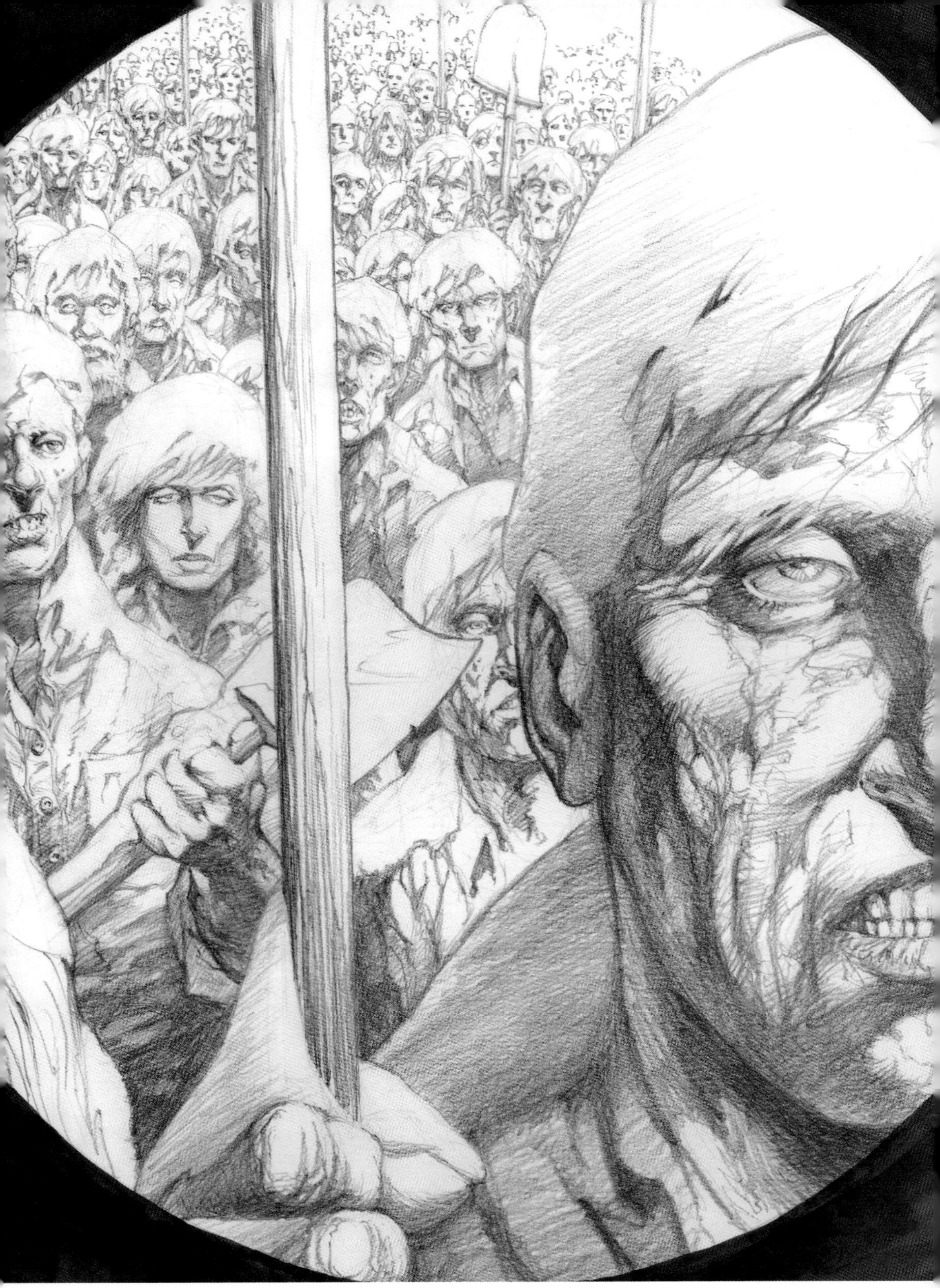

When we first began working on *City of Others*, it was remarkable to see Bernie's raw pencils as they came in. It's incredibly rare to see such fine detail work on a comic-book page anymore, and Bernie was pulling out all the stops. As the series progressed and the first issue hit the stands, we immediately began receiving requests to show just the pencilied line art as a bonus feature to the comic. We all liked that idea, but since there was limited space in the individual issues, we decided to save this feature for the series collection. I still think this is one of the most incredibly beautiful drawings I have ever seen, subject matter aside.

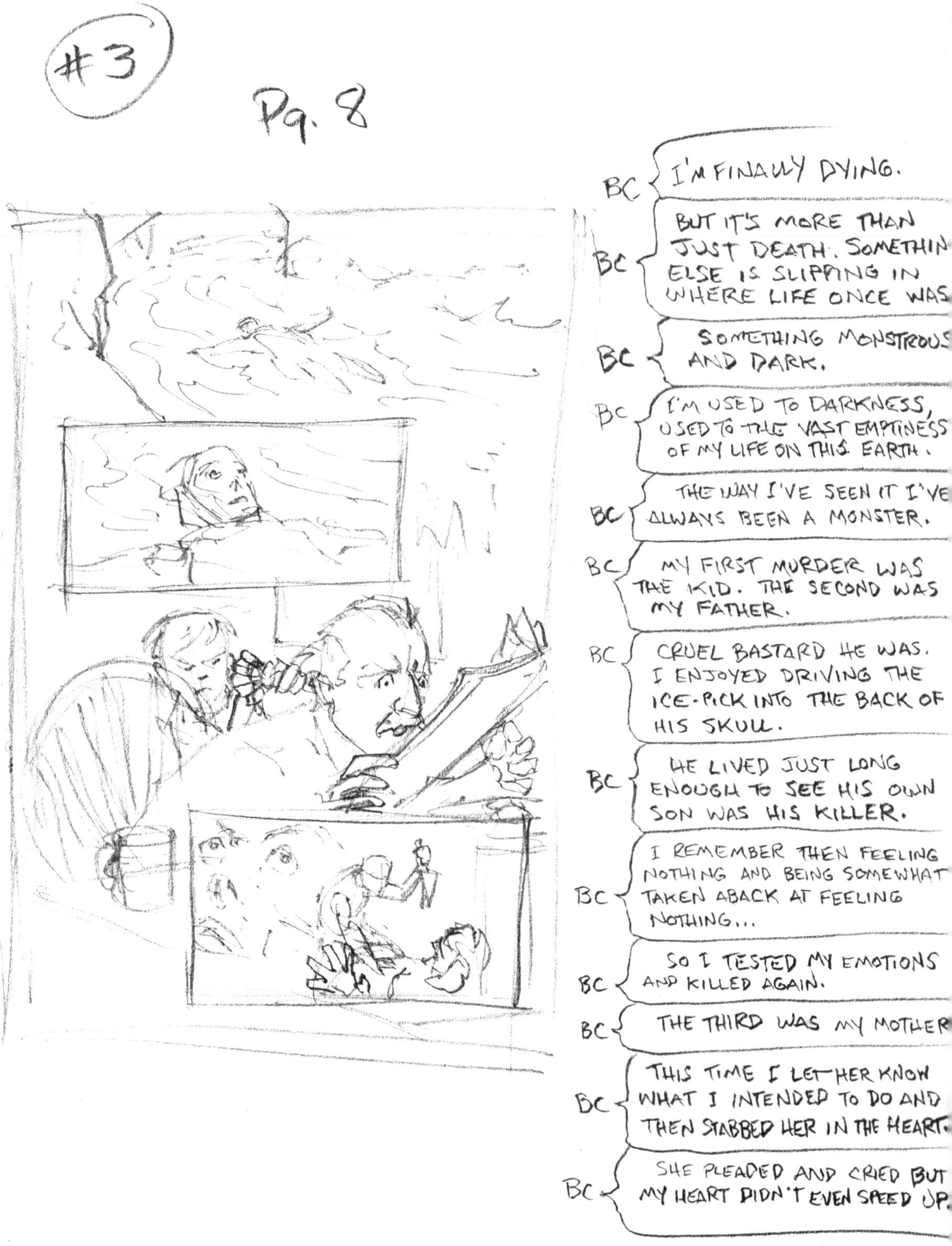
#3
Pg. 8
BC I'M FINALLY DYING.
BC BUT IT'S MORE THAN JUST DEATH. SOMETHIN ELSE IS SLIPPING IN WHERE LIFE ONCE WAS.
BC SOMETHING MONSTROUS AND DARK.
BC I'M USED TO DARKNESS, USED TO THE VAST EMPTINESS OF MY LIFE ON THIS EARTH.
BC THE WAY I'VE SEEN IT I'VE ALWAYS BEEN A MONSTER.
BC MY FIRST MURDER WAS THE KID. THE SECOND WAS MY FATHER.
BC CRUEL BASTARD HE WAS. I ENJOYED DRIVING THE ICE-PICK INTO THE BACK OF HIS SKULL.
BC HE LIVED JUST LONG ENOUGH TO SEE HIS OWN SON WAS HIS KILLER.
BC I REMEMBER THEN FEELING NOTHING AND BEING SOMEWHAT TAKEN ABACK AT FEELING NOTHING...
BC SO I TESTED MY EMOTIONS AND KILLED AGAIN.
BC THE THIRD WAS MY MOTHER
BC THIS TIME I LET HER KNOW WHAT I INTENDED TO DO AND THEN STABBED HER IN THE HEART.
BC SHE PLEADED AND CRIED BUT MY HEART DIDN'T EVEN SPEED UP.

Another great treat for this editor was learning Bernie's working process. Because Steve Niles and I both wanted to showcase Bernie's great visual storytelling, we came up with an interesting way to script the series. Bernie and Steve worked together on the general story outline for each series, then Steve would script it out to twenty-two story pages. Since the series allowed for twenty-six story pages per issue, this gave Bernie free rein to expand the scenes he was most compelled by and develop them with spreads or larger panels.

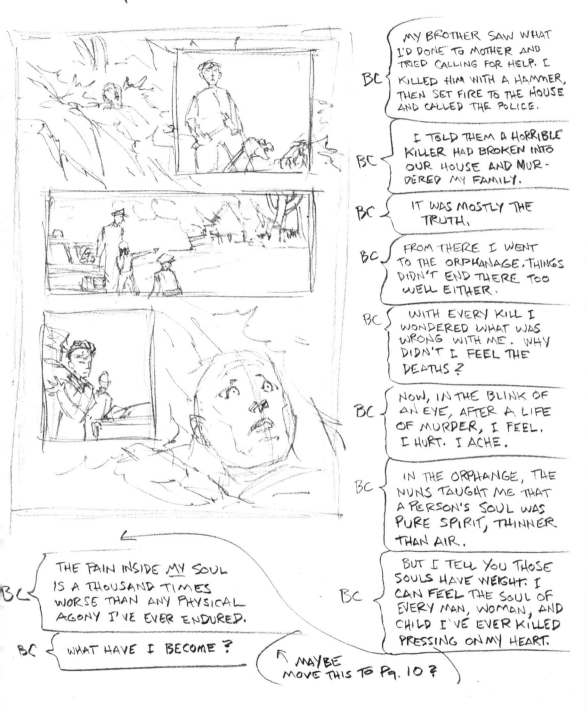

BC MY BROTHER SAW WHAT I'D DONE TO MOTHER AND TRIED CALLING FOR HELP. I KILLED HIM WITH A HAMMER, THEN SET FIRE TO THE HOUSE AND CALLED THE POLICE.

BC I TOLD THEM A HORRIBLE KILLER HAD BROKEN INTO OUR HOUSE AND MURDERED MY FAMILY.

BC IT WAS MOSTLY THE TRUTH.

BC FROM THERE I WENT TO THE ORPHANAGE. THINGS DIDN'T END THERE TOO WELL EITHER.

BC WITH EVERY KILL I WONDERED WHAT WAS WRONG WITH ME. WHY DIDN'T I FEEL THE DEATHS?

BC NOW, IN THE BLINK OF AN EYE, AFTER A LIFE OF MURDER, I FEEL. I HURT. I ACHE.

BC IN THE ORPHANGE, THE NUNS TAUGHT ME THAT A PERSON'S SOUL WAS PURE SPIRIT, THINNER THAN AIR.

BC THE PAIN INSIDE MY SOUL IS A THOUSAND TIMES WORSE THAN ANY PHYSICAL AGONY I'VE EVER ENDURED.

BC BUT I TELL YOU THOSE SOULS HAVE WEIGHT. I CAN FEEL THE SOUL OF EVERY MAN, WOMAN, AND CHILD I'VE EVER KILLED PRESSING ON MY HEART.

BC WHAT HAVE I BECOME?

↑ MAYBE MOVE THIS TO Pg. 10?

Part of Bernie's process is adapting the script into layouts like the ones seen on this page from issue #3. Thumbnail sketches like this are commonly used by artists as they start work on a new script, but this also gave Bernie the chance to play with the placement for key scenes as he decided which plot points deserved more room on the page.

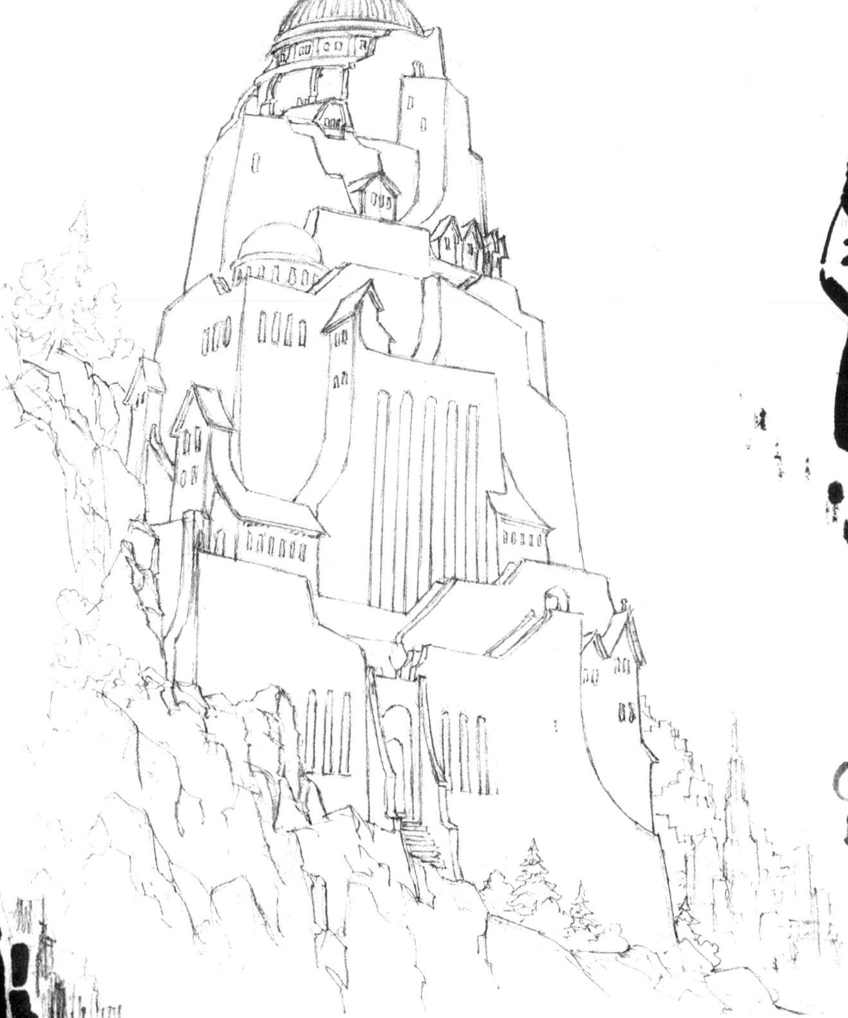

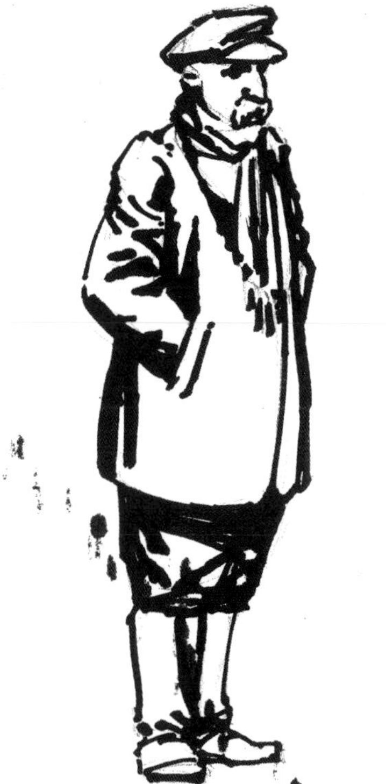

COASTAL
EDDIE

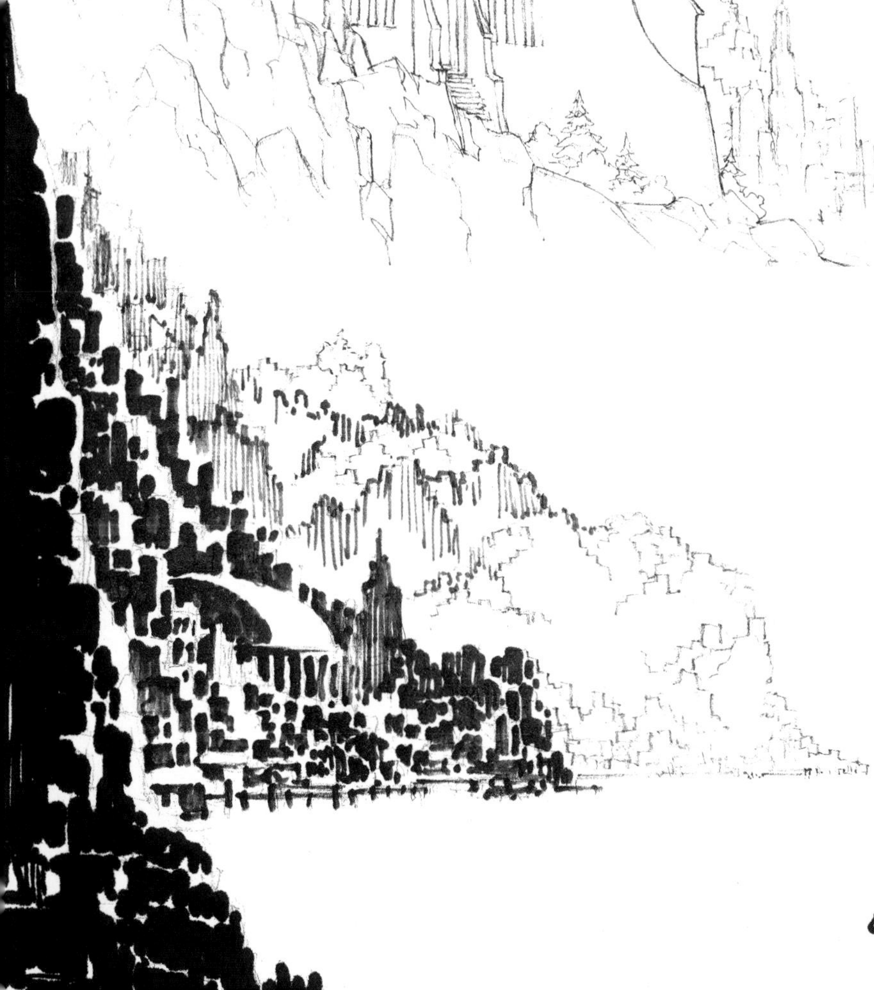

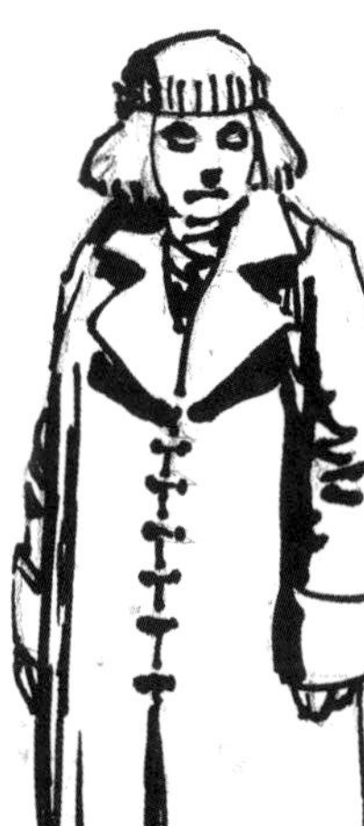

OFFSHORE
FLO

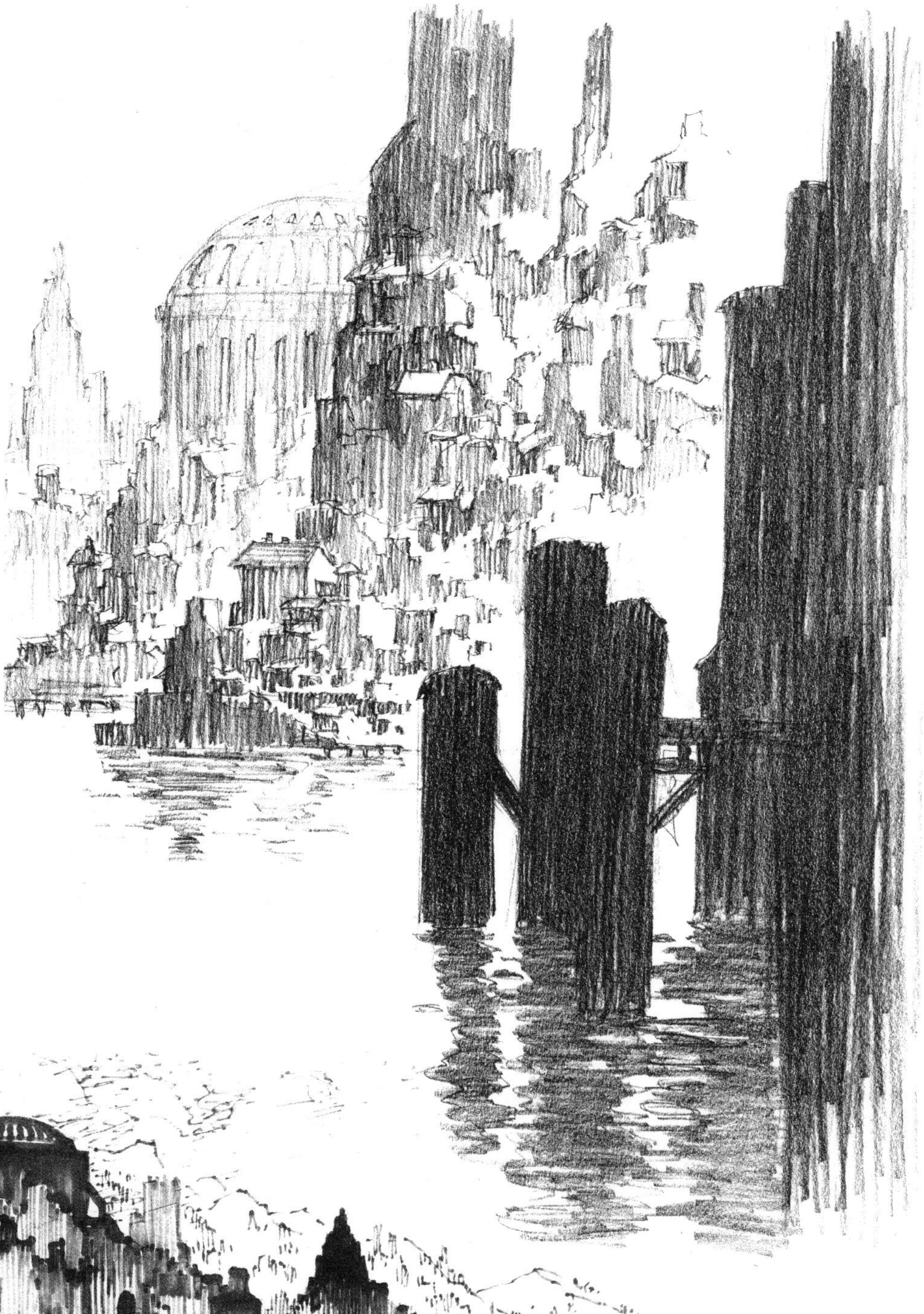

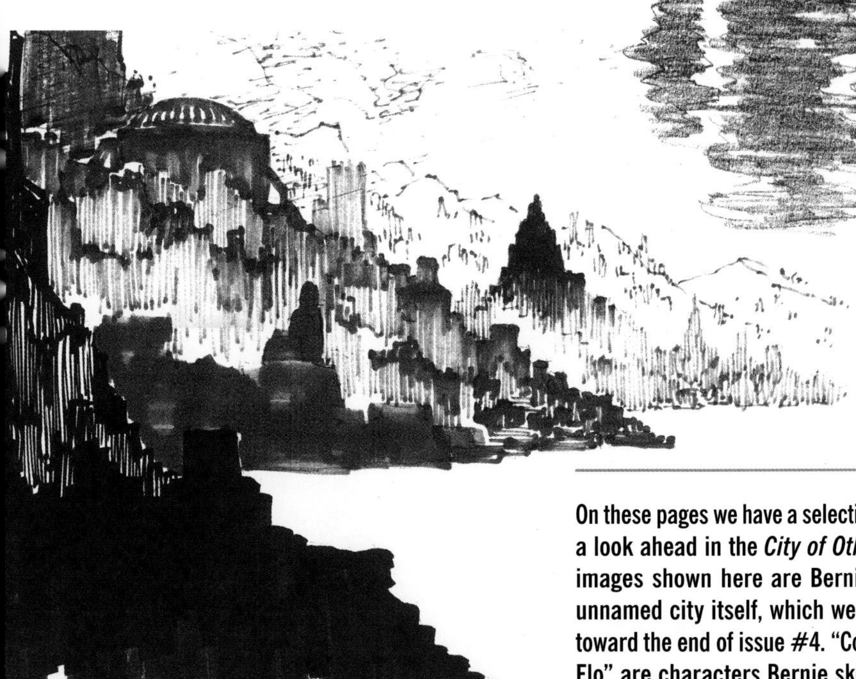

On these pages we have a selection of sketches that suggest a look ahead in the *City of Others* story. The landscape images shown here are Bernie's early sketches of the unnamed city itself, which we finally get a good look at toward the end of issue #4. "Coastal Eddy" and "Offshore Flo" are characters Bernie sketched just for fun and to make a play on words. Keep your eyes peeled, though—you never know when they might turn up in *City of Others*.

CRIMINAL MACABRE

IN 2003 THE CREATIVE TEAM BEHIND THE *30 DAYS OF NIGHT* COMICS SERIES—NOW A MAJOR MOTION PICTURE—LAUNCHED A NEW SERIES OF OCCULT DETECTIVE STORIES FEATURING THE MONSTROUSLY HARD-BOILED CAL MCDONALD. A PILL-POPPING ALCOHOLIC REPROBATE, CAL IS THE ONLY LINE OF DEFENSE BETWEEN LOS ANGELES AND A GROWING HORDE OF ZOMBIES, VAMPIRES, AND WEREWOLVES!

CRIMINAL MACABRE: A CAL MCDONALD MYSTERY

Steve Niles and Ben Templesmith

Recently relocated to Los Angeles, investigator of the weird Cal McDonald finds himself in police custody, implicated in a case involving the elite of L.A.

ISBN 978-1-56971-935-0 | $14.95

CRIMINAL MACABRE: LAST TRAIN TO DEADSVILLE

Steve Niles and Kelley Jones

Cal McDonald thinks he's seen it all, at least until a couple of rampaging rednecks bust through his door. Thus begins Cal's most spine-chilling case yet, as these Beverly Hellbillies take him down a trail of terror into the heart of a Southern California backwater brimming with monsters and mullets.

ISBN 978-1-59307-107-3 | $14.95

CRIMINAL MACABRE: TWO RED EYES

Steve Niles and Kyle Hotz

After a nasty case of police brutality, Cal ends up fighting for his life in the intensive care unit and wakes up days later . . . sober. And what's Cal been missing since he went under? Only the most horrifying convergence of sheer monster power ever to emigrate from the old world. Cal McDonald, meet Nosferatu.

ISBN 978-1-59307-843-0 | $12.95

CRIMINAL MACABRE: SUPERNATURAL FREAK MACHINE

Steve Niles and Kelley Jones

When an old enemy Cal sent to prison escapes, his sights are set on exacting cold revenge on the guy who put him there. And it looks like he'll have to cut through everyone Cal loves to get to him . . .

ISBN 978-1-59307-731-0 | $17.95

CRIMINAL MACABRE: THE COMPLETE CAL MCDONALD STORIES (novel)

Steve Niles

Collected for the first time in one book, these are the long-out-of-print prose adventures of the most unconventional detective of all time.

ISBN 978-1-59582-118-8 | $12.95

AVAILABLE AT YOUR LOCAL COMICS SHOP OR BOOKSTORE! • To find a comics shop in your area, call 1-888-266-4226.

For more information or to order direct visit darkhorse.com or call 1-800-862-0052 Mon.–Fri. 9 AM to 5 PM Pacific Time. Prices and availability subject to change without notice.

DARK HORSE BOOKS *drawing on your nightmares*

darkhorse.com

ALSO FROM STEVE NILES

FUSED
THINK LIKE A MACHINE

FUSED: THINK LIKE A MACHINE

Steve Niles, Josh Medors, and Peter Repovski

Mark Haggerty was a promising young robotics engineer with a smart, sexy wife and a bright future just within his grasp, until his body became fused with an experimental robot suit during a routine testing session!

ISBN 978-1-59307-263-6 | $12.95

THE NAIL
ROB ZOMBIE STEVE NILES

THE NAIL

Rob Zombie, Steve Niles, Nat Jones, and Jay Fotos

A semi-pro wrestler, Hauser tours the country performing at small-time arenas. But after a fateful night when he and his family run afoul of a bloodthirsty gang of Satanic bikers stalking the North Dakota Badlands, he's a lone man fighting for the survival of his loved ones in a no-holds-barred standoff against the forces of Hell itself!

ISBN 978-1-59307-173-8 | $14.95

FUSED
CANNED HEAT!

FUSED: CANNED HEAT

Steve Niles, Paul Lee, Ben Templesmith, and Brad Rader

Trapped inside a body that's not his own, and suddenly the unwilling pawn in a deadly struggle between obsessive egos and misguided military forces, Mark Haggerty's life is forever changed. With his human body consumed more each day by the Cy-bot suit, and the most dangerous elements in the world closing in around him, Mark's only recourse is to keep fighting—until he gets his life back.

ISBN 978-1-59307-192-9 | $12.95

FREAKS
of the
HEARTLAND

FREAKS OF THE HEARTLAND

Steve Niles and Greg Ruth

Under the weathered skies of America's heartland, and in the wounded hearts of every family in one tiny rural town, a terrible secret has been kept for too many years. Now, a young boy named Trevor must try to keep his younger brother Will from falling victim to the worst fears of a troubled town that can't begin to understand the tragic secret that binds its families together.

ISBN 978-1-59307-029-8 | $17.95

AVAILABLE AT YOUR LOCAL COMICS SHOP OR BOOKSTORE! • To find a comics shop in your area, call 1-888-266-4226.

For more information or to order direct visit darkhorse.com or call 1-800-862-0052 Mon.–Fri. 9 AM to 5 PM Pacific Time. Prices and availability subject to change without notice.

DARK HORSE COMICS *drawing on your nightmares*

darkhorse.com

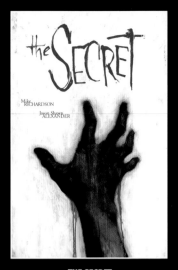
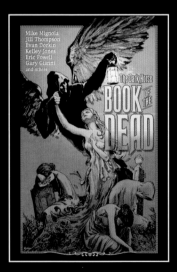
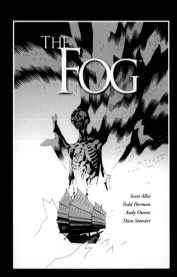